A BODY IN A BATHHOUSE

A BODY IN A

BATHHOUSE

A Mitch O'Reilly Mystery

Brad Shreve

ISBN: 978-0-578-47944-6

Published by Beeson Press

Edited by Alana Garrigues

Cover design by UmeWorks, LLC - *umeworks.com*

Visit *bradsheve.com*

For Maurice,
my husband and biggest fan.

Acknowledgements

Many thanks to the following for their
contributions to this book:
Alana Garrigues, Denise Shiozawa,
Betty Paieda, Dee Masters, Nuna Bosler,
Brian Haney, Lee Ann Hart,
Anna Elizabeth Berrington, Mike Buttitta, Deb Reynolds,
and my friends at the South Bay Creative Writers Group.

A BODY IN A BATHHOUSE

One

"This case will be good for both of us," Eve said. "If we get my client off, we look like heroes. If we don't, he's just another Mexican in prison who'll be forgotten."

"You're one cold-hearted bitch."

"Just honest, Mitch."

Attorney Eve Aiken and I had worked together twice before. Once, I took pictures of a drug-abusing father in a custody battle. The second case involved a Pomeranian and suspicious bite marks.

"He's probably an illegal. That'll make it harder for us." She pulled her gray suit jacket off, revealing a low-cut, black shell top. The skin above her breasts and down her arms was rough, wrinkled, and splotchy, making her look far beyond her fifty years. "I'll give you the quick and dirty."

I cocked my head and smirked. "Quick and dirty is the way I like it."

She glared. "You probably know about the murder at that gay bathhouse yesterday."

"It may surprise you to know there is no gay underground to disseminate information."

"Don't you watch the news?"

Before I could answer, a bell on the main door handle jingled. I rolled my desk chair to see the front of my store, Eye Spy Supplies. My twin sister, Josie, was showing up for work an hour late.

My desk, tucked in the corner of the cramped storeroom, was one of those heavy-as-hell, gray metal types the government used for decades after World War II. I placed my arm back on it, bumping a pile of paperwork to the floor where it mingled with more papers sorted in no particular order.

Eve scowled as she combed my shabby storeroom office, with its dimmed fluorescent lighting and dark wood paneling. Stacked boxes slanted, ready to fall at any moment. A stool next to the desk barely balanced a mountain of bills on top, all stamped "past due." I casually took a book off my desk and placed it on the pile. I had opened the store to be my own boss and get out of detective work. My plan was failing miserably. I still didn't make enough from the store to stop being a private investigator, and I didn't make enough as an investigator to close the store.

"You were saying?" I urged Eve on.

"A man was killed yesterday morning at the Club Silver Lake bathhouse," she said. "Familiar with it?"

Familiar? It had been almost five years since I'd been inside, but I would never shake the lure of sheer self-indulgence that consumed my life after I left the army.

"I've heard of it. What happened?"

"A man by the name of Victor Verboom had his throat slashed while in a steam room. They have a suspect in custody—Ernesto Torres, a jilted lover who swears he didn't do it. I'm defending him. That's why I need your help."

"Given your feelings towards 'the gays,' I'm surprised you took the case."

"I work with you, don't I? Anyway, it doesn't matter which way the wind blows, as long as the cash is green." She slid forward on my turquoise thrift-store couch and leaned toward me. "They found Verboom's body at 3:00 a.m. Apparently, he has a huge house in the hills, but he was known to sleep at the bathhouse several nights a week. Can you imagine?"

I could, but didn't say so. "What's his story?"

"He was a staff writer for some TV comedy I don't watch. It's in the file." She opened a manila folder that was in her lap. "Let's see, it's a show called *Don't Do That!* You ever see it?"

"I don't watch much TV, but I can't imagine you watching a sitcom. Is it even possible for you to crack a smile?"

Eve's lips turned down, and she furrowed her brow. In an attempt to lean back, she forgot she was seated too far forward, which caused her to slump on the couch flailing her raised hands. Grunting and clearly embarrassed, she scooched up in her seat and straightened her gray, stained skirt. I was forced to grit my teeth and look away to maintain self-control.

She brushed aside a strand of her thin, black hair and crossed her arms. "Do you want this job, O'Reilly?"

"I'll quit with the witty banter."

"Witty? Don't flatter yourself." She paused. "I already told you my client and the victim were screwing around. What I didn't tell you is that Torres works there. Talk about a job with benefits—when the cops questioned people at the club, Torres freaked out and ran. When they reached him, they did a quick search and found meth on him."

"Is he a dealer?"

"Nah. He didn't have much, just enough for a misdemeanor, but they're holding him anyway as a person of interest for the murder. Some of the other men said they heard the two arguing about a breakup. But unless they find something more to charge him with, he'll be out in the morning."

"So… minor drug possession, no felony charges. Why are you here? What's in it for you?"

"Trent Nakos, the club manager, hired me to be there during questioning. He wants me to ensure Torres doesn't get charged for the crime."

"How's the manager play into this?"

"I don't know, and I don't care. He's the one who's paying my fees. They may have something going on too. It's hard to keep up with you people."

"You're not making it easy for me to hold back on the witty banter."

Eve groaned and brushed another strand of hair behind one ear. Her face looked as if she had once been beautiful, highlighted by dark brown, almond-shaped eyes. But the years had not been kind. Deep creases across her forehead and crow's feet around her eyes revealed a lifetime of bad decisions.

"You're scheduled to meet the club manager at 12:30."

"Presumptuous of you to schedule a meeting on my behalf, don't you think?"

"You'll find a way to make it."

"I will," I smiled. "I'm honored you'd think to hire me."

"Cut the bullshit, O'Reilly. I'm here because you're cheap, and you know it. Too cheap, I'd say. It makes you look like a goddamned fool. Unprofessional."

"You flatter me, Eve, but we haven't talked about my rates."

"Don't have to. You're getting what you charged for the Pomeranian case," she said.

I caught myself raising my hand to pound my fist and set it back on the desk. "That was not a murder investigation."

She looked around the room. "You can't afford to pass this up."

"And you can't afford to pay anyone with more experience. I guess we're stuck with each other."

"Here's the file." She tossed it on my desk. "The police detective handling the case is Dirk Turner. The file should have everything you need. Torres cleaned the place. I can't imagine a more disgusting job than cleaning a gay men's bathhouse. Filthy."

"Don't knock it until you try it."

She raised a palm toward me. "That's a hard pass. No one in there would be interested in this." She ran her hand along her body seductively.

I chuckled. "I think that's the first time I've heard you say something funny."

"Be serious. Remember, O'Reilly, this could put us both on the map. We've got nothing to lose." She stood and grabbed her purse. "Call me as soon as you know something. And remember, you report to me—and me only."

"It was a pleasure to see you again, Eve." I extended my arm to shake her hand.

"More bullshit," she said. "You're only happy to see me because you need the money."

"I said it was a pleasure seeing you. I didn't qualify why."

Eve walked out, the smell of bourbon wafting behind. I followed and watched as her tired moss-colored Mercedes bounced across the minefield we call a parking lot. I looked around the tiny strip mall, breathed deeply, and slowly let it out. The Los Angeles air had turned the beige, chipped adobe exterior an ashy gray. Reddish-brown stains streamed like dried blood from the rusting gutters and drainpipes. The front of the plaza had a diner that closed years ago, yet a *Now Open* sign still hung on the door.

I reentered the store and found Josie seated behind the cash register, reading *Cosmo* and texting.

"Good morning, sunshine," I said. "Nice to see you're up bright and early."

Without raising her head, she looked at me out of the corner of her eye. "Don't start. I'm only a little late."

"An hour isn't 'a little late.' Most places would fire you with that attitude."

"This isn't most places, Lil' Bro."

Josie was born fifteen minutes before me, which made me forever her "Lil' Bro." But she was right. My store wasn't like most places. Most business owners didn't have a sister willing to take a day off from her primary job to help her brother without pay.

"You have yet to mention my hair," she said. "I changed it over a week ago."

"We haven't seen each other in over a week. It looks great. What did you do to it?"

"I had it cropped." She ran her fingers down one side. "They say us big, beautiful women look better with our hair cropped. It emphasizes the face, or something like that."

I widened my eyes and grinned. "Well, I must say it's absolutely stunning."

"Hmph." She crossed her arms. "Don't be a smart ass. Some detective you are to not even notice."

"It's hard keeping up with you."

My sister, Josephine O'Reilly Baxter Weichselbaum, was always changing her look from one week to the next. Like me, she inherited our Mexican mother's stark black hair. However, unlike the rough, pale skin I got from our Irish father, her skin is light brown, smooth, and flawless.

I scanned the items in the display cases to take mental note of what I might need to order. Eye Spy Supplies carries the latest surveillance equipment, computer monitoring devices, GPS trackers, and bug detectors. There was more in my inventory than I'd ever sell.

Josie stood and tapped on the glass case. A smile spread across her face. "I wish you had come out with me last night. I had the best time and met the cutest guy. I might see him again."

"That'd be a first."

Josie laughed. "I'm not that bad. We haven't partied together in a long time. I am a lady now."

"Since your last divorce, you've been everything but a lady."

She cackled and gave me a hard push on my shoulder that nearly knocked me to the floor. "It'd be nice to hear you say you've gone out for a change."

I tensed up. "You know I have no interest in dating."

"Who's talking about dating? Have dinner. Get laid."

"I get laid plenty, and when I do, the last thing on my mind is to call my sister."

"Hooking up off the internet doesn't count. You don't even know those guys' names."

"That's the way I like it."

She hopped off the stool, laid her hands on the display case, and bounced. It was too much energy for so early in the day. "Come on. Let's go out tonight—the two of us conquering the world of hot, single men, just like old times."

"Your enthusiasm is more than I can handle."

The bouncing stopped, and her shoulders slumped. "Lil' Bro, I love you, but you need to start living again, or you'll end up a lonely old man."

"I'll chance it."

It was a tired discussion that'd been replayed a thousand times since I moved back to Los Angeles. She thought my life was boring. I found solace in the mundane.

"Hey, why'd you ask me to cover for you? I thought you weren't going to be in the store today,"

"I wasn't. I came to pick up flyers to post on bulletin boards around town."

"That sounds like a waste of time."

"Probably, but it's the only advertising I can afford. Then Eve called, and my plans changed. I still need you here. Turns out, I've got an appointment at 12:30."

Josie hopped back on the stool, laid an elbow on the glass case, and leaned forward while resting her chin on her fist. "I heard you talking about murder. That's exciting."

"And yet we talk about hair and getting laid before you mention what could be the biggest case in my career."

"Tell me about it," she said. "I want all the gritty details."

"Some TV comedy writer had his throat cut at Club Silver Lake."

"Ick, that's gross. What show?"

"I don't remember." I looked in the folder. "It's called *Don't Do That!*"

Josie squealed. "I love that show. It's about this little boy who lives in Dubuque, Iowa, who's always causing mischief. Guess what the adults keep telling him?"

"Don't do that?"

"That's right." She shrieked. "Oh—my—god—that never gets old."

I slapped the folder shut and rolled my eyes. "I can't imagine why I don't watch television."

She snickered. "How freaky is it that the murder was at that bathhouse you go to?"

"Used to go to. I haven't been there in years."

"Thank God." She pursed her lips. "You're starting a big case, and I have bad news. I have to be at the office tomorrow. I can't help you here."

"That figures, but thanks."

Josie worked as an executive assistant for my former employer, Regency Investigative Services, the largest detective agency in California. I had worked for her boss, Nat Phelps, while I was earning my PI license. He was the only man I'd ever known who has never had a good day in his life. It was a long two years.

"You know what we need?" I said. "We need a natural disaster. The insurance would pay off this place, and I'd be done with it."

"Where's a good earthquake when you need one?"

I walked into my office to study the case and prepare myself to go back into the bathhouse I'd sworn never to reenter.

Two

LA traffic was a bitch along Santa Monica Boulevard. My blood pressure got a kick in the ass in the record-breaking 101-degree heat, and I couldn't stop my Honda's broken air conditioner from blowing warm air. After almost sideswiping several cars, I pulled onto a side street and parked under a large shade tree to read the last pages of the files Eve had given me and watch news reports of the murder on my cell phone. I reached the bathhouse forty minutes late.

Club Silver Lake was on Sunset and Santa Monica Boulevards, right where they merge. Its name came from the Silver Lake neighborhood where it was located, and it was within walking distance from my place.

The front entrance had no sign or banner. It was in an old, single-story stucco building painted light gray with white trim. One mini palm tree in a large blue pot sat on each side of the entrance. Unless someone was looking, they'd never know it was there. Men found it through word of mouth and the internet.

The bathhouse was usually open twenty-four hours, but a handwritten sign said *Club Opens at 2*. I knocked twice. No response. I banged louder until the door cracked open.

"What the fuck do you want?"

"I have an appointment with Trent Nakos."

"Are you the private eye?"

"Yes."

"You're late."

The door creaked open.

Inside, everything looked different. They had brightened the dingy entryway by painting the walls sage. Two rust-colored mid-century tufted chairs faced the front door, and laminate wood flooring had replaced the tattered black carpeting.

The attendant shut the door and walked behind the counter. "Wait a sec, I'll page Trent."

The announcement echoed from the back.

"He thought you were a no-show. He went in the back to help the guys get shit together to reopen. I'm Seth." We fist bumped.

I couldn't stop staring at him. His milky white skin and gangly body reminded me of a corpse. He had bushy black hair poking out in every direction, an extension of the spiderweb, skull, and snake tattoos covering his neck and arms. His paper-thin white tank top showed the tats didn't end at his extremities; they covered his entire upper body. I always wondered where guys like him found jobs.

The only two things to read in the lobby were a couple of signs outlining the club's code of conduct and a list of fees. By the time the phone rang ten minutes later, I had them all memorized.

"Trent's stuck in the bathroom. Come on back."

Stuck in the bathroom? I didn't know what he meant, and I wasn't sure I wanted to find out. When we entered the back, my eyes watered and my nose burned. It had been years since I was a regular, but I was certain it had never smelled so strongly of bleach. The air had always been a mix of sweat, meth, and poppers.

Trent Nakos, the club's manager, was using a plumber's snake to clean out a toilet. A pile of slimy items covered in sewage lay on the floor next to him.

"Here he is," Seth said, pointing at Trent, "the head shit in charge." He chuckled and walked back to the front.

"Mitch O'Reilly? I'm Trent. I'd shake your hand, but I doubt you'd appreciate it." He laughed.

He turned to face me, and my eyes bugged out like a horny cartoon wolf. A red skintight tank top hugged every muscle of his torso. His powerful thighs filled his shorts, which sported a hefty package. Even the yellow dishwashing gloves he wore made him look sexy—in a kinky way. His body was beautiful, but his broad smile grabbed me the most. The corner of his lip raised a little higher on the left. He had the look of a mischievous child who had found his Christmas presents hidden in a closet.

"I apologize for keeping you waiting. I figured you weren't coming."

"Traffic," I mumbled.

"Uh huh. This is LA. There's always traffic. Would you mind grabbing that trash can and dragging it over here?"

I did as he asked.

"This toilet overflowed after one of my guys used it. When he flushed, it wasn't just the one that backed up. They all did. The disadvantage of working in an old building. I've got them all so busy getting everything else into shape, this was left for me." He nodded toward the pile on the floor. "All of that crap down the pipes makes you wonder… I had to snake each one. Let me get rid of this and then we can talk."

He tossed the last gob of sludge in the can. "Let's go to my office. Hope you don't mind waiting while I take a quick shower."

One of his employees walked past, and Trent asked him to take the trash out back and throw it in the dumpster. "Toss everything, garbage can and all. You don't want to clean that thing out."

The same sage walls and laminate flooring that were in the lobby continued into Trent's office. The tufted chairs also matched the ones up front. Four picture frames with enlarged prints of comic book characters hung behind his desk—Spider-Man, Thor, Wolverine, and Captain America. I stood in front of them, admiring the artwork, before taking a seat. I tried to shake the image of him showering out of my head.

"I love the pictures," I said when he walked in the room.

"Aren't those great? They were at that flea market on Fairfax, and I fell in love. Only twenty-five each, so I had to have them. I've got a couple more at home."

He didn't look like a comic book geek. His slim waist and muscular upper body didn't fit the stereotype. In my line of work, I'd learned to be careful about making assumptions, but still, he caught me off guard. He was charming and playful. "Twenty-five bucks? You got a deal."

Trent sat at his desk, rested his chin on his fist, and flashed a mischievous grin. I struggled to look away from the rich golden eyes that complimented his olive skin. His wavy auburn hair looked tousled but never moved. I guessed he spent time each morning nursing each strand in place for that perfect disheveled look.

He stared through me while stroking his scruffy chin. I debated whether he was flirting or looking past me in deep thought. If he caught me checking him out, he didn't let on.

I broke the silence. "You've been under a lot of stress the past couple of days so we should get the questions out of the way."

"Yes. Let's talk while touring the facility. We're reopening soon, and for my sanity, I need one last walk-through. Follow me."

We stepped into a TV lounge area. My eyes watered again.

"Sorry about the smell," Trent said. "We're taking advantage of the downtime to do some heavy-duty cleaning. I thought the scent would be gone by now."

I nodded at the seating area. "Nice furniture. Like in the lobby."

"They're identical, except these are covered in plastic. That makes them funny because they make farting sounds when the guys stand up. Some don't appreciate the joke, but the plastic makes it easier to clean after hundreds of naked asses have been on them."

I grinned.

They had also renovated the back of the club, while giving it a different personality from the front lobby and

Trent's office. The once-black walls were steel gray, and the black cement floors had been resurfaced with large, dark red tiles. I found it odd—it didn't look the same, but it felt the same. I shrugged my shoulders and blinked my eyes to stop my heart from racing and my skin from tingling.

"Let's start in the sauna where he was murdered," I directed. "Did he rent a room that night?"

"Yes, he always does. Room twenty-two is… was… his favorite, so we tried to keep it open for him. I'll take you there after we see the sauna. The police cleared both. They took the tape down, but it'll be awhile before I rent that room. It'd feel disrespectful."

We walked through a narrow hall with many rooms on each side until we reached the sauna. Trent unlocked the door.

"Look inside. We haven't turned it back on. We'll have our guests use just the one in the back for a while. It's bigger anyway."

The small standard redwood sauna looked built more for a home than a spa. The wall next to the door was smooth, and benches ran along the other three sides, except for the corner opposite the entrance, where the heater with hot rocks stood.

"The cops were thorough. I doubt you'll find much."

"How was he when he was found?"

His lower lip quivered. "He was naked on a mat, face down on the floor, with his ass to the door. He looked as if everything was fine, except for all the blood. The police took the mat for evidence. There was no sign of a struggle, so they think someone came in behind him. They say he most likely never saw who did it."

I smirked. "Not that he could tell us, anyway."

Trent's face went blank.

"Sorry. Too soon."

It was strange. The bright fluorescent lights in the club made it look lewder than with them dimmed. The spartan walls, floors, and hallway were cold and uninviting.

"Were there any men in these rooms that night?"

"No, not in this wing. It was so late we didn't have much business. These were empty."

"Could anyone have used the exit at the end of the hallway?"

"Someone could have, but no one did. It would have sounded the alarm. That didn't happen."

"You said you'd take me to his room next?"

Trent locked the sauna and escorted me to room twenty-two. He opened the door, and I stepped in. He followed, closing it behind us. The warmth of his body inches from mine caused my neck and back to tingle. I took several deep breaths. "Can you open the door? The lighting was better."

He did as I asked and stepped out into the hall. His face flushed, and he used his arm to wipe tears from his eyes. The room had a typical claustrophobic bathhouse design with a bed, a television, a small table, and a single light bulb.

"This is one of our deluxe rooms," he stammered. "It's a little bigger to fit a double bed, plus it has the larger flat-screen TV."

I scoured the floor, baseboards, and under the bed on my knees, but I found nothing of interest. "You're sure Ernesto Torres is innocent?"

"Ernesto is innocent. They have the wrong man. Most of my staff disagrees, but there's no way he could have done it. Gabe wants me to let it go."

"Gabe?"

"Gabe Quinto. The owner. He's willing to let Ernesto hang and doesn't care if he's not guilty. He wants this out of the news ASAP."

"Which is why you're the one left paying to defend Ernesto."

"Exactly. As if I can afford it."

I stood up. "Is Gabe here?"

"He flew in yesterday as soon as I called him, but he already flew back to our home office in Chicago this morning. Have you ever been to Chicago?"

"I changed planes at O'Hare once."

"It's a beautiful city. You should go sometime and spend a few days. The Field Museum of Natural History, the Museum of Science and Industry, the Shedd Aquarium, and the Sears Tower—except it's not the Sears Tower anymore. Now it's the Williams Tower, or the Wallace Tower, or something like that. Maybe it's the—"

"Sorry to interrupt." I leaned against the doorjamb. "So, who do you think did it?"

"It wasn't Ernesto, I'll swear to that. It's inconceivable. I've never known a more sweet, amiable soul in my life. He's like a little brother. I tried to convince the police not to take him, but they wouldn't budge. I worry about him sitting in jail right now. He's so easy to take advantage of, and everyone knows what happens in prison. Did you ever watched that show *Oz*? The guys in prison were hot… but scary, and they kept killing each other. It can't be that bad, but it's what sticks in my mind."

I wondered if it really was that difficult for him to stay on topic, or whether was he being evasive. While Trent locked the door, I surveyed the area.

"Tell me more about Victor Verboom."

"He was one of our best guests... he came no less than four nights a week, and I think he slept most of the time. A lot of guys check in only to have a place to sleep. At thirty-five dollars for eight hours, our rooms are cheaper than a Motel 6. Granted, we're not The Ritz-Carlton, but it's good for some rest. Victor had money. A lot of it. So, that wasn't an issue for him, but he was always here." He paused. "I never thought how sad it'd be to have nowhere to go than here. To think in all of LA, the best they can do is a bathhouse. Guys used to stay at the Y. Do they still have rooms to stay there?"

"No clue."

"Hmm. I'm curious." He smiled and rubbed his fingers on his temples. "Now the YMCA song will be in my head the rest of the day." He chuckled.

"Thanks a lot. Now it'll be in mine." I didn't chuckle.

"What an era that was, huh? Discos. Great dance music. I like all the oldies. Wham!, ABBA, you name it. Imagine being there—with the curly hair and tight blue jeans, the leisure suits and gold chains. Wow, what an era that was. Sometimes I—"

"Victor won Emmys and had a house in the hills. With all his money, why would he sleep here instead of a hotel room?"

"Sorry, I keep getting distracted. My mind is running in a hundred directions today, and I'm still shook up. Supposedly, Victor and his partner, Warren Barone, weren't getting along. Maybe Victor wanted to be away from home."

"But again, why here? If he just wanted to get out of the house, why come to a bathhouse to sleep?"

"My guess is he didn't want to be alone. He was comfortable here. Well, that, and he was always horny. He may have slept a lot of the time, but maybe he also wanted to keep his options open. Come on. Plenty more to see."

"Do you have any evidence to back up Ernesto's innocence?" I asked.

Trent stopped. He turned his head as if trying to hide his tears. He brushed them off with his wrist.

I crossed my arms and exhaled.

"I don't," he said. "But the police don't have enough to prove he's guilty. Eve Aiken said that they will have to release him soon unless they find more evidence. Wait until you see how small Ernesto is. Victor was twice his size."

"It doesn't take strength or size to walk up behind someone and slit their throat."

"Ugh. I'd rather not think about the details."

We stepped into the main hallway, next to a weight room and a hot tub. Trent excused himself to speak with two men who were cleaning the floors. They spent as much time laughing as talking. After a few minutes, Trent and I continued down the hall to a sliding glass door overlooking a pool terrace. He stepped outside and waved for me to follow.

"It's hot out here, but it's not too bad under this umbrella." He sat.

I sat down too, but the umbrella didn't help. Between the heat and the humidity, our bodies were instantly drenched with sweat. His soaked T-shirt clung tighter to his chiseled abs and massive chest, revealing large, plump nipples.

The patio was nice, a real upgrade from when I'd last been in the bathhouse. Light gray pebbled pavement surrounded an oval-shaped pool. Tropical plants and palms hugged the privacy fence, shading a multitude of white lounge chairs.

"It looks like a country club back here."

"Happy to hear you say so. We did a total renovation last year. A little paint here, new flooring there. We've got to keep up with the competition. Attendance has been spiraling downward for years."

"How many bathhouses are in LA?"

"Four of us left. Business is hurting at most clubs nationwide. The internet is killing us."

"How's that?"

"Think about it. You drive to a bathhouse. Then, you pay a fee. Then, you hope to find someone you're attracted to. Then, you hope they find you attractive. Then, you hope you're into the same things. Then, you figure out who's the top and who's the bottom, etcetera, etcetera. On the net, you can log into a hookup site with thousands of profiles. All your questions are answered, and within thirty minutes, you're getting laid. That's hard to compete with. It's why we renovated. But it's not enough. We have to find some way to get back to the heyday of the '70s, when going to a bathhouse was an event, when it offered real entertainment, like a private concert with Bette. It sure would be nice to get her back for a night."

"Bette? Midler?"

"Yeah, Barry Manilow too. They both started in bathhouses. Obviously, they're out of our league these days, but we're hoping to find that level of talent. The next Bette or Barry. Or a top-of-the-line DJ. Speaking of which, we're talking with some great DJs for an event we're organizing. Hot go-go boys too. I'll let you know once we confirm a date."

The uneasy feeling being there after so long was surprising. I was worried the awkwardness overpowering me would be worse when surrounded by naked men again.

"Anyway," Trent continued, "the changes made a little difference. We're not getting the traffic we hoped, but business is up." He stood and fanned his face with his palm. "We've been out here too long. We'll get heatstroke. Let's wrap up the tour."

When we stepped inside, the air conditioning blasted across my skin, and it gave me goose bumps. We continued our walk into another lounge area. A pool table with dark mahogany rails and a scarlet red cloth was the centerpiece of the room. One wall had an electric dartboard, and in the corner of the room, there was a faux fireplace with a mantle that matched the table.

"Nice setup, huh?" Trent said. "Part of creating an 'experience' means making it as hospitable as possible."

"It's definitely luxurious." I had to get him back on track. "Let's get back to Monday morning. Tell me what was going on at the time of the murder."

"It was quiet, as it usually is at that time. There's too many distractions the rest of the week, so I'm always here to take care of paperwork and inventory. I was in my office when it all went down. An out-of-towner named Clark something-or-other found Victor in the sauna and screamed. It would've been nice if he had come to the office and told us discreetly, but I guess I've never stumbled on a dead body before."

"Most people haven't."

I grabbed a pool stick and banked a stripe into a side pocket. Not a bad shot for someone who rarely plays the game.

"Very good," Trent grabbed a stick, planted it on the floor, and leaned his hips against the table. "When Ernesto saw Victor lying there, he lost it. Victor was the love of his life. He collapsed... I thought he might hurt himself." He looked down and ran his hand across his forehead. "That's another reason I know it wasn't him. He'd have to be a good actor to react the way he did. I sat on the floor and held him while Seth called the police."

"How long had they been seeing each other?"

"About six months. Ernesto was in love. It was sweet, but to be honest, I think Victor was using him. I experienced that once when I fell for a man who treated me like royalty. We were together a long time before I found out he was doing the same with half of West Hollywood."

"We've got a lot to cover. I need you to—"

"I adored that man, but he ripped out my heart and stomped on it. As long as I live, I'll never understand…"

He droned on about past loves. I leaned against the pool table next to him and did my best to hide my frustration. Finally, he stopped. "Sorry, distracted again. Where was I?" He stroked his stubbled chin. "Oh yeah. I wanted to warn Ernesto about being in a relationship like that, but when I heard Victor and Warren were struggling to keep their relationship alive, I thought maybe Victor was sincere."

"You let your employees fraternize with your customers?"

"Not while they're here. We could get charged with prostitution, but what they do on their own time is none of our business. I guess I let Victor and Ernesto cross the line a little, but Ernesto seemed so happy."

"How many people were working at the time of the murder?"

"Three of us. Ernesto, Seth, and me."

"Seth is the cashier?"

"He's the office supervisor. He's been putting in extra hours because we're short-staffed. Also, the guys at the front desk are more than cashiers. They monitor the place, track our guests' checkout times, and distribute towels and keys. When things get rough, they act as bouncers. They really run this place, not me."

"So, Seth was working the front. You were doing paperwork in your office. And where was Ernesto? He's a janitor, right?"

"We call them room attendants. He was doing his job. Washing laundry, cleaning rooms."

"Can you recall anything odd that night? Anyone or anything out of the ordinary?"

"You mean other than finding a dead body?"

"Obviously."

Trent hesitated, locked his hands behind his back, and looked up at the ceiling. "Warren Barone was here. That's unusual. He doesn't come often, and I've never seen him at the same time as Victor. They had been together twenty years and had an open relationship, so I don't think Ernesto was an issue. But who knows what their rules were? You know—what's allowed and what's not. I don't believe in open relationships. You either love someone, or you don't. There's no gray area."

"What can you tell me about Warren?"

"Not much. As I said, he wasn't one of our regulars. It's so rare he's here that I wouldn't know him except for his relationship with Victor. He has a floral shop on Melrose. Talk with Seth. He knows more about what goes on than I do."

We left the lounge via a large open area with a tiered floor and three giant TVs on the wall. "This is what we call the playground. Over here," Trent pointed at the TVs, "we show porn twenty-four seven." He turned and faced two human-sized cages with handcuffs and chains dangling from the ceiling. "The bondage crowd loves those." We kept walking, into a hallway flanked with black leather curtains along one side. "Behind those is the dark room. When the club opens, the lights go out and its pure darkness. Guys like to walk through the maze and maybe feel something good along the way."

"I prefer to see the person I'm having sex with," I said.

"So do I, but we don't pass judgment around here."

"I'll keep my mouth shut."

Trent laughed. "I'll resist making a crude comment to that."

It wasn't a funny statement, but I gave him a courtesy laugh and decided it was time to come out to him. We had built a good rapport, but I sensed if he knew I was gay, I could get him to let his guard down even more.

"Did I say I used to come here about five years ago?"

He stopped, looked at me with a toothy grin. "You didn't mention you're gay."

"It never came up. Besides, you've been flirting so much I assumed you knew."

"I sensed it, but my gaydar is terrible." He chuckled. "I flirt with everyone. It's not like your business card says 'Mitch O'Reilly, Gay Detective.' Why don't we see you around?"

"I did a couple of tours in the army, and when I got back, I took a break for a while. I hung out here sometimes but got busy when I entered the workforce."

"The military? Your hotness level just skyrocketed. What did you do?"

"I was an MP."

"Military police?" He opened his arms wide. "A soldier and a cop all rolled into one? Bonus points. I knew a guy once who was—"

I howled, but quickly regained my composure.

"Thanks, I'm flattered. What you've done around here is impressive. It's not the dingy place I used to come to."

"Let me take you through the rest of the club before we open our doors." He grabbed my wrist and pulled me along. We weren't holding hands, but he had my wrist and that was enough to send a charge running through my body. I'd been with plenty of hot men over the years, but this was something else, and it had to stop. I pulled my arm down, and he released his grip. He gave me a puzzled look, but continued walking. We passed through another playground filled with a mix of slings and chains. I thought there was little I didn't know, but some of the play toys puzzled me. I had no clue how to use them. Trent guided me through a quick view of the larger sauna and the showers, and finally, we returned to his office where I took a seat.

"Let me see what's going on out front and send Seth back to talk with you. He'll be able to give you the full scoop on what goes on around here."

Three

After closing the office door, Seth Snider, the office supervisor, took Trent's seat behind the desk, kicked his neon green Chucks on the desktop, put his hands behind his head and said, "Ernesto did it."

Wow. I had planned to relax and break the ice, but he went straight for the jugular.

"Hey, I love the guy, but there's no doubt that little shit killed Victor."

I fixated on Seth's elongated earlobes and wondered if it had hurt to stretch the holes that far. He was cocky, but charismatic enough to get away with it. However, pointing his finger at Ernesto and showing no empathy floored me.

"What makes you so sure?" I asked.

He leaned forward in his chair and laid his arms flat on the desk. "He's too fucking emotional. Can't control himself. When he's sad, we all know it. When he's angry, we all know it. When he's happy, we all know it. And when he's in love… the whole world knows it." He shrugged. "Ernesto is cute and has an adorable ass. He would be the perfect boy toy if he could just shut up. That was all Victor wanted, but Ernesto was head over heels, talking about how it was 'true love,' and they were 'meant

to be,' and shit like that. Once a guy starts clinging like
Velcro, it's time to get the fuck away. Victor and Warren
were together for twenty years. He didn't need to put up
with Ernesto's insecure bullshit. He should have cut that
boy loose long ago."

Seth's bluntness seemed harsh, especially since his
smile never left his face.

"Trent says the rumor is Victor and Warren weren't
getting along."

"That's no rumor. That's common knowledge. The latest
is that Victor and Warren were trying to work things out. I
guess that's why Victor broke it off with Ernesto."

It was impossible to look away from his ears—like
trying to look away from a car wreck. "Is that what they
were arguing about? Victor broke up with him?"

"It's what Ernesto says. It's why I think he did it. He
went *muy loco*."

"Let's back up ear—uh, here. Can you detail for me
what happened Monday morning?"

"You mean Sunday night."

I was puzzled for a second, then understood why he had
corrected me. It was a matter of perspective. "Okay, what
do you remember from Sunday night at 3:00 a.m.?"

He leaned back further in Trent's chair. "It was pretty slow. Not many guys here."

"How many?"

"Eleven total. Eight guests, three employees. I'm guessing we're all suspects, huh?"

"Uh-huh," I muttered. "Did you hear Victor and Ernesto fighting?"

Seth laughed. "Shit, everyone heard it."

"What was said?"

"I don't know. I don't want to hear that mess, but they were loud."

"Did you see Victor interact with anyone else that night?"

"Not really." He paused and raised a finger. "There was someone. He and some other guy got all pissy at each other. Some big Latin dude. Big guy—built like a football player. His name was Gus or something." Seth stroked his chin and eyed the ceiling. "It was Gustavo. Like I said, he was a husky guy."

My eyes darted away from his ears and focused on the large ring dangling from his nostrils. Should I look at his nose or his ears? It had to be one or the other. I chose the nose, hoping it'd appear as if I was looking in his eyes.

Every few seconds, I'd catch myself darting back to his lobes. "How long have you worked here?"

"Three years."

"Like it?"

"It's a pretty fucked-up job, but fun. Not where I thought I'd be at twenty-two." He raised his arms and spread them out. "You know. Big dreams and all."

"Where'd you work before ear... err, here?"

"I was part-time bagging groceries while taking classes at Barstow Community College. Talk about shitty jobs."

"You in school now?"

"Hell no. I'm having too much fucking fun."

Seth leaned forward and pushed papers across the desk. "Here's the guest log from that night. The cops have a copy too. I doubt it's legal giving it to you—client privacy and all."

I thanked him and pointed at the papers in front of me. "Anything you can tell me about the guys on the list?"

"Not much. Some of them were regulars, but it wasn't my normal shift. Denny quit, and we couldn't find anyone to take his shift. I volunteered to pull a double for the extra cash. The only ones I know on the list—besides Victor— are Christian Freeman and Warren Barone."

"Who's Christian Freeman?"

"A friend of mine. We go way back. Now he's a dancer at Euphoria in West Hollywood—fucking hot, and everyone wants him. Hanging with him increases my property value."

"How often does he come here?"

"If I work the late shift, he sometimes comes to hang out and shit until I get off work."

"Did he know Victor?"

"If he did, they wouldn't have hooked up… if that's what you're asking. Christian is a pretty boy who's into pretty boys. Victor was in his forties."

"What about Warren? How well do you know him?"

"He comes in sometimes. We've talked, but not a lot. Warren and Victor had an open relationship, but Warren must've got it on with guys somewhere else—on the net or a different bathhouse." He shrugged. "Who knows? He may not have hooked up much. Victor was a slut, but I don't think Warren is. That's how it goes in open relationships. One guy wants to fuck around, and the other goes along to make him happy. Eventually shit hits the fan. That's why I avoid relationships—all that fucking baggage, having to worry about someone else, and care what they think, and watch what you say or do. That bullshit's not for me."

As a man who avoids relationships, I understood where
he was coming from. There had been no one special in my
life since leaving the military five years prior. There were
rare moments I'd entertained the idea. The reality was I
didn't want to be in a relationship, even though I felt like I
should want to be in one.

"Is it possible Warren killed Victor?" I asked.

"Possible he wanted to, but not possible he did. He
wasn't here when Victor was killed. It's there on the guest
log. Warren left a half hour before the murder."

"How many security cameras are there?"

He held up two fingers. "One facing the front door and
one facing the cash register. If there were any more, we'd
be out of business. It freaks guys enough that they can't use
an alias when they sign in. Stupid ass law says they have to
use their real name. That's bullshit." He put his feet back
on the desk and tossed a thumb drive on the desk. "There's
a copy of the videos on there."

"Did anyone act strange or look suspicious to you?"

He shrugged again. "They were all shitting themselves
trying to see what was going on. Except for three guys who
got the fuck out of here. I guess they didn't want to be
around when the news cameras showed up."

"You let them leave?"

"I ain't no fucking cop. Wasn't my business to make them stay. The ones that stayed around were held by the cops until they were questioned."

Trent stuck his head in. "Sorry to interrupt, gents, but we're opening soon."

"Can I hold onto him just a few more minutes?" I said. "I haven't seen the laundry room. Mind if I have Seth take me?"

"Sure. But please don't take too long."

I followed Seth back to the laundry room where the police found the knife that was used to kill Victor. The floor was plain gray concrete, except in the back of the room where there was a tiled utility nook with a floor drain. There were three industrial washing machines and dryers. And there were towels. Lots and lots of towels stacked on metal racks with wheels.

"Where was the knife found?" I asked.

"In the middle here." He patted a hand on the top of a pile of towels.

The rack was the one closest to the door. I thumbed through the towels as if the weapon would still be there. I got on my knees to look under the rack and around the baseboards. There was nothing of interest on the white walls. After I paced the room a couple of times, I looked at Seth, and he shrugged.

"Did anything seem out of place to you?"

"No, it's just a laundry room. I didn't even come in here until the cops brought me in after they found the knife."

I paced a couple more times.

"I better get up front before Trent has a coronary," he said. "He's nervous as hell about reopening. I don't think he wants to hear all the questions. Doesn't bother me. I'll tell them it's none of their fucking business."

We returned to the lobby.

Trent raised his arms and announced, "Time to dim the lights and cue up the music."

"Thank you both for your time. We'll be in touch. Good luck today."

"Thanks." Seth put one hand on my shoulder. "By the way, Mitch, stretching my earlobes didn't hurt, but the nose ring stung like hell."

I chuckled and exited as a small group of men entered. The bathhouse was back in business.

Four

My legs shivered from cold despite the thick warm blood rising from the floorboard. I gasped for air, struggling with the seatbelt, as it grew tighter across my chest. My ribs felt like they were collapsing. By the time the blood reached my neck, I was hyperventilating. I lifted my head, refusing to accept my fate as I tasted the fluid on my lips and choked as it drained down my throat. Once all hope seemed lost, the door across from me ripped off its hinges, and the blood rushed from the vehicle.

Jackson reached in his arm to pull me out.

The seatbelt released its grip and fell to the floor. I stretched to grasp his hand. Our fingers nearly touched… when I woke up from the nightmare.

My body and sheets were covered in sweat.

By begging, I convinced Josie to open the store for me, but her car wasn't there when I pulled in at 10:00 a.m.

Frank, the homeless man who sleeps in my doorway, lay there snoring. As usual, I had to wake him to get in the door. I shook his leg a couple of times, gave him a dollar when he sat up, and he took off down the sidewalk with his shopping cart. I unlocked the door as Josie pulled up to the store in her yellow Volkswagen bug.

"Hope you're happy, asshole," she huffed past me. "I told you I needed to be in the office. I'm running out of diseases to lie about. Nat didn't yell, but I could tell he was pissed."

"And here you are. Thank you." As I hugged her, she kept her arms straight and at her sides. "You know I wouldn't ask if I didn't have to. Someone has to run the store."

"It wasn't my idea to quit my job to open this place, asshole." She looked down and started texting. "Why am I here?"

"Eve called this morning. Trent, the club manager who hired her, is on his way with Ernesto Torres. He's the guy who I'm supposed to prove is innocent. Ernesto was released after a forty-eight-hour hold because the DA says the police don't have enough evidence to keep him. I have to question the guy. I promise we'll be done by noon... or should be."

"Well, asshole, how nice you're allowing me to go back to my job for at least half the day."

"You could have told me no, rather than standing here and calling me 'asshole' every five seconds."

"You're right," she said. "But then I wouldn't get to call you an asshole, which I enjoy very much." Her tone was light, but there was still tension in her voice. She was pissed and had a right to be. She gazed out at the parking lot as a red Jeep Wrangler pulled up. "Your client's here." She returned to her texting. Trent stepped out and came inside.

"How's it going?" he asked, as he held out his wrists. "Since the police let Ernesto go, are you ready to cuff me?" He chuckled.

Josie placed a hand to her lips and giggled. She never giggled.

Handcuffs? Interesting. I grinned. "Nope. Not enough evidence on you yet. You're a free man for now. Did you forget Ernesto?"

"His grandma insists they go to church after this. A friend is driving them. They should be here any minute."

Josie's eyes didn't leave Trent. I half expected her to clasp her hands across her breasts and bat her eyes. "My brother failed to introduce us. I'm Josie."

"Hi, Josie. Mitch didn't mention he had such a beautiful sister." He gently shook her hand.

"You're right," I said. "You do flirt with anyone."

"Is that a dig at me?" Josie protested.

"No, just an observation about him."

I walked Trent back to my office, forgetting I hadn't cleaned it. Books, paperwork, and clothes covered the couch. Grabbing items by the handful, I tossed them on top of boxes and my file cabinet. He wrinkled his nose but was polite enough not to say anything. I motioned for him to take a seat.

"I joked about you cuffing me, but it wouldn't be so bad," he said. "Between us, I hate that bathhouse. A life behind bars may be a better option."

"What would you do?"

"I'm a writer. Science fiction."

"I don't think I've ever met a writer before. What have you published?"

He gave a half-hearted smile and bowed his head. "Nothing yet. So far, I've sold a few short stories and have written two novels that no one will publish. I'm working on another one. The bathhouse doesn't pay a ton, but it's enough to pay the bills. I work long hours, but I set my own schedule, so I have time to write. I knew a writer who had two full-time jobs. He was talented, but died before getting a book published. I don't want to be that guy."

"I never would've pictured you as a science fiction writer."

"Oh, really?" He leaned back, crossed his arms, and taunted. "Why not?"

I hesitated. "You don't look like the type. You—"

Trent waved his finger. "Now, now, you're about to list stereotypes, aren't you? Should I have buckteeth, wear a beanie, and live in my mother's basement?"

"Point taken."

"Does it help that I still live in my mother's house?"

"Really?"

"She left it to me when she died four years ago. It was paid off, but a huge chunk of my income goes to pay the property taxes."

I smiled awkwardly. "I hate to change the subject, but I have a question for you before Ernesto gets here. Last night, I watched the surveillance videos Seth gave me. He kept disappearing. Moving off camera."

"He was probably just sitting on the stool at the window into the bathhouse area. That's where guests can exchange towels and get change for the snack machines. Sometimes the guys like to hang out there and talk with him. The camera's pointed at the cash register, so that window is out of view."

"I'm most concerned about the timing, though," I said. "He vanished off camera soon before Victor was found dead. Do you remember him leaving the counter around that time?"

"No, but he lets me know when he's going to the bathroom or somewhere. Anytime he's away from the front desk area, he gives me a heads up so I can cover for him." He brushed a hand aside. "The last person you have to worry about is Seth."

"Hmm."

"I went along to pick Ernesto up," Trent said. "He didn't look good coming out of jail—run-down and tired. He says everyone left him alone, but he couldn't sleep."

"I'm sure he was terrified if he's never been there before."

"He's a good kid, never been in trouble."

We made small talk, and he kept telling his long tales. I didn't mind. He was playful and silly—exactly the type of guy who would normally get on my nerves. But he didn't.

When Ernesto and his grandmother arrived, Josie pointed them toward my office. I stood and shook their hands. They both sat on the couch with Trent.

"Where is your friend?" Trent asked.

"She in the car," Ernesto said. "She wants to hear the radio."

"This is Mitch—he's the one Eve told you she hired to help. He's okay. He's a good guy," Trent reassured him.

"Hello, Ms. Torres," I said.

She smiled and nodded her head. "Hello. I'm Lupe. I know only little English."

I smiled back. "*Yo no hablo español.*"

"*Entiendo.* Uh, I understand."

Seth's use of the term "boy toy" was a good characterization of Ernesto. He wasn't much taller than five feet, with a thin yet toned body. His tight chest muscles were noticeable at the top of his frayed, light blue scrub shirt. His hair, combed high in a bouffant style, was a look I wished hadn't come back.

I allowed Trent to have a brief conversation to calm him down, but Ernesto never stopped rocking back and forth. I ended their talk when Trent went off on one of his never-ending stories.

"Trent, I'd like you and Ms. Torres to step out front," I said. "It'd be easier for me and Ernesto to focus with no distractions."

Trent's eyes widened. "Are you sure?"

I nodded. Trent held out his hand and helped Lupe to her feet. Ernesto spoke to her in Spanish. She stopped, leered at me for a moment, then followed Trent out.

I closed the door. "Ernesto, you may have answered these questions for the police, but you need to repeat them for me."

He ran a hand through his jet-black hair from his forehead down to the nape of his neck. He pouted and lowered his eyes, unable or unwilling to look directly at me. I hit hard right out of the gate to break down any walls.

"Did you kill Victor?"

He jerked his head up, eyes wide, and yelled, "No! No! Why would I do that?"

His grandmother swung the door open. She had a tall frame and towered over me, her brow furrowed, her hands firmly planted on her hips.

Ernesto said, "*Abuela. Abuela. Está bien. Está bien. Por favor.*"

She patted her grandson's shoulder, then turned and grimaced at me, huffed, and stormed out.

"I'm sorry, Ernesto. Because I work for your attorney, I must assume you're innocent, but as an investigator, I had to ask."

Ernesto gazed downward again and muttered, "No. I no killed him."

"Is it true that Victor broke up with you?"

"He had to break up with me. Warren made him."

"Did he tell you that?"

Ernesto wrapped his arms around himself, and his rocking quickened. Barely audible, he hummed to himself. He raised his head and looked at me. Tears leaked from his bloodshot eyes.

"I loved him. I never hurt him. I wasn't even close to the sauna when he was killed."

"Do you know what time Victor went to the sauna?"

He shook his head. "No. I see him leave his room maybe ten minutes before he die." He placed his face in his palms. "If I loves him, why would I kill him?"

"It's called a crime of passion—when you're so angry with someone you love that you kill them."

"Don't talk down to me. My *inglés* may not be good, but I'm no stupid."

His English was fine, but his accent made it hard for me to understand. My initial goal was to aggravate him enough to get him to open up, but asking bluntly if he had killed Victor may have been a bad move. My inexperience in cases like this was showing. Ernesto covered his ears with his hands and shook his head. I decided to back off, hoping it wasn't too late to get him to trust me.

I leaned back. "I'm sorry this is hard. Trent said you and Victor were very close. I'm sorry for your loss. Where were you when they found his body?"

"In laundry room. I was there most of the night. The earlier crew left all the dirty bedding for me. They think because I work third shift, I don't do nothing."

"I'm sure that sucks." I smiled. "Did anyone see you in there? In the laundry room?"

"*No sé.* I don't know. I was busy loading sheets in the washers and dryers. The door was open, so anybody could see me, but I didn't see no one."

"Can you think of anyone who might have wanted Victor dead?"

"No. Everybody loved Victor." He paused. "Except Warren."

"Why Warren?"

"They didn't get along so good. Victor loved me. He was going to leave Warren." More tears rolled down his face, and his hands trembled. "Warren is no good. He made Victor sad. That's why Victor want to leave him for me."

"Do you know anyone else who would want to kill Victor?"

"You already ask that."

"I'm sorry to ask again."

He trembled more with each question. "I said no."

"I understand it's hard to talk about this, but I'm trying to help you. When I asked who would want to kill Victor, you said Warren didn't love Victor. Did you know Warren wasn't in the club when Victor was murdered?"

"*Sí.*"

"Of course that means Warren couldn't kill him." I paused. "I'm going to ask again because I want you to think about it. Who do you think might want to kill Victor?"

"I don't know. I don't know."

He pounded one fist on the arm of the couch and clutched the side of his leg with the other. As I opened my mouth to speak, Ernesto jumped to his feet and walked to the door. Instead of leaving, he turned and paced back and forth in front of me. When he stopped, he raised his head and looked at me with pouted lips, then plopped himself on the couch.

I drew a heavy sigh and said, "Of course you don't."

"You are like Eve. She *no es agradable tampoco.*"

I shook my head. "I don't understand."

"She is not nice either. If Trent hire you to defend me, don't you have to be nice to me?"

"You've gone through a lot, so I'm trying to be easy on you, but you don't need nice. You need someone who can get the police off your back."

He nodded, then raised his head and snorted two times. There was no point in questioning him further. Like Seth had warned me, Ernesto was high strung. And I had blown my opportunity by pushing too hard.

"I'll have more questions for you," I said. "Right now, I think it's best to let you go get some rest."

I opened the door and walked Trent, Ernesto, and Lupe outside. They said their goodbyes, and Ernesto and his grandmother drove off with her friend. Trent folded his arms and sat on the hood of my car.

"We heard everything. You were tough on him."

"How old are you, Trent?"

"Twenty-five. Why?"

"I knew you weren't much older than Ernesto, and I thought it was strange you call him a kid. Now I get it."

"Yeah, he is a kid. He had it rough growing up. His father was nonexistent, and his mom died when he was young. His grandma raised him all alone. She struggled to earn enough to feed two people. He's emotionally stunted. You just saw it in action."

We stood smiling at each other, but neither said a word. I debated inviting Trent to lunch, but I had to let Josie get to her job. We shook hands, and he drove off. It was for the best.

Five

I swung by Subway on my way to lift weights. As I sat in the gym parking lot eating a foot-long roast beef sandwich, I thought to myself that I shouldn't be sitting in the gym parking lot eating a foot-long roast beef sandwich. After scarfing down the sub, I belched a few times... which hurt my bloated stomach. At thirty years old, not working out was starting to show. I had accepted I wouldn't see my perfectly tight abs again, but I still wanted to get rid of the little pooch belly before it got out of hand. Exhausted, I dozed off in the car until 9:00 p.m. Too late for a workout, but the perfect time to hit the clubs.

Because they had alibis, I had already scratched off four bathhouse customers from the suspect list. They were all together having sex in the playroom at the time of the murder.

Christian Freeman wasn't high on my list of suspects, but I knew where to find him and every name on the guest list from Sunday night was worth a second look.

Trance music, which I hate, blared into the streets from the club. Since I hadn't been dancing in West Hollywood since college, walking into Euphoria was surreal. The faces were different, but nothing had changed.

The bartender yelled over the music, "What can I get for you?"

"A Rolling Rock," I yelled back. I gave him my credit card and told him I'd run a tab.

Near the bar was a platform where a go-go boy was dancing. He was young, scrawny, and pasty white, with a red mohawk. The crowd paid no attention, and he frowned. I made a mental note to tip him on my way out.

Further back in the bar, another dancer dominated the crowd's attention. I recognized his rich, dark, perfectly defined body from Club Silver Lake's security videos. What got him the most attention was what he was packing below. His thong had to have been custom-made. It wasn't possible for him to fit into something off the shelf.

"Is that Christian?" I yelled at the bartender.

"If you're asking, you must be from out of town or you don't get out much," he hollered back.

"Touché," I replied. "What's his usual?"

"A tequila shot with a Corona chaser."

"Set them up for me for his next break," I said, thinking it might be necessary to loosen him up before questioning.

I grabbed the three drinks—his tequila and chaser, and my beer—and moved to a table near Christian. He rolled his magnificent stomach, then turned and shook his bubble butt at the crowd. Cheers drowned out the music as he played with his honey-colored thong—pulling it down just enough to throw them into a frenzy, then raising it again to groans of disappointment. His face was rugged yet boyish with a wide smile and deep dimples. The bucks were flying.

Christian stepped off the platform as I downed the last of my beer. I grabbed his drinks and rushed behind him, through the rows of sweaty men, to the back of the bar. I was too slow. He entered his dressing room before I could catch him.

I knocked.

The door opened. "What?"

"I ordered these for you."

He took the tequila shot from my hand and downed it, then grabbed the beer. "Thanks," he snapped and closed the door.

I knocked again.

The door flew open. "Thanks for the drinks," he shouted, "but I'm on break and need my space."

I held out my hand to shake. "Hi, Christian. I'm Mitch O'Reilly. I——"

I narrowly escaped him cutting off my hand as he slammed the door shut.

I was shocked that he actually opened the door when I knocked again, and I stuck out my foot so he couldn't slam it again. "Not to disappoint you, but I'm not here as a fan. I'm the private investigator hired to look into Victor Verboom's murder."

He took the business card I held out and tossed it to the floor. The room was nothing more than a closet with a single wooden chair and a bookcase stacked with clothing.

"What do you want?"

"You were at Club Silver Lake the night he was murdered."

"Yeah. What of it?" His voice was smoky.

"I'm meeting with all the suspects."

He turned his head quickly. "I'm a suspect?"

"You were there, weren't you?"

"Uh, yes." He looked back and forth through the club and took a step back. "I'll put some clothes on, and we'll go to my car. Meet me out front."

I wasn't on the sidewalk long before he trotted out wearing jeans and a white tank top. He motioned for me to follow him to a light blue Mustang. It looked new. "When I can't get any peace in there, I come out here on my breaks."

"Nice car. Not a bad ride for a nightclub dancer. You must do pretty well on that platform."

"Screw the car. What do you want?"

"I just have a few questions for you." I pulled out my notepad. "Records show you signed in at the bathhouse at 2:24 a.m. and left around 6:15 a.m. Most of the men left earlier. Why did you hang around so long after the body was found?"

"I was one of the first guys the cops talked to, but I was waiting for my friend Seth to get off work. He was the last to leave."

"How well did you know the victim?"

"He hit on me a few times, but I didn't know him. He practically lived at the bathhouse, so I'd seen him around."

"How long had you known him?"

He turned to look directly at me. His eyes were fierce. "Do you not listen? I already said I didn't know him." He got defensive fast… to think I had almost put off talking to him.

"Fine, you didn't 'know' him. When did you first meet him?"

"When I started hanging out at the bathhouse with Seth, I became aware of him, but I never 'met' him."

"What was your relationship with him?"

"Relationship?" He rolled his eyes. "There was no relationship. Look at me. Do you think I need to hook up with some old man? He looked good for his age and all, but I ain't into all that daddy shit."

"Old man? He was only in his forties."

"Whatever."

"Listen, you can define 'relationship' and 'met' and 'knew' however you want, but at the very least, I know you spoke with him. Witnesses saw you arguing with him in the bathhouse that night."

Christian mumbled, "There was no argument. He grabbed at me, and I told him it better be the last time."

"The last time or what?" I prodded.

He slammed his hand on the steering wheel. "It's just an expression. He wouldn't stop grabbing my dick, so I told him to cut it out."

"Did you ever see Victor outside of Club Silver Lake?"

"Only in the parking lot getting in or out of his car."

I sat and stared at him—not for the view, which was damn fine, but to keep him on edge. He squirmed and blinked repeatedly as perspiration streamed into his eyes.

"Quit eyeing me or I'll demand a tip. Look, I already told the cops. I saw nothing that night because I didn't come out of my room."

"If you didn't come out of your room, how did Victor grab your dick?"

"You seem to know everything," he said. "Look at your notes. Does it tell you in there I went and took a piss?"

"What time?"

"If I need to take a piss, I take a piss. No reason to check the clock to make sure the time is right."

"Did you want to get laid that night?"

"No, trust me. If I'd wanted to, I would have. I wasn't desperate. There's not much to choose from that late." He pointed at his chest. "I have the luxury of being picky, you know."

"Of course," I fought rolling my eyes. "If you weren't having sex, why were you in a room?"

"Stop playing with me. If you talked to Seth, you know we hang out when he gets off work. He gives me a room to lie down, maybe take a nap until he's ready to go. If I'm horny enough, I come out to get laid, but not often."

"Is there anyone who can vouch that you stayed in your room?"

The horn blew when he threw his fist down, hitting the center of the steering wheel. "How can someone vouch that I was alone?" He shook his head.

"Sometimes Seth leaves the front desk. Did he come to your room that night?"

He grimaced and rolled his head. "Seth is my friend. The thought of screwing him is disgusting. Some friends with benefits ain't a bad thing, but there's certain friends—close friends—you don't cross that line with. Besides, you've seen him. Do you really think he's my type?"

"I didn't ask if you had sex. I asked if he came to your room. I was hoping you would come up with something that'd take you off the list of suspects."

Lowering his head to the wheel, he grasped it as if to rip it out. "I'm still a suspect?"

"Everyone's a suspect… until they're not."

"That's crazy. I got to get back inside. How do I get off being a suspect?"

"Either confess," I paused for effect, "or wait until we catch the right guy."

"I've got nothing to confess."

"Then you don't need to worry."

I got out of the car and walked away—no goodbye, no looking back. He was on the defensive, and I intended to keep it that way.

◆◆◆

It had been a stressful few days, and I needed relief. I'd been running high on the horniness scale since meeting with Christian. He was one of those rare exceptions where a smug attitude didn't detract from his sexiness.

I logged onto some porn and tried to take matters into my own hands, but it wasn't happening. Cumming alone wouldn't cut it. I needed another body to service and be serviced.

No one stood out as I debated who to call. Each person who came to mind bored me. I wanted someone new, so I logged into studs4studs.com. As usual, there were some good options, but I'd scroll past each opportunity to see if someone better would log on. By midnight, I'd been reading profiles for over ninety minutes. The internet's a dangerous place for time management.

Someone finally caught my eye as I was getting ready to log off. It was rare for me to see an unfamiliar face that I was interested in.

The man's name was Giovanni. Italian. I wasn't sure I'd ever done an Italian guy before. He was forty-five, tan, with rich, dark eyes and curly salt-and-pepper hair. He didn't have any dick shots, but the rest of his body wasn't bad at all.

I was typing to greet him when he beat me to it.

"*Ciao.*"

My fingers were on the keyboard to respond when another message popped up.

"What are you into?"

Straight and to the point with no unnecessary conversation.

At 2:00 a.m. I told Giovanni it was time to leave. Before stepping out, he turned and leaned in to kiss me.

I placed a hand on his chest. "Thanks, but you need to go. I need sleep."

He put his hands on my shoulders and kissed each of my cheeks too quickly for me to protest. Once he was gone, I closed the door and went straight to bed.

Six

Beneath the white canopy, white folding chairs were marked off with white pylons, tied together with white rope. White blossoms hung from each pylon. A white lattice archway sheltered the minister. Victor Verboom's service on the beach looked more like a wedding than a funeral.

My intention had been to arrive early in order to case the place and discreetly ask a question or two. I'd forgotten to account for the construction on Santa Monica Boulevard, even though it had been going on for years. Although I was fifteen minutes late, the service hadn't started.

I grabbed a sugar cookie off the snack table and took a seat in the back row. The cool and gusty morning had been a welcome change, but by noon the sweltering heat and humidity were back. I loosened my tie and undid the top buttons of my shirt in a futile attempt to gain comfort. Like most of the crowd, I fanned myself with the memorial program.

The minister's old microphone and portable speaker garbled her words, making her almost unintelligible. Combined with the thunder of the waves behind her, I couldn't understand a thing.

Her violet hair was pinned up in a bun, with loose strands fluttering around her forehead. She grabbed the podium several times in what looked like an attempt to keep from falling down. I guessed it was heat exhaustion due to her thick, oversized black robe. I was certain the heavy rainbow stole around her neck didn't help.

"It is fitting we gather here today, upon this shore, to honor the passing of a loved one—a man who loved the sand, the sea, and the sunsets."

If he was so into sunsets, why time the service under the highest sun? Likely because the minister had many more bodies to stand over, I figured. They make a bundle off funerals. Weddings too.

Scriptwriting had earned Victor a fine reputation and the admiration of the Hollywood muckety-mucks. It was a small ceremony, but attendees included a mix of actors that even I recognized. Most of the crowd wore Hawaiian shirts, apparently Victor's preferred style. I stuck out with my black slacks, dress shirt, and maroon tie. Had I known the dress code, I would've worn sandals. My loafers were filled with sand.

It took a few minutes for me to realize Victor was in the white ceramic jar up at the front. I had been too distracted by his partner, Warren Barone, to notice. Warren's sobs made it even more challenging to understand the minister. A ginger bear, his red hair and beard framed a round, pink, freckled face.

The minister had never met Victor. It was obvious from her hesitation and vague stories. I figured she probably had a quickie checklist of questions to ask family members before the service:

What were his hobbies? Check.
What made him laugh? Check.
What were his favorite Bible verses? Check.
What was his name again?

She did a decent job of summarizing his life. I learned a few things that hadn't been listed on Victor's Wikipedia bio, including that he first studied air conditioning and refrigeration repair after graduating high school in Barstow, California. Once he had earned his certification, he changed direction and moved to LA with dreams of writing instead. He became an avid surfer, hitting the waves every morning. The man survived five years of near starvation as a struggling artist. He was making arrangements to move back to Barstow when he got the call that he had sold his first script.

After twenty minutes of dancing her way through the memorial, the moment I had been dreading arrived.

"Is there anyone who would care to say a few words about the deceased?" the minister asked. This was the part of the service where I usually left, but I had to stay in case someone shared relevant information.

Warren held back his tears for a moment, took a heavy breath, and stepped forward. Just then, the snack table was overrun by seagulls. Several mourners jumped up and flapped their programs to shoo them away. One older—yet still muscular—actor picked up his chair and waved it at the birds, spraying sand from the chair's legs into my hair… and the hair of everyone else sitting in the back rows. It ruined the food he was trying to save. The gulls backed off, defeated, but stood squawking a few feet away. The actor's name escaped me. He was an "oh-yeah-that-guy" celebrity.

After the bird attack, Warren mopped the perspiration from his head with a handkerchief and proceeded to the front. His Tommy Bahama shirt was pressed and well fitting on his tall, heavyset body.

"Victor—" he started, having reached the makeshift pulpit, but he blubbered and couldn't go on. A friend escorted him back to his seat.

After Warren's failed attempt, several people Victor had worked with over the years came marching up, one after another, each saying the same thing. Those who spoke the longest had the least to say. Forty minutes passed, and judging by how often the minister checked her watch, her time was running out. There was a lull when no one walked to the front to speak. Assuming that portion of the service was finally done, she started for the podium, ready to wrap things up.

Instead, a young woman walked forward, her mid-length sandy blonde hair lashing at her face. She wore a tight black dress with shoulder straps. Apparently, she hadn't gotten the Hawaiian shirt memo either. She cleared her throat before speaking.

"Um. Hello." She blushed and lowered her head. "Good afternoon. I'm Heather Verboom. Thank you for being here for my father—"

She paused and allowed the gasps and chatter to quiet down. She stunned the crowd. Even Warren Barone stopped crying and sat with his mouth open. There was murmuring, and it became apparent that it was a surprise to everyone that Victor had a daughter. When the voices died down, Heather continued talking. She said that although she wasn't raised by her dad, she still loved him and was thankful for the years they had spent together. She spoke for more than five minutes.

When the mystery daughter stepped away, the minister rose again, but Warren waved her back. When he reached the podium for a second try, he clasped his hands behind his back, froze, and cried again. Two men linked their arms with his and escorted him down the beach. The service swiftly ended with a "blessed be," and the minister stumbled across the sand toward the parking lot, dropping her portable speaker along the way. On her way to a wedding or another funeral, no doubt.

The small crowd broke into smaller groups, discussing how wonderful Victor had been. His daughter was left to mourn alone, except for a scrawny young man with waist-length chestnut brown hair. He wore a gray and a white shirt frayed at the cuffs and collar. He had removed his black tie and draped it over his shoulder.

"Good afternoon, Ms. Verboom," I said as we shook hands. "I'm sorry to meet you on such a somber occasion. My sincere condolences. I'm Mitch O'Reilly." She stood mute while she looked over the business card I gave her.

"Um… uh. Thank you. Please, call me Heather. Ms. Verboom makes me sound old. This is my fiancé, Kelvin Daniels."

He looked my way and nodded. The wind blew Heather's hair across Kelvin's face, and it kept getting caught behind his glasses. The concept of standing upwind from her was beyond him.

"Were you a friend of my father?"

"He sounds like a great guy, but I never met him. I've been hired to investigate his murder."

Heather wrapped an arm around Kelvin. "Oh my. The thought of how awful it must have been during his final moments makes me ill. Didn't they catch the killer? Ernesto something-or-other? I heard they let him go free. I don't understand."

"The police deemed him 'a person of interest,' but there wasn't sufficient evidence to charge him. I want to make sure they catch the right guy and are able to build a solid case against whoever did it."

"I see." Her speech became short and rapid. "I hope they get whoever did it. I have chills knowing he's still out there."

"Can we schedule some time to meet tomorrow? I don't want to intrude any more today than I already have, but I do want to talk soon. You might have information that could help crack the case."

"We can't," Kelvin butted in. "We're leaving right after this to go home to Riverside. I want to beat traffic."

"There's never a good time to beat traffic in LA." I smiled. They offered blank stares in return. I cleared my throat. "It's important for us to talk. Can we meet before you leave?"

Heather looked at Kelvin. He shrugged.

"That'd be okay, I think. Kelvin wants to walk to the pier before we leave. He's never seen it."

"There's a nice little coffee shop around the corner. Would an hour give you enough time?"

Heather looked at Kelvin again. "That should be enough."

I gave them the name of the coffee shop, then grabbed a bottle of water and roamed around, hoping to hear something useful.

The group thinned soon enough, and Warren returned to the canopy. His flushed face dripped with sweat, and he gasped for air. He wiped his eyes and brow before reaching out to shake my hand.

"I don't believe we've met. Did you work with Victor?"

I stood, grinning like a fool, while I debated whether to bring up the investigation. "Mr. Barone. I am so sorry to hold you up at this difficult time. Can we talk for a minute?"

He puffed several times and wheezed as he spoke. "Thank you for coming to Victor's service. He had so many friends. I appreciate you being here."

"Mr. Barone, I need to speak to you about Victor." I bit my lip, knowing that what I was about to say wouldn't be well received. "I'd like to discuss how he died."

"Are you a reporter?" He gave me no chance to respond. "My God. Have you no ethics? This is a memorial service."

"No, sir. I apologize for not introducing myself. I'm a private investigator looking into Victor's death."

"You're the one who keeps calling me?"

"I have tried to reach you several times, yes."

Warren lunged forward but was held back by two friends who linked their elbows with his. "There's nothing to investigate. That little slut, Ernesto, killed Vic. End of story. They'll find enough evidence soon enough. If you call me again, I'll have the police arrest you for harassment." He turned away and nodded toward the street. "I want out of here."

It would take a lot to get him to open up after that blunder.

As I was leaving, a woman approached from behind, whispered my name, and placed her hand on the back of my arm.

"Excuse me. I could not clearly hear you, but believe you told Warren you are a detective. Am I correct?"

She was tall, slender, and pale. She wore white pants, a blue and white striped mariner shirt, and a white sailor hat pinned cockeyed on her head. Her gray hair was in a shoulder-length bob with bangs cropped at her eyebrows.

"I am Pam Hernandez, Victor's sister." Her lipstick matched her blood red ascot. I wasn't sure if she was trying to be cute or had bad taste. It took an effort to squelch a laugh.

She gestured to the broad-shouldered man standing next to her. "This is my husband, Rodrigo."

He extended his hand and gave a firm, painful shake. We nodded at each other and said, "How's it going?"—the noncommittal greeting men give each other. He had a baritone voice that was hot and sexy.

"Call me Rod," he said.

Rod seemed familiar and looked uneasy as I eyed him longer than necessary. His weathered face was softened by a neatly trimmed goatee that framed his wide cheekbones and deep dimples.

"We noticed Warren cursing at you, so I have been waiting to speak with you," she said. "I do not know how much help I can be, but I would love to discuss putting him behind bars."

"'Him' who? Warren?" Something about the way she spoke irritated me, but I couldn't put a finger on it.

"Yes. For twenty years, I have not been able to stand that man. He has always been a gold digger, and now that they are older, he decided to get Victor out of the picture." A single tear rolled down her cheek. She dabbed it with a tissue. "May I ask who you are working for?"

"The attorney representing Ernesto Torres."

"He thinks it was Warren, too?"

"No, that's not what I said. *She* doesn't know who murdered your brother, but—and this is just between us— the club manager doesn't think it was Ernesto. That's why he hired her."

"I agree. It was not this Ernesto fellow. It was Warren. You can be sure of that. Did you see what a spectacle he made of himself? He did a fine acting job but did not fool us. Did he, Rodrigo?"

Rod chuckled nervously. "No, he didn't. The mortgage on Victor's Hollywood Hills home was paid off, and there's no telling how much his life insurance was worth. Now it's going to Warren."

"We do not know that," Pam corrected him. "Some may go to Heather." She grimaced. "Lord knows my darling niece could use it, but I fear what will happen when her Kelvin gets his hands on it. He will fritter it away on drugs and alcohol."

"He has a problem?"

"He certainly seems the type. We tried to speak with her earlier, but he dragged her away after we said 'hello.' He acts as if someone will steal her." Pam eyed the invisible watch on her wrist and grasped my arm. "Oh dear. We really must run. I would love to invite you to dinner at our home on Wednesday so we may speak further."

"Wednesday works for me. But are you sure you don't have time to discuss this sooner? This is about your brother's murder. A lot can happen in four days."

"We are busy with previous commitments. I am sure you understand. Is 6:30 good for you?"

"6:30 works." Her brother had just died. I didn't understand.

It was only after I shook Rod's hand that I remembered why he looked familiar. He had been in the bathhouse security video. I should have caught the last name. He checked in under the first name Gustavo--the name of the man Seth Snider said had a fight with Victor at Club Silver Lake. It looked like dinner on Wednesday was going to be interesting.

Seven

Whistles and catcalls greeted me as I approached my car in the parking lot above the beach. I was going to drop off my tie and switch my sand filled loafers for a pair of tennis shoes. I ignored them until someone called my name. Trent Nakos pulled up beside me in his Jeep. The top was down, and Ernesto sat in the passenger seat.

Trent beamed with his toothy grin, looking very Californian under the blazing sun with the wind in his thick brown hair.

"Can't you tell when a guy is whistling at you?" he laughed.

"I'm flattered."

Ernesto looked as if he was trying to hide from the world. His baggy black jeans and oversized t-shirt swallowed his body. He pulled a Dodgers cap low over his brows. He wouldn't make eye contact.

"Are you out for a day at the beach, or is this not a coincidence?"

"He thought he wouldn't be welcome at the funeral, but wanted to see it," Trent said. "We watched what we could from up here. It wasn't much. We saw Warren get escorted down the beach away from the service and later try to rip your head off."

"Emotions are high at times like these."

Ernesto wiped his eyes, raised his head, and glanced at me. "You see what I say? Warren *es peligroso*. He no should be on the streets for killing Victor."

"*Peligroso?*"

"He's dangerous," Trent said. "Ernesto says he's dangerous."

"*Sí.*"

"We're heading for lunch. Care to join us?"

"I'd love to, but not this time."

"Oh, come on. You may learn something about the case. Right, Ernesto?"

"*Sí.*"

"I have an appointment in a few minutes."

"Your loss!"

As I stood alone, watching them drive off, I agreed it was.

The coffee shop bustled. The only table we could grab was next to the pickup counter, steps away from the hall leading to the bathrooms. It offered no privacy but was better than standing.

Bob! Your large iced coffee!

"You have questions for us?" Heather said.

"Since you have a time crunch, I'll make this fast." I took a sip of my coffee. "Everyone seemed shocked when you spoke at the funeral."

"Well, my dad wasn't part of my life. He moved here to LA the year I was born, and I never saw him. Most of his friends and colleagues didn't know about me. Obviously…"

"When did he become—"

A woman bumped into me, causing me to spill coffee on Kelvin's shirt.

"Asswipe!" he wailed. Saying nothing more, he stormed off to the bathroom. Once he was out of sight, Heather stretched her neck and rolled her head.

"When did you find out your father died?"

"My Aunt Pam called me Monday morning." Tears streamed down her cheeks. "My dad and I were just getting close. I called him a couple of years ago and asked if we could meet."

"Why did you decide to reach out?"

Sara! Small nonfat mocha latte!

"Why'd you call him?" I asked again.

"I never gave it much thought until Mom died. I wanted to be part of a family again. He said he was grateful I called."

The crowd grew. A man and a little girl stood with their hands on the counter at the pickup area. The two of them would shuffle and mumble whenever someone reached around them to grab their drinks, feeling entitled to the space. Three teenage girls chatted and laughed loud enough to fill the whole shop. Two college-aged men and a woman in her sixties stared into their cell phones, oblivious to the world around them. Another man, bald, with a bushy mustache, and dressed in a three-piece suit, bellowed into his phone about a difficult employee, revealing details of the troublemaker's personnel files.

"You said you and your father were just getting close. How long did it take to develop that relationship?"

Kelvin came back, holding out the front of his shirt. "Green donkey dicks. It's stained for good."

I ignored his problem and continued talking with Heather. "I asked how you and your father became close."

"The first year it felt kind of weird anytime we'd get together. But then this past year was better. We bonded, you know. I'm blessed he was in my life. It's hard to

believe we finally built a relationship, and now he's gone."
She planted her face in her palms. Kelvin rolled his eyes.

"Kelvin, did you know Mr. Verboom?"

"Yes."

"Did you have a good relationship? Did you know him
well?"

He huffed.

"Yes, and yes."

"How long have you and Heather been together? When
did you get engaged?"

"Together—three years. Engaged—six months."

"Not much of a talker, are you?"

"No." He kept looking over his shoulder.

"You seem nervous."

"I don't want any more dunder-fucking drinks spilled on
me."

Marcie! Cinnamon spice latte!

"Heather, how well do you know Warren?"

"Oh, we never met him. They were together for a long
time, but Dad said they didn't get along. He told me they
were breaking up and didn't want to get me involved.
Warren didn't even know about me. Well, I guess he did,
but he didn't know I was coming to see Dad."

A man wearing khaki shorts and a Greenpeace shirt towered over us, waiting in line for the bathroom. A little girl rushing to get her blended drink knocked him off balance. He fell into the back of Kelvin's head, which caused Kelvin's iced tea to fall on his lap.

"What is wrong with you, butt-munch?" he grumbled.

Heather shuddered and shielded her eyes with her hands. Kelvin glared at her, tearing past the Greenpeace man to the bathroom. I fumbled with my coffee sleeve while waiting for her to regain her composure.

"What did your father say about Warren or any of his friends?"

"Not much, you know. He made sure Warren and I were never in the same place at the same time. He never said why other than they weren't happy together. He said Warren had gotten hard to live with."

Kelvin gave a loud sigh, screaming for acknowledgment that he'd returned, and plopped his ass back in his seat. The paper towels did little to dry his pants.

"How often did you see your father?" I asked.

"Once a month or so." She turned toward Kelvin for confirmation, and he shrugged. "Sometimes more. He'd drive out to see us, or we'd drive here. He took us to Chinatown maybe a month ago. Not a good visit."

"Why not?"

Kelvin jumped in. "Because he pissed me off. He got on my case about my job. The jackoff said I'm not good enough for his daughter. Right to my face."

"The mystery is over," I said. "The man can speak a complete sentence."

"Fuck you, ass-biter."

Lucy! Large cappuccino!

"Where do you work?"

"At a Speedster Mart." He looked around some more. "It's too crowded here. This is chaos."

"Heather, what else would you do when you were in town?"

"All sorts of things. We ate out every meal. He took us whale watching, horseback riding near the Hollywood sign. We went to Broadway shows, and concerts at the Hollywood Bowl. Why? I don't understand what this—"

Kelvin tapped his wrist. Heather started, "Mr. O'Reilly, we—"

Jonathon! Small vanilla latte!

"Where were you at 3:00 a.m. on Monday?" I said.

"Let's go," Kelvin said. "This is getting ridiculous."

"What's ridiculous?" I asked.

"You're interrogating us, treating us like we did it." He scanned the crowd, leaned toward me, and said, "Why would we be in a bathhouse? She's a woman, and I'm no fag."

I wanted to kick the bastard's teeth in, but that wouldn't have helped the case any. I couldn't let my personal feelings get in the way with Kelvin. He wasn't in the club's surveillance videos, and his name wasn't on the guest log, but I still didn't trust him.

"Are you willing to answer the question? Where were you at 3:00 a.m. Monday?"

"In bed," Heather answered.

"Was Kelvin with you?"

He waved a fist. "You bet your sweet ass." He stood and pulled his keys out of his pocket. "Let's go. We're done."

"Okay." She looked at me.

Maxwell! Green tea smoothie!

"Did you ever go to your father's house?"

"Only once, when Warren was out town… two or three months ago. Dad's place is nice, but we were afraid to touch anything. It's too froufrou. We didn't want to sit because everything looked expensive."

Kelvin tapped his leg with his keys.

"Where was Warren?"

"Dad never said."

"So, you never met him?"

"Uh—"

"She already said no. Come on." He grabbed her arm.

"We've never even seen him except for in photos, Mr. O'Reilly."

Kelvin took Heather's elbow and pulled her.

"Thank you again for trying to find who's guilty," she managed to add before he dragged her out the door.

"I'll do the best I can," I said to no one in particular.

Eight

Eye Spy Supplies reflected my aversion to cleaning, and while Josie was great with customers, she was no help when it came to keeping the store tidy. I spent most of the morning between customers getting the place in shape. As usual, that gave me plenty of opportunity to touch up.

The smears and smudges on the glass display cases hadn't seen a cleaning cloth in weeks. I'd bought them from a jeweler's going out of business sale. The black frame with brass trim complemented the ancient oak wood paneling on the walls.

Since the funeral, I had tried reaching Warren Barone, Victor Verboom's partner, several times by phone. He never returned my calls. I paused between cleaning and helping customers to call him twice, and each time the line went silent without ever ringing.

Some browsers dropped in—mostly teenagers who laughed at seeing themselves on a monitor from a camera hidden inside a teddy bear. It was a hit for giggles but had yet to help line the cash drawer. The only thing they gave me was a headache, so after thirty minutes I chased their asses away.

I made three sales.

A mom bought computer monitoring software to keep her children from watching porn. Her rigid posture and lack of expression made me sympathize with the kids. It was likely the net was the only sex education they got.

A couple came in that had a problem with a neighbor kid vandalizing their yard. They bought two plastic rocks with hidden cameras to catch the little bastard. That was my biggest sale of the day.

My last customer, a chubby guy, wore a tweed jacket far too heavy for the hottest part of the afternoon.

"I've been so good to her. I treat her like a queen, and she deserves it." Scraps of tissue stuck in his scruff as he dabbed at the spittle on his cheeks and chin. "She is a queen, but all she does is break my heart. Over and over again."

"I understand," I said, trying to appear sympathetic.

The shirttails of his oversized gray shirt pulled out each time he tried stuffing them back into his stained powder blue slacks. "I don't want to track her. I really don't, because I'm not the sneaky type. I'm trusting. I am, but she's left me no choice and I hate it."

"I understand."

The bell on the front door jingled, and a man walked in wearing a camel-colored suit coat. His head of thick, coarse

caramel hair was trimmed and combed to one side. When I
tried stopping Mr. Spittle to greet him, the newcomer
pursed his lips and gave the okay sign. Anyone could spot
him as a cop. My experience as a detective was
unnecessary.

"I'm so angry. I'm so mad," Mr. Spittle continued. "It's
like she doesn't see how much I love her." He bowed his
head. "Or, she doesn't care."

"I understand."

"Thank God someone does." He placed his clammy
palm in mine and shook my hand.

The police officer stepped to a display case on the
opposite side of the store and scrutinized the pepper spray
and stun guns.

"Sorry to take so much of your afternoon. You have
another customer." He turned to the officer. "I won't be
long. I'm wrapping up now."

He asked to go over the GPS trackers for the third time.
Had I offered life advice, I would have said to dump his
girlfriend. She couldn't deserve what he must have been
putting her through, but I kept my mouth shut. I made my
money selling products, not supplying therapy. My advice
was limited to the best model to buy.

After painstaking consideration, he chose the Eavesdropper 222. It was my cheapest model, so I encouraged him to buy a voice-activated hidden recorder too. He promised he'd come back, and I believed him.

As soon as the anxious Mr. Spittle stepped outside, the other guy introduced himself. My instincts were right.

"Mr. O'Reilly, I'm Detective Dirk Turner with LAPD. I'm the investigator assigned to the Verboom murder. We need to talk." His voice was flat, and he stood straight and rigid, a scowl on his face.

"Hello, Detective. It's a surprise to see you. Should we go in my office?"

"That's unnecessary. This won't take long." Each time he shut his mouth, his bushy mustache curled between his lips as if he were eating the hair off his face. "This isn't a social visit. Our department got a call from Mr. Verboom's partner, Warren Barone. Typically, I wouldn't be tasked with talking to you about it, but since there's been lots of press over this incident, here I am."

"The media thrive on lascivious stories like pretty Latin boys murdering Hollywood bigwigs," I said. "The killing having been in a bathhouse is a reporter's wet dream."

"Mr. Barone wants to file a harassment charge against you. You approached the grieving man at his partner's memorial service?"

I nodded.

"It was a tasteless move, and he wasn't pleased with it. That, or the repeated messages you've left."

"Sir, at the risk of being out of line, I haven't badgered him. The memorial was bad judgment. And yes, I've called him once or twice a day since then, but that doesn't qualify as harassment in my book."

Detective Turner shrugged his shoulders and tugged on the knot in his tie. "Of course you're right, which is why I'm here. I'm not going to bust your chops, just to ask you to back off. We told him there wasn't enough for him to charge you, so consider this more of a courtesy call. The man has anger issues. He gets riled, and the walls go up. That makes my job harder. As a professional, I hope you'll let the dust settle so we can both do what we need to do."

"I appreciate your candor and your patience." I stepped in the back, grabbed two bottles of water, and handed him one. "It's my responsibility to talk with him, though, and he's my prime suspect."

He crossed his arms. "Oh? Care to share something, Mr. O'Reilly? He wasn't there, but if you've got anything that implicates him, you know that you're obligated to tell me."

"Sir, I know the law, and I'm no fool. A spouse is usually the number one suspect is all. Plus, the guy has serious financial problems, and a lot to gain from Victor's death."

Detective Turner tilted back and took several big gulps of water. He leaned back so far I expected his five-and-a-half-foot body to hit the floor. He gasped when he pulled the bottle from his mouth.

"As long as you're here," I said, "any more information you can give about the case?"

"We agree Mr. Barone is a suspect, but only because he has much to gain. It seems unlikely. You should know your client is still the target of our investigation. All things point to Mr. Torres, but he's free until we have solid evidence. He had both motive and access to the victim. Plus, they found the weapon in the laundry room where he works most of the night. It's all circumstantial though."

"Anything on the knife?"

"No time yet to get DNA results back, but I don't expect they'll show anything. The killer wore gloves." He polished off his water and tossed it across the counter into the trash.

"Not surprisingly, there were dozens of fingerprints in the laundry, which all the employees go into for one thing or another."

"What about the surgical gloves they wear when cleaning?"

"The trash was full of them, but none had traces of blood. Forensics checked, and so far only a few have prints. They belonged to Mr. Torres, of course, and a couple of other room attendants who weren't working that night. There are a few other leads and tests we're running, but nothing I can share. Got another water back there?"

When I reached in my mini fridge and discovered only one bottle, I rolled my eyes. I was lucky he was looking out the window.

"Mr. O'Reilly, do you have anything for me?"

I thought about it. I didn't have much to tell him, other than who looked suspicious and why. Things I was sure Detective Turner had already established in the first hours of his investigation.

The sauna where Victor was murdered had been accessible to all eleven men there at the time. It would have taken mere seconds to stuff a knife between towels in a laundry room with an open door.

Among those in the bathhouse at the time, Ernesto and Rod both knew the victim, and both had arguments with him minutes before the murder. Christian said he didn't know Victor, but they had argued too.

My last suspect was Seth Snider. He knew the place as well as Ernesto, and his only alibi was Trent, who was in his office. The video couldn't substantiate Seth's movements that night since he was out of camera range for twelve minutes. I couldn't figure out a motive for him though. There seemed to be no connection between them, other than that Victor was a regular.

Detective Turner stared at me. My expressions must have made it obvious a lot had raced through my mind in those few seconds since asking the question.

"Sir, there are at least six guys off the hook," I said. "Two of them were in a room together. Some of the others there confirmed they went into the room, but no one saw them come out until the shit hit the fan. Then there's the four guys who were all together in the playroom. Uh, you know. Playing?"

The detective stroked his mustache. "Hmm. Yes, the orgy."

"I don't know if four men make an orgy. I've heard of four-ways, but never of a five-way. Maybe five makes an orgy? I don't know if there's an official rule."

He glared. "Of the four men participating in—uh— playing as you say, the only one who left was Clark, the man who found the body. The others said he screamed less than a minute after leaving the group. That wasn't enough time to kill Victor, run to the laundry room to hide the knife, then back to the sauna to pretend he had discovered the body."

"That's what I have too," I said. "I wish I had more. I've got leads but no evidence. The fingerprints info is news to me. Beyond that, I know who was there from the video feed Seth gave me, and that's it."

"Well, if you have nothing for me, I have plenty of other things to do." He gave me his card. "Please leave Mr. Barone alone for a while. It's your right to ask questions, but it's his right to decline comment. I'm sure you'll ignore my request, but if he calls us again, know that we will reconsider the harassment thing. Have another water?"

"No, that was the last one, sir. I promise you I won't harass him."

Detective Turner left an hour before closing. Enough time to finish polishing the brass trim on the display cases and try to reach Warren again.

Nine

Everything around me was darkness, except for pulsating lights that blinded me. Screeching sounds followed by loud bangs accompanied each pulse. Sometimes, time would slow to allow a few seconds between each flash, and then speed up to a near constant light. The longer the flash, the louder the sound. It was intolerable.

I couldn't back away. I had no traction in the void. The sounds raised to a higher pitch, and I squeezed my eyes tight, but it was as if I had no lids. I covered my ears and screamed. My quaking body felt ready to explode when the void became engulfed in one last flash and a final boom. I floated in silent darkness.

I awoke to find myself lying in sheets soaked in sweat.

I tossed my cell phone on the couch and muttered to myself. It was the fifth message I had left on Warren Barone's voicemail, and I knew he wouldn't return my calls. I had to go straight to the source.

The heat and humidity during the drive to see Warren burned my skin. It was a short trip to his flower shop, but my shirt was soaked. When I reached the parking lot, I opened my shirt and flapped it to create a breeze, hoping to keep it from clinging to my body. It was a wasted effort.

The shop was triangular. The front of the store was a wall of glass doors which opened onto Melrose Avenue, an area where Beverly Hills and West Hollywood meet, while two sides of the mossy green cinder block building came to a point in the back.

Melrose was full of independent boutiques, trendy cafes, and chic wine bars. Stores offered everything from elegant party gowns to hip skirts for clubbing to shredded blue jeans, all for around the same price. It was where celebrities and the LA elite went when they felt like slumming it. I hated it.

Warren's flower shop had tilted wooden boxes filled with flowers of every color bursting toward the sidewalk. On top of the building the store name, Bloomers, was spread across the ass of a woman bending over picking flowers. Exposing her bloomers, of course.

I buttoned my shirt and entered the store. I was met with a loud and overenthusiastic greeting that made me jump. A young brunette holding a fistful of daisies smiled. *Darcy* was embroidered on her mint green apron.

"How may I help you?" she squealed.

"Hi, Darcy. I'm looking for Warren Barone."

She frowned and knitted her brow. "Oh, I'm sorry. He's off until next week, but I'm a supervisor. Can I help?"

"No. It's important I speak to him. It's a personal matter. Can we talk privately?"

"My coworker is on break, so as long as you don't mind that I have to keep an eye on the store." She motioned for me to follow. We stopped in the doorway to the storeroom. She leaned toward me and asked, "How personal?"

"If I could say, then it wouldn't be personal, would it?" She rubbed her hands and bounced on her toes. "So, it's a secret?"

"Well, in a way, yes."

"What's the secret?"

"If it's a secret then... didn't we go over this? How can I reach Mr. Barone?"

An older woman sifted through a row of bouquets. She wore a light blue unitard and a baggy gray T-shirt with *Namaste* printed on the front. "Young lady, would you help me?"

"Of course. One moment, ma'am," Darcy called over, then looked at me. "Warren calls to check in at least once a day. I can give him a message."

"Plumeria. I'm looking for plumeria. Do you have any?" the old woman butted in.

"Do you know if he's grieving at home?"

Darcy leaned against the doorframe. "You could try him there, I guess. To be honest, I'm not sure." She looked at the woman. "Ma'am, I don't think I have plumeria, but I'd be happy to check. It'll be just a moment. My coworker is on break." She turned back to me. "Anything more I can help you with? Did you want me to give him a message?"

I flashed my license. "I'm a detective investigating Victor Verboom's murder. It's imperative I speak to Mr. Barone."

"Are you really a detective?"

"Yes."

"Let me see your ID again."

I handed it to her.

"You're not a real detective. You're a PI."

I scowled.

Namaste rambled. "Do you have any lilac? I'm staying with my daughter. She has three cats, and I cannot take the smells of cat piss one more day. I'd love some lilac."

"Since you're not a real detective, and you don't seem to have a message for my boss, I don't have to answer your questions." Darcy turned away from me and practically skipped across the store. "Yes, I believe I have lilac." She looked in a cooler near the cash register.

I wondered if she was covering for Warren, or if she really didn't know where he was.

"No lilac, ma'am. No plumeria either."

"What kind of flower shop has no flowers?" Namaste grumbled.

"I have lots of flowers, but I don't have any lilac or plumeria." Darcy sighed, crossed her arms, and glared at me. "You're still here?" she growled.

"It's true, you don't have to answer me," I said. "But I'm trying to help Mr. Barone."

"You're sure you don't have plumeria?"

"Yes, I'm sure, ma'am."

"If I go to a larger florist, they'll have plumeria."

Darcy walked over to me as quietly as she could, so as not to draw attention to our conversation. "Warren said the police arrested Victor's murderer."

"The investigation is ongoing, and it's important to speak with all witnesses—especially Mr. Barone. We need all the information we can get."

"Who is *we*?"

"Me and the person who hired me—an attorney representing the club manager." I didn't bother to mention Trent's intent was to prove Ernesto's innocence.

"Club Silver Lake?" She crinkled her nose. "My friend Gabriel went there. He left after fifteen minutes. He said that place is super sleazy and disgusting. Why would I help?"

"It's not for everyone, but Warren goes there sometimes," I said.

She rolled her eyes. "Your point being?" She exhaled. "Sorry, but I can't help you."

My neck muscles tensed, and I could feel my face turn red. I was getting nowhere, and I was frustrated I'd driven in the heat for nothing.

"Here are some dahlias," Namaste said. "How lovely. I should get these."

"They won't work for what you need," Darcy said. "They have no scent."

"Well, shoot. They sure are pretty. Plumeria has a nice smell."

I pursed my lips, shrugged my shoulders, and tried again. "Darcy, I appreciate you don't know where he is, but can you tell me anything that may help with the investigation? With the killer still out there, people's lives are at stake."

She bowed her head and dangled her arms. "Warren likes to gamble. He spends a lot of time in the desert. That's probably where he is now."

"Palm Springs? Vegas?"

"I'm really not sure."

It was a small concession, but at least I had something. I rubbed my palms. What to ask next?

"Could you check one more time on that plumeria?" Namaste knew how to get on my nerves.

"No, ma'am," Darcy said. "I—"

"How many times has she said she doesn't have plumeria?" I shouted. "No plumeria. What do you not understand?"

The two women gaped at me wide-eyed, their mouths open.

"I apologize for this man's rude behavior. I have sweet peas. They have a lovely scent." Darcy showed Namaste a large bouquet of sweet peas and told her she'd be right back. She then stomped over to me with her hands clenched.

"You, sir, must go now." Darcy pointed toward the sidewalk.

"I was rude, and I'm sorry. I'll pay for the woman's flowers. Can I ask you one more—"

"No, you may not. I've told you plenty. I can't help you anymore."

"Will it help if I buy something?"

"If you buy anything, you'll have flowers. They may brighten your day, but they won't get you any information."

"I don't need flowers."

"Then you should go."

I gave her my business card, knowing she wouldn't call.

Ten

Josie called my cell.

"Hi, Josie."

"Hey, Lil' Bro. What's up?"

"I'm just nursing my wounds after having my ass handed to me by a teenage girl."

"What?"

"Never mind. I'm headed to the Hollywood Hills. You?"

"Pick me up. I've got nothing to do."

"I don't know, Josie. It's for business—I'm looking for the murder victim's partner."

"I'll stay in the car… I won't cause any trouble. Promise. We can get drinks after."

"Where are you?"

"The Abbey. I just had lunch."

"On my way." I regretted the words as soon as they came out of my mouth.

We drove the winding roads through the Hollywood Hills for a while before finding Warren and Victor's home on Gentle Slope Road. There was nothing gentle about it. From the hilltop, the slope angled sharply down, past the house and beyond. It was too narrow to park on the curb, but a small driveway that led to the garage left just enough space to pull to the side. The home was sleek, modern, and shaped like a cube. It was painted bright white with a pair of cobalt blue glass front doors.

"You stay here," I ordered Josie.

I rang the doorbell twice and waited a minute between each ring. Nothing—no movement, no answer. I tried Warren's cell phone, but he didn't pick up, and I didn't hear it in the house.

When I turned to get back in the car, Josie wasn't there. She had run across the driveway to the side of the house. I made a quick dash and caught her descending a steep stone staircase leading underneath the main floor of the house.

"What are you doing?"

"Being a good detective." She continued down the dangerous steps.

"What the hell does that mean?"

"I want to see if he's down here."

"Nothing is down there. The hill is too steep. Good detectives don't snoop in a tight skirt and heels."

The house was supported by three large stilts buried in the hillside. A concrete slab lay beneath the main house, and a small basement had been built into the hill. Next to the door, there was a single window—which Josie was climbing into.

"Get out of there," I said in a hushed tone.

"Come to the door. I'll let you in," she replied too loudly.

"Open the door and get your ass out here."

She opened the door as requested but refused to leave. "What are we looking for?"

"Right now, we're looking at five to ten for breaking and entering."

"We didn't break in. The window was open. We're only entering."

I shook my head. "I'm sure the cops will see it that way." Knowing Josie wasn't going anywhere until she'd accomplished her superspy mission, I stepped inside to a small storage space and laundry room. She was sitting on a box putting her shoes back on. It's difficult to climb in windows while wearing heels.

She started up the stairs and wrested her wrist free when I grabbed it.

"Get down here," I whispered. "I knew I'd regret bringing you."

She ignored me, and I chased her up the wide stairs. There were no rails, so we stretched our hands to the walls to keep our balance. At the top step, an open door offered a view of the kitchen.

"Josie, what are you doing?"

"You're the detective—you tell me. Shouldn't we look around for clues or something?"

I cupped her chin, looked into her eyes then bowed my head in defeat. "We're not getting out of here unless I drag you by your hair, are we?"

Her hair bobbed as she jumped up and down, clapping her hands and laughing.

"Fine. In that case, stay here. Don't move. Don't touch anything." I used my shirttail to cover my hands and fumbled through the kitchen. "Aha." I grabbed four plastic freezer bags from a cabinet and handed two to Josie. "Put one on each hand. We can't leave fingerprints."

"How the hell am I supposed to do anything with these on?"

"You're resourceful. Figure it out. Don't move an inch until I'm back. I have to go downstairs to wipe off our fingerprints."

From the basement, I could hear Josie ambling above, ignoring my orders. I used a washcloth that had been hanging off the dryer door to wipe the windowsills and other areas we may have touched.

When I stepped back into the kitchen, Josie popped out of a hallway.

"There's no one home," she said. "You can stop whispering."

"What you're about to hear will hardly be a whisper."

"Chill out, Lil' Bro. You said it—I'm not leaving until we find something. You need to solve this case. Ooooh… do you think this guy did it?"

"He's one of many suspects. He wasn't in the bathhouse when Victor was killed, but most homicides are done within the family, and he had a lot to gain."

"Maybe we'll find a check stub that shows he hired a hitman!" She sounded excited. This wasn't going to end well. "Come." I followed her to a bedroom. "Look. That bed is messy, and there's a full basket of laundry. There's another messy bed and a full basket of laundry in the other bedroom. I deduce that these two were not sleeping together."

"Everyone knows they weren't getting along." I found too much joy in bursting her bubble.

"Well, I didn't. Why didn't you say so?" She huffed and marched down the hall. "I'd never stay married to someone who won't sleep with me. That's when I know it's time to serve up the divorce papers." She froze in front of the archway leading into the living room. "Look at this place. The furniture is fabulous."

The room was white. The walls, fireplace, plush carpeting, extra-long circular couch, chairs that leaned too far back, and coffee table were all white. I could see where Warren got his inspiration for the memorial service.

"Too modern. Too funky. No color."

Josie walked to the couch and picked up two pillows—one bright red, the other bright yellow. "Not true. These accents and the tchotchkes on the shelves are vibrant."

"What's a tchotchke?"

"It's a knickknack."

"Why not just say knickknack?"

"You're impossible." She threw the pillows back on the couch. "They need to take away your gay card. You have no sense of style."

Further down the hall, we walked past the kitchen and into the den, which had coral walls and sandy-colored tightly woven carpeting. An overstuffed chair was tucked into the corner, next to a wall of glass overlooking the canyon. A brown, extra-long tufted leather couch stretched across one wall.

"Come on, I see the office," she said, opening a set of French doors off the den. She stepped in. Based on the floor plan in my head, I surmised the office was tucked behind the garage. It was decorated with heavy matching oak desks and a pair of computers. A caramel-colored rug lay on cedar flooring. Cheap curtains darkened the only window in the room.

"Since we're here, let's see what we can find," I said.

Josie squealed and clapped her hands. "I knew you'd come around."

"I don't know what we're looking for, so check anything and everything." I picked the desk with Bloomers invoices on it. "I'll take this desk. You look through that one. Be careful, we— Josie, what are you doing?"

Her hands were bare. The freezer bags were off, and she was sliding paperwork into one of them.

"We'll go to my place, have drinks, and go through this," she said.

"No. No. No. We're not taking anything. Everything must look undisturbed. It can't be obvious we were here."

"Too late for that, but okay." She dumped everything back on the desk. "Happy now?"

"Only if you know where it all goes."

"No clue."

"Fine. Just… move stuff around and make the piles look natural."

I pulled out my cell phone and took random pictures of papers on Warren's desk, moving piles slightly to get pics of the items underneath. Both desktops were cluttered and out of place in the otherwise immaculate home.

Josie looked at the mess she'd recreated. "All better now. You want me taking pictures too?"

"Yes."

After five minutes of clicking and sorting through the piles, I asked, "Have you found anything?"

"To be honest, I'm not sure what to look for. But this is fun. PI work is so nosy."

"You mean being a spy is fun. Breaking and entering and rummaging through personal items is not normal investigative work. PI work is boring if you want to keep your license."

I kept rummaging. All I saw were a bunch of receipts, bills, and credit card offers. Each piece of paper looked the same as the last. Finally, I struck gold. Buried under the mound of paperwork was a document with the words *Life Insurance Policy* written across the top. I started snapping pictures as quickly as I could, when a whirring sound came from the garage.

"Come on," I rushed out of the office and held out a hand to urge Josie to come.

Josie held up one finger. "Just a sec. A couple more pics."

"Now." The whirring sound stopped, and the gears switched direction. The garage door was closing. "He's coming."

I tried to grab her sleeve, but Josie pulled her arm away before I could grasp it. Warren entered the hall, and Josie dropped to the opposite side of a desk while I ducked behind a chair.

"Hello?" Warren called out as he stepped into the den. "Anyone here?"

I wondered who he was yelling for, then remembered my car out front.

He walked down the hall, and we started toward the front door, but he doubled back into the office. I hid behind the kitchen island and lost sight of Josie.

"Helloooooo."

Warren changed direction again and turned into the kitchen. I curled myself in a ball as tight as possible.

"Anyone here?"

He had to be an idiot to call out looking for an intruder. When he left the kitchen and walked toward the bedrooms, I bolted down the stairs, but Josie wasn't anywhere to be seen.

I snuck back up the stairs and found her flattened against the wall in the den. She nodded when I pointed to the front door. We tiptoed toward it when a door creaked open. We froze in the silence that followed until the sound of a toilet lid clanking on porcelain gave us the break we needed. We rushed to the foyer to escape out the front door.

Out of nowhere, Lady Gaga sang "*Boys Boys Boys.*"

"Holy shit," Josie said too loud. She pulled out her phone, looked at the display, and answered. "Sorry, Tom. Can't talk right now." I snatched the phone out of her hand and shoved it into my pocket.

"Who's there?" Warren called.

As we rushed out the door, I could hear Warren huffing and puffing up the hall.

When we reached the car, I pushed Josie into her seat, ran around, jumped behind the wheel, turned the key, and hit the gas. In the rearview mirror, I could see Warren in the middle of the road, watching us drive away.

Josie laughed. "Sometimes I amaze myself. What a blast. I broke a heel, by the way. You owe me a new pair."

"To hell with the shoes. That's your fault."

"I hope he didn't get your license plate before he came into the house."

"If he did, I'm screwed."

◆◆◆

I took the elevator to Josie's condo in the Fairfax District. Her place was in one of the newer complexes that had popped up around the traditionally Jewish neighborhood near the Farmers Market.

Josie and her second husband, Cal Weichselbaum, had bought the condominium four years earlier, just six months before their divorce. They met at one of those speed dating events, the kind where each person gets three minutes to talk with a possible future mate before moving on to the next hopeful candidate. Josie went on a dare and ended up marrying Cal two months later. He was a film editor for a major television studio just around the corner from their place. One day, Josie came home and found Cal in bed with two of his interns. Even my open-minded sister had her limits.

She won the condo in the settlement, though it's not really accurate to say she won. The mortgage was far more than she could afford, but she was proud of it. Her credit card debt was enormous. She wasn't much better than me with money management. She was just lucky enough to earn more.

Josie plopped onto her red loveseat. There was a bottle of tequila on the turquoise marble counter in her kitchen. I grabbed two shot glasses and salt from the cupboard and found limes in her stainless steel refrigerator. I placed the ingredients on a TV tray, took it into the living room, and set it on the floor in front of her. She had no coffee table.

Her condo complex was popular with the younger middle management crowd known for overextending themselves. Her place was on the third—and top—floor. It had high ceilings, skylights, big windows, and an open concept. The kitchen counter was raised to allow for a breakfast bar overlooking the living room. She had no stools.

Cal had taken most of the furniture, leaving the place sparse. She had no dining table or chairs, and the living room had only the loveseat and one matching recliner. A small flat-screen TV hung on the wall. In her bedroom, where she did most of her entertaining, were a queen mattress on the floor and a white lacquer dresser. She had crammed her extensive clothing collection in the closet, leaving its sliding mirrored doors unable to close.

I poured us some shots, and we downed them right away. Josie put her laptop on the TV tray, and I spread out on the floor on my stomach. We downloaded the photos from our phones onto our computers and started the tedious task of going through them one by one, searching for anything that might be useful. Because my pics were of

Warren's desk, much of the paperwork looked familiar. It was apparent his store was struggling. He had one overdue notice after another, several from collection agencies. Beyond that, it was boring—theater ticket stubs, restaurant receipts, and Post-It notes with scribbles that made no sense without a frame of reference.

I looked up at Josie. "How's it coming over there?"

"Forget what I said earlier, Lil' Bro. If this is detective work, I don't envy you. This is boring. There's pictures here and a lot of notes and stuff. There are memos signed by celebrities that I wish I grabbed—probably worth good money. There…"

Josie continued to rant about the nothingness in her pics when I found the series I was keeping an eye out for—two forms with *Kvasir Life Insurance Company* across the bottom.

"Josie, I found the two policies with Victor's signature on them."

She clapped her hands. "Who are they made out to?"

"That's the problem. There's a vacation brochure to the U.S. Virgin Islands on top. It covers everything except the signature and part of the dates. I had to snap the pics fast when the garage door opened. I thought I captured more of the documents." I banged my head on the keyboard a couple of times. "Damn! The dates are worthless. On one, you can see 08/03/2 and then it cuts off. It's this millennium, but it could be any year. The other is worse." I squinted my eyes as if that would change what was in the photo. "The only date showing is 10/. It's got the month, and that's it. No day or year. It could have been signed around the time of Moses for all I know."

"Now you're being ridiculous."

"It's that helpful. From these, there's no way to tell when they were signed or who benefits from Victor's passing."

The loveseat shook as she bounced giddily. "We could break into his house again." Whatever look was on my face caused her to sigh. "It was just a suggestion. Whose names do you think are on them?"

"My guess is one is for Warren, but the other could be for anybody—Heather, Pam, Darcy."

"Who's Darcy?"

"Just a girl. She works for Warren at the flower shop."

Josie clasped her hands and bounced again. "Victor was having an affair with Warren's employee?"

I shook my head. "Josie, enough. I was being flippant."

"Well, stop it. You got me excited. You know I love a good scandal."

"You are working for me Wednesday, right?"

She closed her laptop. "Yes, I'll be there."

"Thanks, I'm meeting Victor's personal assistant on Wednesday. Maybe he'll have some answers. Pour me one more shot before I go."

Eleven

Historic Westlake Park, situated outside downtown, was an idyllic getaway for turn-of-the-century Angelenos, the preferred term for LA residents. It was a haven for city dwellers seeking outdoor concerts, dancing, pleasant strolls along the palm-lined sidewalks, or a lazy sail on the small lake. In the early days of Los Angeles, the region's richest citizens flocked to the neighborhood to build their mansions and posh hotels.

But much to the dismay of local residents, business leaders got their way in the 1930s and extended Wilshire Boulevard, splitting the park grounds in two. The community was further outraged in the 1940s when William Randolph Hearst convinced the city to rename the park after his favorite wartime hero, General Douglas MacArthur. That marked the end of the park's heyday and the beginning of its decline, with each decade worse than the last.

Ultimately, MacArthur Park had become the site to buy illegal goods, from crack to fake IDs, as well as grassy spots for the homeless to rest. The city's attempt to revitalize it had been half-hearted and the onetime oasis

was as unpleasant as the Richard Harris song named after
it.

Someone left a cake out in the rain…

...and it had melted all over the place.

Ernesto Torres lived with his grandmother, Lupe, on
South Westlake Avenue, three blocks from the park. I had
scheduled to meet Eve Aiken there so we could question
Ernesto together. For once, I arrived at our appointment on
time, but no one answered when I rang the buzzer. Eve
waved me over to wait with her in her car.

"He's running late," she said. "He called when he and
his grandmother were getting on the Red Line. I have no
idea where he was, so there's no goddamn way to know
when they'll get off. They should've been here ten minutes
ago. Who arrives late to an appointment at their own
house? It'll be dark when we come out of their place, and
those people will have stolen our cars."

"I'm not sure who 'those people' are, but our cars will
be fine. I need to run to the bank. Why don't you walk over
there with me while we're waiting? You can browse the
shops. It might help you relax."

"You're not getting me out there to be robbed or assaulted. This whole area went downhill when these Mexicans moved in. Do you have any idea what the crime rate is around here?"

"Not everyone who's Hispanic is Mexican, Eve. And you know as well as I do that this community fell onto hard times long before immigrants from the south arrived. They could afford to set up here because it was already in a slump." I swung the car door open and set a foot on the curb. "Come on… get a little culture. Stretch your legs. It'll be okay if we're across the street from the park. We'll be right there when they reach the station. There are worse places than this."

"And there's a reason I don't go to those places either." She motioned me to climb back in. "Stay here. I'm perfectly happy in my own culture."

"Fine, I'll stay." I slammed the door and crossed my arms. "You're missing a lot in this world. Folks around here may not have much money, but it's a thriving neighborhood." I debated whether or not to make it personal and decided I had nothing to lose. "My name may be O'Reilly, but I'm half Mexican and proud of it. So, I suggest you tread lightly with the 'those people' digs."

"We're here on business, let's talk business," she said. "Give me an update. Where do we stand?"

"I'm still working through the suspects, but things are moving along."

"If you've got nothing, say you've got nothing."

I knew she wouldn't take it well if I admitted that was true. Warren Barone's gambling was an issue, but as yet insignificant in connection to the case. The life insurance was a big story, but not one I could tell. She'd be an accessory if she knew of my breaking and entering, and I'd end up fired or in jail. I needed to think of something to report if I wanted to stay on the case.

"There's a rumor around town that Victor had two life insurance policies."

"Rumor? All you've got is a rumor? Whose names are on them?"

"I'm looking into that." Nothing worthwhile came to mind. "Warren Barone likes to gamble—he's a gambler."

"You gave me a list of four men besides Ernesto who could've murdered Victor, and one of them—Warren— wasn't even there at the time of the murder. Since then, you've learned the brother-in-law, who was at the club that night, is gay and may be on the down low about it. Then again, this is Los Angeles. For all we know, he may have his wife's blessing or encouragement to 'explore his sexual energy and feelings' or some hippy-dippy shit like that. Then there's this kind-of-maybe insurance thing and a man who gambles? Goddammit, what am I paying you for, Mitch?"

"These things take a while."

"The police took O.J. Simpson into custody five days after Nicole was murdered, and that investigation was effing sloppy. They already had Ernesto jailed once, they don't need much to lock him up again. This should be easy, Mitch. I'm not asking you to solve the case—just to take the heat off my client. But goddammit, don't waste my time. All I want is something on each of the other suspects to cast enough doubt and show that he wasn't the only possible killer. That's it, nothing more—here comes the son of a bitch now."

Ernesto and Lupe Torres shuffled up the sidewalk. They carried three plastic bags in each of their hands. We met them on the stoop leading up to their building.

"*Lo siento.*"

"*Mi abuela* say she's sorry," Ernesto said. He jiggled the keys in the lock. "When we came out of the Metro station, she demanded we shop the 99¢ Only Store." He opened the security door and raised his hands. "See? We got lots of stuff."

I took Lupe's bags before we climbed the stairs to their second story apartment.

"The store is three blocks away," Eve whispered loud enough for anyone listening to hear. "That flake couldn't go tomorrow?"

"*Trabajas para* Trent."

"She say you work for Trent," Ernesto explained. "Means you had to wait."

I glared a warning at Eve to keep quiet and let me do the talking.

Lupe had decked the apartment's nickel-colored walls with yellowed photographs of varying sizes. On the wall opposite the front entry, a passageway led to the kitchen on one side and a walnut door on the other. Between the two hung a three-foot-tall crucifix with a European Jesus. He had blue eyes, and his light skin and brown hair had dabs of blood-red paint.

Lupe led us into the kitchen and set a teapot on the stove. Eve, Ernesto, and I sat at her oval-shaped kitchen table with a pink faux marble top and chrome trim on the sides.

"Are you okay?" I placed a hand on Ernesto's shoulder. "You were upset the last time we met. I still have more questions, but I want to make sure you're ready to talk to me."

He nodded. "I'm now better. I loved Victor so much and want to catch whoever kill him."

Lupe threw a wooden spoon on the counter and walked out.

"What's wrong with your grandma?"

"I never tell her I'm gay before, not even when in jail. She no find out until she saw the news of my release, and it made her cry. *Abuela* is religious, and I think she is more embarrassed than sad. She goes to Mass five times a week and prays all the time. She only go to confession once since the news, and that's it. She didn't answer when the *padre* called. She's missing Mass right now."

Eve blew out a long stream of air. "Sorry your Grandma's upset, but we have to ask you some questions, and we need you to answer them." She stormed to the window and peered at the street, stomped back, and sat. "It's still there," she muttered.

"I need you to be very specific," I told him. "You want us to find Victor's killer, and we want to help. We can only do that if you stay focused and answer my questions. Understand?"

"*Sí.*"

"You said you were in the laundry room when you heard the scream. How long had you been there before they found his body?"

"Only three, maybe five, minutes. First, I cleaned room eighty-seven. It's a sling room, and they are really large. It was dirty, like they had a big party in there. Seth, he told me it was bad, and I got to make it sparkle. I thought that's kind of funny, but he seem mad about it. I just finished and went back to the laundry room."

"Seth schedules your cleaning?"

"Most of the time right when a guest leave, the desk person tells me what room checked out so I can go clean it. On Fridays and Saturdays, it's very full. There's a waitlist for rooms, so I have to turn them fast. They usually have three of us when there are that many men."

"You said it wasn't busy that night," Eve said. "Hardly anyone was there."

"No, not many, but the afternoon was crazy because we had Sordid Bear Sunday. We get lots of big men, and the attendants leave all the dirty rooms. Because it's slow Sunday nights, they think I got nothing to do but clean their rooms and do their laundry. It's not fair, but Trent and the guys up front leave me alone because of no one waiting, and they know I work hard."

"Did Seth say why you should clean that room?" I asked.

"No, I guess someone wanted it later, but I don't know for sure because of what happened to Victor."

"Did you see Rod Hernandez around that time?"

"Who is he?"

"He's a big guy. Broad. Uh, large. A big, thick man? Rugged-looking with a goatee? You may know him as Gustavo."

"The one who talks sexy? I heard his voice. So nice. He didn't stay long. He cruised some, but I never saw anybody with him. When he—"

The teapot screamed. Lupe rushed to the stove and grabbed the handle.

"*Ay. Caliente. Está muy caliente.*" She blew on her hand. "*Dios mío.*"

Ernesto jumped from his seat and grabbed Lupe's wrists. Eve brushed him away and pulled his grandmother's hands to the sink. She snapped, "Sit your ass back down, Ernesto. Keep answering Mitch's questions."

He stayed nearby to watch until Eve held Lupe's palms under cold water. Then he shuffled back to his chair.

"*Lo siento*," he said. "I'm sorry. I was saying I was in room eighty-seven. Someone tell you that man and Victor had a fight, *si*? They yelled, and when I came out that man went to his room mad. I tried to talk to Victor, but he told me to go away, so I went back to room eighty-seven."

"Did this happen before or after you two argued?"

"Was before. Maybe ten minutes. Everybody say no one talked to Victor after me."

He sobbed into his palms, and tears dropped onto the table. Lupe turned. She frowned and clasped her hands to her breasts, but then marched out with a scowl. Eve impatiently walked to the window. "It's still there."

She plopped on her chair and laid her arms down. She looked at me and rolled her eyes.

"*Lo siento. No más hablar*," Ernesto said, rubbing his eyes. "I don't want to talk no more."

"But we haven't even talked about Warren or Christian yet. Please, Ernesto. You must try. You need to tell us what they did that night."

He pulled his fists from his face and set them on his lap. "Warren yelled at Victor, Christian yelled at him, that man with the sexy voice yelled at him, and I did too. Everyone yelled at Victor. He wasn't happy, and I'm sad he died like that. Christian got angry with him early in the night. He checked into room thirty-something, and I can see that hall from the laundry. When Victor saw me watching Christian get mad at him, he looked embarrassed and went away."

"Victor left? Where did he go?"

"I don't know right then. Too much cleaning. He just was someplace else."

"Did Christian and Victor know each other? Have you seen them talk before?"

"Christian never talks to nobody. He stay in his room to wait for Seth to finish work. Sometimes he comes out and cruises, but he usually go back all alone. He's at the bathhouse a lot, but I didn't know he was there that night until he was mad and called Victor names. 'Old troll,' he said. That was not nice. I did not see Christian again until after they found Victor in the sauna."

"You told me that you think Warren is the killer," Eve said. "What did you see that makes you think so?"

"Victor hated him. That's why he loved me. Warren was bad to him."

Eve slammed her palm to her forehead. "Goddammit, Ernesto. You keep repeating that. We get the point. You don't like him, blah, blah, blah. He's a bad man, blah, blah,

blah. Fine then, Warren's a prick. See? Mitch is nodding his head. *Comprende?*"

He squinted and bared his teeth.

"Don't be a bitch, Eve," I said.

She raised an eyebrow and slackened her mouth. She walked to the window and looked out. Again. "It's still there."

I held a palm to Eve, warning her to back off. "She's sorry. We're frustrated is all. We need to find out who murdered him so that the police don't come back to arrest you, and you keep telling us Warren did it, but you won't say how. Do you know?"

"No, no, no." He lowered his head. "Warren was there a long time. I think he stayed after the Sordid Bear Party was over and waited until Victor showed up. They went into room twenty-two, and I cried when I stood by the door. They were talking. I couldn't hear what they say but heard my name sometimes. I couldn't stay longer because I had to go back to work. After that, I didn't see Warren again. I know I didn't kill Victor. And he was the only one who I know was mad and could do that to him."

"You know Warren left the bathhouse before Victor was murdered, right?"

"*Sí*. He wasn't there when everyone ran to the sauna or when the police got there. He was gone."

"Then why do you keep saying he did it? How did Warren murder Victor when he wasn't there? He left thirty minutes before, which is why we're asking for details. Did you see anything that night that we can take to the police that proves he did it?"

He kept his eyes lowered, and tears rolled down both cheeks. "He did killed him. I know he did, but I don't know how. He is a bad man, and he was angry that Victor loved me. He did murder him."

Eve pushed her chair back and stood with her hands on her hips. "Here we go again. Is there anything else you have to say before we leave?"

He shook his head. "That's it."

On the front stoop, Eve crossed and uncrossed her arms as she darted her eyes up and down the street. "We got him to cut the Warren crap for a few minutes, but that's it. Did you get anything out of this meeting? Seemed like a goddamn waste of time to me."

"First, look, and you'll see your Mercedes is still there. Second, yes, I was sick of his whining too, but he gave a clearer picture of events. I never expected Ernesto to be the one to clear things up and give a better timeline."

As I climbed into my car, I heard Eve yell from down the block.

"Goddammit! Those bastards took my hubcaps."

I knew I shouldn't, but I broke out laughing.

Twelve

The television studio lot was a maze of sound stages, adobe offices, and warehouses. Despite the guard's directions to Victor's former office, I meandered the narrow drive for fifteen minutes before finding the right bungalow. It was nestled in a small shady spot ten steps up from the driveway. One week had passed since Victor died, and I had an appointment with his assistant. The door to the office was open, so I stepped inside and introduced myself.

"Hello. I'm Mitch O'Reilly, the private investigator looking into Victor's murder."

His eyes bored through me until finally, I saw the light of recognition. "Yes. My apologies. I pride myself in being proficient in my job, but being here alone without Mr. Verboom has me a bit befuddled. I'm Abraham Horowitz."

His hand swallowed mine when we shook. He was intimidating. He stood seven feet tall, with wide shoulders and a thick torso. I'd estimate him to be in his late thirties. His white shirt fit at the shoulders but was loose at the waist. It was tucked yet baggy, causing it to flop over his olive slacks pressed with flawless creases.

He motioned for me to take a seat. The ultra-modern office furniture matched the interior of Victor's home, but with brighter colors. I sat on a chair with a red circular cushion and yellow tassels, with a back shaped like a sunflower. The seat was soft on my ass, but the chair back's twists and turns dug into my spine. It was designed for style, not comfort.

The desk, made of solid glass, had a flat top that curled down at the sides and flowed to the floor like a waterfall. Abraham's chair had a beechwood back, and legs so thin it looked as if it floated on air. Supporting a man his size defied the laws of physics.

"My apologies for the mess," he said, stuffing books into boxes. "I've been getting Mr. Verboom's effects in order, and I am devastated. Determining which items go to the writing staff, and what I should send to his home, is quite an undertaking."

His golden hair was cut short on the sides, but long on the top. As he placed each book in a box, his hair would fall in his face, and then flip back into position when he stood.

"If you think this is a mess, come see my office," I said.

He laughed far louder and longer than my comment called for. A man well versed in schmoozing Hollywood executives.

The place was immaculate. Paperwork was stacked neatly on his desk, books were shelved and ordered, and not a picture frame was askew.

"Mr. Verboom abhorred clutter. That's why we're— why we were—compatible." He paused a few seconds, looked at the ceiling, and sighed. "What may I do for you?"

"Abe, you may—"

"Abraham."

"Excuse me?"

He pushed his round wire-rimmed glasses to the bridge of his nose. "Abraham. You called me Abe. My name is Abraham."

"Sorry. Like I said on the phone, I'm investigating Victor's murder."

"You must have heard the many kind words about Mr. Verboom at the memorial service. I noticed you sitting there in the back. Everyone loved him." Abraham leaned forward and whispered unnecessarily. "I'm certain it was a random act of violence. How else can you explain it?"

I whispered back. "Random acts are rare. They're just the ones that make the news. There's almost always a motive."

"In that case, was it Ernesto?"

"Could be. But I'm not entirely convinced it was him. You say people liked your boss, but we all have someone we don't get along with."

"That's true. Let me see." He sat down, clasped his hands, and placed his elbows on the desk. I cringed, waiting for the spindly chair legs or the glass top to crack beneath his weight. "You heard he won several Emmys. Perhaps one of the losing nominees?"

What an asinine response. It frustrated me not being able to say so.

"Anything's possible. Good start. Don't edit. Just say whatever comes to mind. As his assistant, you kept track of him at all times. Are there any specific people you can think of who he rubbed the wrong way? Someone he worked with?"

"There's not one person who I can imagine would kill Mr. Verboom."

"I'm not asking who killed him. Just some names of people he wasn't the best of friends with."

"There is one man who came by on a regular basis, but Mr. Verboom handled his appointments himself. I did think it was odd that he never officially introduced us. I did worry he might have gotten himself into something that could tarnish his reputation." He turned his head to gaze at the trees out the window.

"What can you tell me about him?" I said.

Abraham continued to look outside. "He's strikingly handsome, and he only comes to mind because Mr. Verboom was so secretive about his visits. He's muscular, young, African-American. Some days they'd spend a good part of the afternoon together." He placed his index finger on his lower lip. "My apologies, but to discuss this with you feels irresponsible. This job requires utmost confidentiality."

"It's not like you can be fired."

He turned back toward me. "You have a point, and I do want to help you catch the culprit. Mr. Verboom would give me two hours for lunch whenever the gentleman came, so I hardly saw him. Occasionally, he'd give me the entire afternoon off. He said he gave the man acting lessons." He giggled into the palm of his hand.

"What's so funny?"

"I watched one of his audition videos. No amount of lessons would be able to help that dreadful thespian."

"I didn't realize Victor taught acting."

"It was rare."

"Other than the lessons, is it possible that Victor had a special arrangement to get him some acting gigs? You know, a little something on the side?"

"I presume you're referring to something sexual. That's terribly underhanded and shows you didn't know him. Why would he do such a thing when he was having relations with Mr. Torres?"

"He'd been with Warren for twenty years but was having a fling with Ernesto. It doesn't seem like monogamy was high on his list of virtues."

"Point taken."

"Is it possible Victor wrote the man's name down somewhere?"

"I wouldn't know where to look." He leaned forward and rested his head on his chin. "Aha! The security guards at the main gate would know. They'd need it to let him pass."

"Can you get it from them?"

Abraham hit a few buttons on the phone and was on for no more than two minutes. "Christian Freeman."

So pretty boy wasn't just an asshole. He was a liar. He had claimed not to know Victor.

"Does the name mean anything to you?" Abraham asked.

"I couldn't really discuss that with you. Discretion is a principal aspect of my position."

He covered his mouth and giggled again. "I'm positively giddy. This is fun."

Truth be told, I was feeling giddy myself. Knowing that Christian had lied was a breakthrough in the case. It definitely raised reasonable doubt about Ernesto being the only one with a motive at the club that night. The investigative moment had created a bond between Abraham and me, which gave me an advantage.

"Do you mind telling me what you know about Ernesto?"

"There's not much to tell. Mr. Verboom brought him in a few times after his lunch. Ernesto is a friendly, timid young man who adored Mr. Verboom. You could see it in his eyes. It's difficult to believe Mr. Torres could have been a killer. I can't imagine he would hurt a fly."

"Where were you when Victor was murdered?"

Abraham chuckled. "Oh, don't worry about me. I was at a family reunion in Sheboygan."

"No problem if I make some calls to validate that?"

"Do you consider me a suspect?"

"Not if you were in Sheboygan." He nodded overdramatically. "There's no problem then."

"I didn't think so. Do you have that audition video you mentioned earlier? It might help to take a look."

"It may still be saved on our system. Give me a moment."

While Abraham clicked away at the keys, I stood up to stretch my legs. I circled the room and stopped at the open door to Victor's office.

"Nuh-uh." Abraham wagged his finger.

After several minutes he sighed and said, "I can't find anything. It's possible he deleted it, knowing how bad it was. If it ever got out, that man would've been the laughingstock of Hollywood. We can access his computer to see if he saved it privately, but it will feel awkward."

In Victor's office, Abraham typed away while I skimmed through an issue of *Variety*. I was halfway through an article about an upcoming musical version of *Saving Private Ryan* when he said he found the files.

"Interesting… There are many more videos of Mr. Freeman than I expected, and there are other names that I don't recognize on several files. Let's play this one." He clicked on a file. "Oh, dear God."

The video presented Christian in all his glory. Even more impressive was Victor taking it with a smile. Christian showed him no mercy.

I grabbed my stomach and laughed out loud. "That's one hell of an audition."

Abraham quickly switched off the screen.

"Hey! That was getting good," I grumbled.

"It is disturbing and most definitely not what I saw before."

Even without the monitor, the video kept running. The sounds of Victor grunting echoed throughout the room. Abraham fumbled with the buttons on the side of the screen, but when he couldn't get the screen back on quickly enough, he turned down the knob on the speaker.

"By the look on your face, I believe you." I suppressed laughing as much as I could, but struggled to keep my composure. "Can you get me copies of all those videos with Christian's name on them?"

He pursed his lips. "Accommodating your prurient interests is not appropriate."

I waved a hand at him. "Chill, Abe. There could be conversations on those that could help my case."

He shut the computer down. "I'm not comfortable providing them to you, but copies will be stored for when I deem it's critical to your investigation. And my name is Abraham, as I told you earlier. It's still not Abe."

"If needed, my employer can get a subpoena."

"I've shown my willingness to work with you and will continue to do so, but I cannot hand over something this personal. If you need to review the videos further, we can come to an agreement without giving you possession."

Our relationship had gone from congenial to combative. I needed to calm myself down before it cost me his cooperation altogether. I grabbed a seat on a couch in front of Victor's desk, paced my breathing, and forced a smile. "Have you met Victor's daughter, Heather, and her boyfriend, Kelvin Daniels?"

Abraham leaned forward and folded his hands. "What a lovely young lady. So bashful yet pretty. You saw her at the funeral. I only met him once. He is such a crude man. I didn't know either of them well. I made arrangements at Mr. Verboom's request for outings—I bought event tickets, made dinner reservations, booked hotel rooms for when they came to town."

"How often did they visit?"

"Once a month or so. They always stayed at the Willoughby Hotel in Hollywood. It's a splendid establishment and was most convenient to Mr. Verboom's home."

"Can you look up when they last stayed?"

"I don't think I—"

I leaned forward and placed my hands on the desk.

"We've already gone down this route, Abraham."

He chortled and checked the calendar app on his phone.

"The last time they stayed there was the weekend before last—Saturday and Sunday night." He paused, snagged a tissue, and wiped his eyes. "That was the night Mr. Verboom died."

I nodded.

"I'm terribly busy, Mr. O'Reilly, and I really must get back to the grindstone." He stood and walked me out. A breeze tousled his hair. "Anything else I can assist you with?"

"One last question, please. Can you tell me anything about Warren Barone?"

He crossed his arms. "There's nothing to say. I hardly know the man."

"When did you become Victor's assistant?"

"Four years ago."

"You're saying that in four years working with Victor, you hardly knew the man he'd been in a relationship with for twenty years?"

"Mr. Verboom mostly kept his personal and his private life separate. I know it's hard to believe based on what we just found on his computer, but that video was as much of a shock to me as it was to you. Mr. Barone rarely came here. When he did, he would say 'hello' and nothing more. Over the past couple of years, Mr. Verboom made fleeting comments about the status of their relationship. He implied there was tension, but I wasn't privy to the details." He paused. "I only asked Mr. Verboom as much as I needed to know to get my job done. I wasn't in the habit of asking unnecessary questions."

"Had he mentioned that he and Mr. Barone were trying to fix things?"

"No."

"Apparently, the ups and downs of their relationship had been the talk of the town, so I thought you, of all people, would know about it."

"I never have been one to listen to tasteless gossip. I do wish I could say more, but Mr. Verboom rarely mentioned Mr. Barone." Abraham stepped back inside and started to close the door.

"Wait—" I said.

"Thank you kindly for your time, Mr. O'Reilly. As I said, I really must go now. I will pay attention to his belongings while I'm packing up, and if there is anything I believe could be useful to your investigation, I'll call you. Do you have a business card I could put in my wallet now?

The studio expects me to collect all of his things and mine and vacate this office by the end of the week, and I want to be sure I don't misplace your number."

"Absolutely." I handed him my card. "Sorry about you losing your job and all. Any prospects?"

"Thank you. I've already found a new employer. I'm now the personal assistant to Mr. Sheen."

"Martin or Charlie?"

"Charlie."

"Good luck with that."

Thirteen

Traffic was at a standstill on Los Feliz Boulevard, and I was already twenty minutes late. If it weren't for the tall, cooling cedars flanking the streets, the heat would've been unbearable. I looked forward to the day I could get the air conditioning fixed.

Once traffic started moving, I turned north on Nottingham Avenue into the Los Feliz neighborhood, where mansions with lush lawns and tree-lined driveways were nestled among the Los Angeles hillsides. My foot heavy on the pedal, the tires squealed as I pulled onto the cobblestone driveway. Pam and Rod Hernandez's Mediterranean style home was extravagant. Three large archways graced the face of the mansion, holding up a balcony that shielded the entryway. Additional balconies on each end of the upper level looked down on the gardens below.

I rang the bell, and Rod opened the large rounded door to greet me with a firm handshake. He was more hospitable than when we had met four days before.

The tiled foyer matched the Mediterranean style of the home, but the rest of the observable rooms were mismatched, as if they had hired a different designer for each one.

Directly ahead, an archway beneath a winding staircase opened to a country western style living room decorated with leather and cowhides.

To my left was a pagoda study with clean lines, mint green walls, and a minimalist bamboo desk facing the foyer. A bonsai tree sat on the desktop, and a black stone slab fountain was placed along the back wall. Water flowed down its façade even though no one was in the room.

To my right was a French country dining room where Pam greeted me and escorted me to a large oval table with ten matching chairs. She was as cordial as she had been on the beach. "Would you mind if we start with dinner right away? Everything is ready."

"Not at all. I'm hungry," I said, rubbing my stomach. "Sorry I'm late."

"I do hope you like seafood. We are having garlic shrimp pasta."

"Seafood sounds fantastic," I lied.

I sat down. The high back chairs were upholstered in custard-colored fabric with long-stemmed pink rose embroidery. Matching curtains framed the large front windows. A rug—with the same floral design—lay underneath the table on the hardwood floor. I was both impressed by how much it must have cost and disgusted by how ugly it was.

"Your home is beautiful. Just the three of us for—"

"Dinner. Yes, just us," Rod cut in.

"I asked because it's so—"

"Large. Yes, the house is too large. Would you care for a drink?" he asked.

"Just a beer if you have—"

Rod stepped into the kitchen as Pam sat across from me. I wondered if Rod was nervous, or if he just had a penchant for cutting people off. He had to know I had watched the club's security video and knew his dirty little secret.

"We have two sons who have moved on to college, Juan who is twenty, and Miguel who is eighteen," Pam said. "The house seems quite big and empty now. I cannot believe how they have grown and become men. I do miss having them here, fighting one minute and laughing the next. You know how siblings are."

"I understand how a home this big would feel empty for just you two," I said.

Pam chuckled.

Rod poured a Sam Adams into a frosted mug and placed it on the table. "I prefer a smaller home now that it's only us, but Pam won't consider it. Too many memories, she says."

She placed a hand to her lips and giggled. "Rodrigo sometimes says that I am a pack rat. I like to keep mementos of everything I have seen or done. This house is just one big memento."

A gray-haired Latina wearing the traditional black and white French maid's outfit brought out our dinner. I didn't think they even made French maid's uniforms aside from trampy Halloween costumes anymore. She spooned pasta from a pot onto our plates while we passed the dinner rolls.

Soon after we began eating, Pam placed her hand on mine. "I love reading mysteries, Mr. O'Reilly, both old and new—Agatha Christie, Josephine Tey, Dick Francis, Sue Grafton. Your career fascinates me. How long have you been a detective?"

"Please, call me Mitch."

She smiled.

"I've been a private investigator for about four years. I spent two years at a large detective agency to earn enough hours to get my license, then left to open a store and work on my own about two years ago. Don't believe the books or the movies. Detective work is boring. I spend most of my time sitting alone in my car for hours on end, following cheating spouses."

"Oh? That sounds dreadful. How disappointing. I wish I hadn't asked."

"I read you own an escrow company, Rod," I changed the subject. "Looks like it's worked out for you."

He hesitated. "It pays the bills."

Pam snorted. She covered her mouth, blushed, and apologized. "Rodrigo is being ridiculously modest. He founded the company when he was only thirty, and it is now the largest on the West Coast. He is still the President and CEO, despite my begging him to retire. I stopped working as a talent coordinator eight years ago. At first, it was wonderful, but now I spend too much time alone. There are so many hobbies we could enjoy together if he would leave. This room is the result of an interior decorating class I took. Is it not lovely?"

"Your place is beautiful, Pam." I chugged my beer.

There was still something about her that irritated me. It wasn't only her highfalutin speech and methodical pace, but the way she said things. I couldn't put my finger on it, but she reminded me of a robot.

"I apologize for bringing this up during dinner," I said, "but in the interest of time, can we talk about your brother?"

Pam dropped her fork and wiped her lips with a white linen napkin. "You are right, it is not appropriate. However, continue if you must."

"You've made it clear how you feel about Warren, so let's come back to him later. Is there anyone besides Warren who you think might have had a conflict with Victor?"

"Everyone loved him," she said. "I cannot imagine who else would have wanted to kill him. However, it is not like we socialized in the same circles. He was—"

"Gay," Rod said. "He was gay."

"My brother was a homosexual. We rarely met at social occasions. I have never been to a gay bar or a bathhouse. Can you imagine?"

Rod clasped his hands and placed them on the table. "Don't misunderstand. It's a simple fact of human nature that we associate with those who are most like us. Wouldn't you agree?"

"So, you're saying you associate only with wealthy couples who live in mansions and own companies?" I asked.

"Oh dear," Pam said. "Rodrigo's position requires him to socialize with people from all walks of life." She placed her hand on his. "Rodrigo, do you still have that lesbian who—"

"Is black too." Rod cut in. "Yes, in accounting. Hard worker."

"Is she not dating that Oriental girl in marketing?"

"You're thinking of Yuna, and they're called Asian, dear."

"Yes, she is the one."

"No, Yuna's not a lesbian. She's married to Wagoner."

"You see?" Pam said. "Rodrigo is a strong proponent of diversity. He even has a midget in the office."

"The correct term is 'little people,'" I said.

Pam flopped her napkin on her lap and crossed her arms. "Oh pooh, I never know what to call people anymore."

"There's no midget," Rod said, "Who are you talking about?"

"You said his name. Wagoner."

"He's not a midget. He's short, but he's no midget."

"Well, excuse me. I do not know what the criteria is to be a midget."

"Again, it's 'little person,'" I reminded them both.

Pam changed the subject and monopolized the discussion during the rest of dinner. She tediously name-dropped every celebrity she'd ever met and told detailed stories about raising her two sons. I was relieved when she directed us to the living room. She and I walked together with her arm locked around mine. Her pace was slow and deliberate.

A large stone fireplace scaled two stories along an outside wall. The room was rustic, with textured sand-colored walls and dark wood beams. A mocha leather couch faced the fireplace, and a large TV hung above it. The seating looked old and worn—worse than the couch in my office I got from Goodwill. But I knew it was purposely "distressed," and very expensive. The entire back wall was glass. It overlooked a pool surrounded by statues of Roman soldiers and naked Greek men. Rod must have had some influence on decorating the patio.

Pam and I sat on the couch. Rod set a beer on the coffee table for me and took a seat on a matching leather chair.

Pam sat up straight and raised her chin. "We should talk about my brother and Warren now."

"You really believe he murdered your brother?"

Rod crossed the room, grabbed a box of tissues, and laid them on the coffee table in front of Pam before sitting back

down. She pulled out three and dabbed them under her
eyes. She shed no visible tears but was too choked up to
speak.

"What she's trying to say," Rod said, "is that it's not just
a belief. It's a certainty. Warren has been taking money
from Victor for years. When their relationship went sour,
and the money train was running out, we have no doubt that
Warren wanted Victor out of the way once and for all."

Pam piped in. "Victor owned his home outright. He
finished paying the mortgage early and invested well. The
inheritance alone—"

"Would feed a small country. There's no telling how
much his life insurance is worth." Rod finished.

"I understand you have issues with Warren," I said. "But
he wasn't there when Victor was murdered, so unless you
have some proof—"

"It was Warren. I can assure you." Pam's face turned
red, her eyes narrowed, and she clenched her fists on her
lap.

"Well, the security video and guest log say otherwise.
Everyone who came and left the bathhouse is on there." I
glanced at Rod, who gave no visible reaction. I didn't
mention Warren had been at Club Silver Lake earlier that
night.

"He must've arranged it then. It wouldn't have been beneath him," Rod said.

"Yes." Pam sat up and leaned toward me. "That is what he did. He hired a hitman. There must have been some unsavory characters there at that time."

"Everyone looks unsavory in a bathhouse," I said.

She crossed her arms and pouted. "Well, how would I know?"

"Do either of you know any of the other men who were in the club that night?" Again, he didn't flinch. The man had nerves of steel.

Pam pulled the tissues away from her face, clutched them, and thrust her hands down on her lap. "How on earth would—"

"It's ridiculous to think we would know," Rod said.

I took a deep sigh.

"You're right. It was a silly question. Did your brother mention if he had made any recent changes to his will or insurance?"

"He was never so crude as to discuss personal matters of that nature." Pam paused. "Oh, my goodness. You are asking because you found a connection between Warren and Victor's money. I was right!"

I held out a hand, leaned back, and shook my head. "Whoa, that's not the case. Just a question is all."

Pam fled the room without excusing herself. I opened my mouth to question Rod.

"No. Not here. Not now." He leaned forward with his arms down and rubbed his hands between his legs. One knee bounced intensely.

"Do I make you nervous, Rod?"

He glared at me, and we sat in silence until Pam returned.

"I apologize for getting so emotional," she said. "I hope you can understand."

Rod relaxed his shoulders and grinned at his wife.

"Of course. Ready to continue?" I asked.

Pam nodded.

"Is there anything you can add that could implicate Warren in any way, other than your belief he's after your brother's money?"

"Unfortunately, no, though I stand by my assertion that he killed my brother," Pam said.

"What about your niece, Heather? She sure shocked everyone."

"Oh, the poor, sweet thing. It was brave of her to go up there. She surprised people because most did not know that

Victor had a daughter. Those who knew of her did not know she had become a part of his life. We may be the only ones there who knew."

"And Warren?"

"Warren knew of her," Rod said, "but as far as we know, he wasn't aware that she'd been in contact with her father. Victor wanted it that way. Since they were on the skids, he shared as little information as possible with Warren. Most nights, he didn't even go home. I laugh when I think of Warren's face when she walked up there. He was watching what may be a big share of his inheritance go down the drain."

"What about Kelvin?"

Pam gritted her teeth. "Kelvin is mean and uncivilized. I am sure you are already aware of that. Victor tried hard to convince Heather to leave him, but she says she is in love. She is such a sweet thing, and he is just horrible to her." Pam dabbed her eyes again. "Her mother, God rest her soul, raised her well."

"Did you see her the night of Victor's death?"

"No, I was not aware that she had been in town until I called her. Victor had wonderful times with Heather, but they did not include us. Or anyone for that matter. He did not want to share her with anyone else, except Kelvin, of course, because she would refuse to come without him. We did visit her at home in Riverside once while we were in the area. I almost cried to see the condition she lives in. Why Victor did not help her is beyond me." Pam turned toward Rod. "Oh honey, we should help. Get her somewhere safe to live. Perhaps with us?"

"We'll discuss this another time," Rod's stern tone implied the discussion was over for good.

"Well, thank you both for your time and insight," I said. "It's time for me to go. I have to get up early to open my store. I promise to be in touch if I have any more questions for you."

Pam and Rod stood. She grabbed my hands. "I wish we had more information to give you. Please, focus your investigation on Warren."

"I only promise I'll watch him, though that's been difficult. He's not easy to track down."

"He's a gambler, Mitch," Rod said. "If you can't find him, you'd best look at the races or the casinos."

"Do you know where he goes?"

"He's got a few favorites, but Victor said he usually goes to Fiesta Springs."

Finally, a piece of useful information. I hadn't gotten much all night. "Appreciate it." I shook Rod's hand. Pam put her arm around mine and walked me to the door.

I turned my key in the ignition and stretched to the glove box for gum to get the taste of seafood out of my mouth when Rod ran up and leaned into the passenger side window. He caught me off guard, and I yelped.

"Give me one of your business cards," he demanded, his forehead creased and a scowl on his face. I obliged. "Tomorrow. I'll call you. We need to meet."

I wanted to appear self-assured. Rod needed to know I had the upper hand, but I couldn't get too cocky. "Call anytime. I'll—"

"If she hears of this, you're a dead man." His eyebrows narrowed, and an eye twitched. He bounced his hand up and down on the doorframe.

"Not really smart to threaten a man who has possession of a video that could turn your life upside down."

"Wait for my call and be ready to meet."

"I'm sure I'll be able to pencil you in."

Rod strolled back in the house. I put the car in drive and checked my GPS for Fiesta Springs Casino. It was over two hours away in Coachella Valley, and it was too late to go. One more thing to add to a busy week.

Fourteen

When I drove up to my store, Frank, the homeless man, was already gone, and Rod Hernandez leaned against his metallic blue Tesla smoking a cigarette.

"Last night you said you'd call for an appointment," I said.

"Sorry for being inconsiderate." He exhaled a lungful of smoke.

"Didn't know you smoked, Rod. Not allowed at home?"

"Some battles aren't worth fighting."

"I'm over an hour late and need to open the store. Can you give me a minute?"

He peered around the plaza. "I've been here over forty minutes, and not a soul has pulled into the parking lot. We have things to discuss." The embers at the end of his cigarette brightened as he took another drag.

When I unlocked the door and stepped in, Rod was at my heels. I turned and put up my hand. "Sorry, but no smoking."

He glared and flicked his lit cigarette out the door. I grabbed the money for the register and rolled up the security gates.

"Okay, Rod. How can I help you? Care to buy something?"

He put one hand on the counter and scribbled in the air with the other. "I'm ready to write you a check."

I shrugged. "What for? I've got some really good products. You ever think about installing hidden security cameras around your home, Rod? They're great for finding out family secrets."

"You know damn well what for. No one, absolutely no one, can find out about the bathhouse." He pulled a checkbook out of his suit pocket.

I had my fun. If I wanted to get any information out of him now, I needed to relax and earn Rod's trust. "I'd love to take your money, but I can't make that promise. There's no way to know where the investigation may lead."

"This is what you want, Mitch?" He looked around. "This dump of a store? Sneaking around and following people for hours on end? It seems like you could use cash right now."

I bit my lower lip. "Dump? You're not winning me over by dissing my place. I made a commitment to a client, and as much as I could use your money, I will stand by it. My promise to you is no one finds out our little secret unless absolutely necessary."

His face flushed. "What does that mean?"

"I'll keep quiet, but you've got to tell me what you know. I swear to you—I have no intention to out you. Crossing that line is against my nature. It's up to each individual to choose when it's the right time for them. Unfortunately, if solving this case and locking up the killer means I have to out you then I will. I'd hate it, but I'd have no choice. Your cooperation can go a long way if you don't want me revealing too much. Have you talked with the—"

"Police? Yes. They scheduled an appointment at my office. The detectives came in suits, no badges. They were discreet and advised me to stay close in case they had any more questions, but said they thought they had everything they needed from me. I'm taking them at their word."

"And you can take me at mine. My client is paying me to find out the truth and gather evidence. I make no assumption of anyone's innocence or guilt. That said, unless you did it, you shouldn't have to worry about me exposing your secret. And if that's the case, you've got a lot bigger problems than me telling the world you were at a bathhouse."

"I'm not confident about your discretion," he said.

"My promise is all I can give." I smiled. "If it makes you feel any better, I'm gay. I came out early, so our circumstances aren't the same, but it was hard. I can't imagine what it would have been like if someone outed me and didn't allow me to do it on my own time. Better?"

"A little, but not much. You didn't have a wife or kids to contend with."

I stepped into my office to make coffee. Rod followed.

"Tell me what happened that night," I said.

"I'm sure you heard that Victor and I argued briefly. It was nothing, really. I was in no position to draw attention to myself, and Victor was not the type to stir up drama in public. Years ago, we bumped into each other at a place in Miami. Victor planned to tell Pam, but he didn't want to hurt her, and I promised I'd never to go to a place like that again. He was disappointed to see me at Club Silver Lake. Called me a liar. We exchanged words but went our separate ways."

"You didn't leave?"

"I had screwed up. I knew Victor liked to spend time at bathhouses around town, and I felt bad about putting him in that position again. I went to my room to collect my thoughts and get my head together, obsessing over the repercussions of what I'd done."

"So, tell me why—"

"Why I went to the bathhouse?" he asked. "You know why."

"Okay. Sex. But why there? Why not just hire an escort?"

"Escorts can be dangerous."

I set the coffee to brew, and Rod and I walked back to the storefront. He placed his hand back on the glass. "Sure, but they're discreet," I said. "No government IDs, no guest log, no security cameras. And it's not like a bathhouse is the safest place either."

"Considering someone killed my brother-in-law a few feet away from me, I can't argue with that. Look, I—never mind. I'm not here to discuss my sex life."

"Oh, but yes, yes you are, Rod. This visit has everything to do with your sex life. That's what drove you to go to that bathhouse. And that's why you're standing here today, trying to pay me off to keep quiet about it." I smiled again. "Just think. If you hadn't been there that night, I'd only know you as the victim's brother-in-law. Instead, here we are, sharing your deepest, darkest secrets."

Rod frowned, looked down at the merchandise and braced his arm above a hairline fracture that ran through the glass. "I had nothing to gain from Victor's death."

"You're married to his sister."

"I can't explain it. I've never gone to the baths here in LA." He slapped his hand on the glass. I was relieved when it held together.

"Pretty bad timing. Where do you go?"

"There's other ways. I uh… I just cruise. You know… places."

"Let me guess. You're into restrooms, is that it? Rest stops? It's the thrill, isn't it, Rod? The danger. The risk. I bet that's what you're into. All you big bankers and money guys, you thrive on risk." I sighed knowing a conversation about where and how he liked to hook up was a dead end. "You're sure Victor never told Pam?"

He lowered his head, placed his hands behind his back, and paced, lifting his head several times to glance out the window. He shook all over.

"I'm certain. I'd know if he had." He snickered. "Do you really think Pam would stay with me?"

"Why wouldn't Victor say anything?"

"I assumed he didn't want to hurt her. Like I said before, when he saw me in Miami, I promised not to do it again. He never saw me in a compromising situation after that until the night he died. Maybe he figured I'd learned my lesson? I don't know. We never talked about it."

"Did you see Warren at the club that night?"

"For a few seconds. We didn't talk, but we nodded when we passed each other."

"Did you see him leave?"

"No, but I wasn't paying attention."

"I'll be upfront with you," I said, "and share that you didn't see him because he left about thirty minutes before the shit hit the fan. Warren wasn't there so he couldn't have killed Victor."

"But—"

"Unless he snuck back in, successfully avoiding both security cameras and the front desk clerk, then magically buzzed himself in through a latched door, Warren didn't kill Victor. We can agree that sounds difficult to pull off, yes?"

"Yes, but—"

"Let's move past this whole 'Warren did it' thing so you can tell me exactly what you saw that night."

"Nothing. I told you everything. I nodded at Warren, argued with Victor, and sat in my room. That's it. I'm just trying to clear my name." He lifted his head and rubbed his temples, his eyes closed.

"I want to help you, Rod. But I can't do that unless you share with me. Where did you bump into Victor?"

"He stepped out of his room when I walked by, grabbed my arm, and admonished me. I couldn't do anything but listen. He said it was a shady place, he'd already warned me once, I'm a married man, I had no business being there… basically rehashing what happened in Miami."

"What did you—"

"Say? That he was right. I know he was right." He slapped the glass again and made me jump. "If this gets out, I'm ruined."

"Not many people are ruined for coming out these days, Rod. At least, not in California."

"I have two boys. And a wife. I don't want to hurt them. See, you don't understand."

"You're right. I understand to a degree, but we're not the same. What happened after your confrontation with Victor?"

"How many times are you going to ask? I went to my room. Then I heard Victor arguing with someone else. He had a thick accent, so I figure it was that guy they arrested. The music was blaring so I couldn't hear their words, but there was definitely some drama. When the fighting stopped, I got dressed. I wanted to get the hell out of there before Victor got out of his room."

"You said earlier that Victor didn't get involved in drama."

"It's not who he is, but things were different that night. He wasn't himself. I knew something was wrong, but I never dreamed he'd end up dead."

"So, you left after you overheard the heated discussion between Victor and the mystery man with an accent?"

"Yes. Well, no. I went to the bathroom."

"Did you notice anything suspicious?" I asked.

"No. There was no one around, except for a guy that works there. He left the bathroom when I went in. Muscular guy—I don't know his name, but he's the manager. You don't forget a man who looks like that. I did my business and was drying my hands when someone screamed about a body. I was terrified, so I ran like hell. I didn't want to be caught up in that mess. It was shortsighted, of course, because the police would catch up with me, but at least I stayed out of sight of the cameras." He looked me in the eyes. "Level with me. Am I a suspect?"

"You're a smart man, Rod. What do you think?" He looked like he was about to pass out. "If it helps, I don't think you did it." I had no idea but wanted to continue earning his trust. "And the manager's name is Trent."

Rod's eyes watered and he trembled. "What do I do now, Mitch?"

"Help me solve the case. If you think of anything else, call me right away. I promise I will not out you unless I have no other choice." Trust was one tactic. Fear was another. Best to leave him with both. "Besides, you need me. If I quit the case, there's no guarantee they won't hire another investigator who isn't so discreet."

Rod rubbed his chin and fixated on the ceiling.

"I've got to go to work," he finally said. "This isn't over. No one can know."

I nodded.

He slammed the door behind him. The bell fell off the knob and hit the floor.

Fifteen

My stomach grumbled while I stared into the microwave. Dried black and brown swirls blanketed the turntable and honey-colored stalactites hung from the top. I pledged to scrub it with bleach before closing, knowing full well it wouldn't happen.

In the two years since I had opened Eye Spy Supplies, I'd become well versed in the fine art of ramen preparation. I kept a stash in my office—Cajun shrimp, beefy mushroom, Oriental surprise—an assortment of choices. In addition, I had a cabinet full of herbs and spices to add a little oomph. I tried to store vegetables in my mini fridge to get some vitamins, but it never stayed cold enough to keep them long.

I went with an old standard and opened a pack of chicken-flavored noodles when the bell I'd put back on the front door jingled. When I leaned back to look out front, my heart raced. Trent Nakos waved a paper bag in the air then dropped it on the counter. His goofy smile was contagious.

"Greetings," he said. "I come bearing gifts."

I put my hands on my chest, leaned back, and inhaled. "Mmm. I haven't had a burger in ages. Thank you. What brings you in?"

"You said you get stuck here all day, so I brought lunch. The thought of you going hungry brought a tear to my eye." He laughed. "Plus, I swung by Ernesto's this morning, and he's not doing so well. He looks bad. Depressed. I'm hoping you have good news."

"There's nothing I can tell you about Ernesto, but come on back, and we can eat."

When we stepped into my office, I raised my hand to Trent's chest to keep him from coming any further. He kept a smile, but his nose turned up, and his eyes darted. I slammed the microwave door and asked him to wait a second. I picked a broom up off the couch and tossed it in the corner, then grabbed several piles of paperwork and put them on my desk. I sat on a cushion at one end of the couch and suggested he join me.

"You didn't need to bother tidying the place. I saw it before. You know, Mitch, I'm sorry to say it, but this place is a dump. You should hire someone."

"I wish I could. It's a challenge to keep it in order, between running the store and the PI work. Always the last priority. But I know it's bad. A professional cleaning is the first thing on my list of expenditures as soon as sales pick up. Sometimes it's like I'm back in the desert in a war zone."

He sat against me, leaving a large gap between himself and the arm at the opposite end of the couch. There was no room for me to slide over, so I bathed in the heat radiating from his body. We leaned over the coffee table and each took a bite of our burger.

From the corner of my eye, I took a good look at him. He was irresistible. I raised my eyes, and he focused on me with his mischievous grin. I played it cool. He said nothing, but his smile didn't fade.

"I know you can't tell me anything specific about the case. But can you at least tell me if the investigation is going well?" He popped a single fry in his mouth. "I am the client, after all." He winked.

"Oh no, you're not getting anything out of me that way." I laughed. "You know I report to Eve Aiken only. But there's nothing to tell, anyway."

He pouted. "I was hoping I could help."

"In that case, I do have a question for you. What can you tell me about Rod Hernandez?"

He gazed at the ceiling for a moment then shook his head. "I don't know him, but the name's familiar. I met a

Hector Hernandez once. Well, more than once." He busted
out a laugh. "I met him in Phoenix, and we—"

"Let me stop you right there. Rod is the big Latino guy
who was there the night of the murder. Barrel chest, broad
shoulders, has a goatee."

"Oh yeah, him." He leered and moved his eyebrows up
and down. "Good looking guy, but I never really met him.
I'd never noticed him before that night, but that doesn't
mean much, except to say that he wasn't a regular. We get
lots of guys through there. Some local, some from out of
town, some every week, some only once. It's hard to keep
track of who's who."

"He says you met in the bathroom."

"I wouldn't say we met. If he says so, then he has a sad
social life." He laughed harder. "I was washing my hands,
and he bumped into me. I excused myself, and he said he
was sorry."

"What'd you talk about?"

"'Excuse me,' and 'I'm sorry.' That's it. What's his
name again?"

"Rod Hernandez. He checked in under his first name,
Gustavo. He goes by his second name, Rodrigo, or Rod.
Do you remember how long after you saw him they found
the body?"

"Not long. I was in my office when the screaming started, so I jumped up and ran toward the sauna. That man, uh… Rod, you said? He and some other guests made a mad dash to grab their things and get out of there. One guy ran straight out the door wearing nothing but his towel. He never came back. We have his wallet and car keys in a locked box. If he took a cab, I don't know how he paid. His clothes are still in my office. Some other guys were too curious to leave. Good for them since they got to make their statements to the police that night. The cops had to track down the others. Who knows where they caught up with them, asking about their night at the bathhouse?"

His amber eyes gleamed, and it was hard not to stare. Their shine brightened whenever he laughed, and the crinkles in the outer corners had become a permanent fixture.

"Did you see Rod before or after Ernesto had a fight with Victor?"

"It was after. About, oh, five or ten minutes after. Probably closer to ten." He paused. "Why are you asking so many questions about him? Do you think this Rod guy murdered Victor?"

"I didn't say that. Just doing my job, gathering information and putting pieces together."

Trent smirked and eyed me sideways. "Something tells me there's a lot more to it than what you're letting on. You haven't asked me about anyone else. You're not giving me the full story. But I get it, you can't."

"Were there any other fights earlier in the evening?"

He scarfed down a big bite from his burger. "There was a lot happening. While we waited for the cops, a couple guys said there was a lot going on with Victor—one fight after another." Trent faced me and smiled like the Cheshire cat. "This is fun. Have I told you I never met a private investigator before?"

"No, but I hear that a lot. Sometimes it's like people think we only exist in movies and paperback novels."

He cocked his head. "Oprah did a show where she interviewed the families who were victims of serial killers. She had a couple of private eyes on there. They talked about best tips to find missing people, way back before the internet was a big thing. None of them were dark and mysterious like in the movies. They were all normal guys, like you. Did you watch it?"

"I don't watch much TV. I never saw Oprah's show."

His mouth dropped and his eyes widened. "Are you kidding me? Everyone watched Oprah. It was a great show.

You watch Ellen, don't you? She's the queen of daytime television. Do you know she's a lesbian?"

I chuckled. "The whole world knows. How do you stay fit when you watch so much TV?"

"Good genes." He ran his hands up and down his torso. "I don't really watch that much. Between the bathhouse, writing, and working out, I don't have much time for the tube. And I rarely eat anything like these burgers and fries." He pulled his shirt up and rubbed his hard stomach. "Not bad, huh?"

"Not too shabby," I stared too long.

"To be honest, I have one guilty pleasure," he said. "It's a comedy about this cute kid named Gilbert from Iowa who's always getting in trouble, and the adults are always telling him—"

"Don't do that?" I cut in.

Trent placed a hand over his mouth and roared. "Yes, *Don't Do That!* That show is so funny. Everyone loves it. I didn't take you for a fan though."

"No, I heard of it. Supposed to be a riot," I tried my best not to sound condescending. "It's the show Victor wrote for."

"I knew he wrote for a hit comedy, but I didn't know it was *Don't Do That!* That's sad. I hope they keep the show

on the air." He looked to the clock on the wall. "You must
be busy running this store and moonlighting as a PI. That's
a lot of work for one guy. Do you normally only investigate
at night?"

"You've seen me during the day, but I try not to. My
sister runs the place on Saturdays, and the store's closed
Sunday and Monday. I'm only here four days a week."

"Still, I'm sure you're busy." He stood. "I should get
going and let you get back to work."

I struggled to come up with a reason for him to stay, and
could feel him gazing down at me as if he was waiting for
an invite. I stood up too quickly and got dizzy. Trent
noticed, put his hand on my shoulder, and asked if I was
okay.

"Just stood up too fast. Thanks for lunch," I said as I
backed away.

"You're welcome. Before I go, I've got something to do.
Hold on."

He walked into the bathroom and left the door open. The
sound of scraping of porcelain echoed from the room.
Curious, I leaned in and caught him over the toilet.

"The water's been running the whole time I've been
here. The chain fell off." He put the lid back on. "We're in
the middle of a drought, you know."

"Thanks. I keep putting it back, but the chain won't stay. I've gotten so I don't even hear it anymore."

"No problem," he replied. We walked to the door. "Are you available tomorrow night? We're having that big party at Club Silver Lake I told you about, the one to remind everyone how fun it can be at the bathhouse. We need to make sure the murder doesn't permanently hurt business. Gabe Quinto is flying in." I gave him a blank stare. "The owner. Anyhow, we'll have dancing, food, strippers. It'll be a grand ol' time. You can't miss it."

"I'll be there."

"Great. Now, I've got to run. I have to help set up… should have left a while ago."

Trent jogged out, climbed into his Jeep, climbed back out, returned to my door, and paused. I wondered what he forgot. He opened it ever so slightly.

"Are you available next Friday night?" he asked. "We'll go out for dinner."

Dinner? I wanted to have dinner with him badly, which is precisely why I couldn't. "Blurring the lines" is what I'd call such behavior. I tried to figure out how to tell him no while softening the blow.

"So sorry, in my line of work it's hard to plan a week out in advance. I never know what's happening from one day to the next. It all depends on where a case may lead."

"You've got to eat sometime. Besides, I may be able to give you more information."

Say no, my mind screamed. *Just say no.*

"All right." My mouth hadn't listened. My first thought was that it was my cock that did the talking, but that wasn't true. I enjoyed being around his energy. It had been awhile since I appreciated being with another man for his company.

"Great, we'll iron out the details," he said.

My eyes were glued to his tight ass as he walked back to his red Jeep and got in. I exhaled as he pulled out of the parking lot and drove down the street. *Don't get hurt*, I told myself.

"Of course it's a date." Josie teased over the phone. "The man brings you lunch and then asks you out for dinner. You're not that naïve, Lil' Bro."

"It's not appropriate. He's the one who hired Eve to defend Ernesto Torres. He is the real client."

"Appropriate?" She clicked her tongue. "Get over yourself and stop trying to find excuses to cancel. Enjoy yourself for a change. I'm excited for you. You should feel it too."

"I've got to go. A car is pulling in."

"Probably just someone asking for directions."

"Bitch." I hung up.

I was disheartened when Pam Hernandez got out of her candy apple red Thunderbird. I'd been hoping for a sale. She was aloof as she sashayed in. She wore a yellow halter dress that ran to her knees and a matching sunhat.

"Good afternoon, Mr. O'Reilly. I hope you enjoyed dinner last night."

"Mr. O'Reilly? Why so formal? Didn't I tell you to call me Mitch?"

Her eyes darted around while she pretended to examine the items in my glass display cases. "Curious items you have. All sorts of contraptions… what about this cute little birdhouse? How peculiar that you would sell it here."

"Not peculiar at all, Pam. It's not a birdhouse."

"What on earth is it?"

"It's a hidden camera. There are cameras or audio recorders in all the regular-looking items you see here—the pens, the clocks, the glasses, the hats. Name anything and I can find it with a camera inside."

"It is rather ironic that you are a PI, yet you sell items that make hiring a detective unnecessary."

I was speechless. She had a point.

Pam placed her silver clutch on the glass case and locked eyes with me. "It is important that we discuss Rodrigo."

"Your husband? I assumed you came to talk about Warren."

"You know why I am here. You have been investigating that place for some time, and you know who was there when my brother was murdered."

"I wouldn't be much of an investigator if I didn't."

She took a final glance at the case then ran a finger along the top while strutting to the next one down. "I do not wish to mince words. You are aware that my husband is gay."

"He is?" Her glare and smirk made it clear my acting abilities weren't convincing. I curbed a chuckle. Rod had wasted a lot of time and effort to keep his wife from knowing the truth. I almost regretted not taking his money.

"It is impressive that you are sticking with the gay code."

"Gay code?"

"Yes, that you will not out another individual. It is admirable, but I cannot allow it to become public that Rodrigo was in that bathhouse when my brother was murdered. How much would you like to stay quiet, Mr. O'Reilly? Maybe I can help you get out of this dump."

If one more person called my place a dump, there'd be another murder to investigate. "I can't accept your money. If he's gay, it's not for me to say."

"Would five thousand be enough?" she asked.

"Five thou ain't much to protect Rod's reputation… or yours."

She stepped back over to her clutch and opened it, pulling out a checkbook. "How much then? What is an acceptable figure?"

"Nothing. I don't know what there is to be quiet about."

"Apparently you are going to continue this charade." She slapped the checkbook on the counter. "Rodrigo was there and is a suspect. I have him followed on a regular basis."

"I'm impressed, Pam. You're keeping it together for a woman who's so nervous."

"Nervous?" She forced a cackle. "What makes you believe I am nervous?"

"You don't go into investigative work without learning a thing or two about reading people."

"I do not know what you mean." She took a deep breath. "My brother told me about Rodrigo's predilection toward men long ago, and I have had Rex Tillerson keep tabs on him ever since. He is a fine detective. You have heard of him, have you not?"

"Rex has been around a while. I hear he's a good PI."

"Indeed he is. He has a fine reputation. Regency Investigative Services is well respected as well. You used to work for them." She paused and looked out the window. "They tell me you were their go-to man for tracking cheating spouses. If I understand correctly, you have never worked a real investigation. Is that true?"

Ouch. That stung. "I don't know what you think qualifies as a 'real investigation,' but I can tell you this. Spying on people is a lot of work."

"Tedious, perhaps, but not one that takes skill. Anyone can sit in a car and take pictures." She walked to another section of the display case and continued to act as if she was interested in the items inside. "I do not mean to insult you. I like you, Mr. O'Reilly. You should take my check and leave Rodrigo out of the picture."

"I won't take your money." Damn, it hurts to have scruples.

"I could call that bathhouse and offer to hire Regency for them. It is most certain it would thrill them to have a real investigator working for them."

"I can assure you I'm a real investigator. You don't get a license by just passing a test."

She positioned herself inches away from me and put her hands in a prayer position. "Work with me," she begged.

"Let me offer you this. If Rod was there that night, I'll try to leave him alone. But there's no guarantee."

"How do I get a guarantee?"

"You can't. Just hope he didn't get himself into a situation that forces me to out him… that is, if he happened to be there."

"It is in your best interest not to let that get out."

"Really? Tell me more about the threat you just made. Wait, let me turn on this audio recording device so I can get it loud and clear."

She turned away and looked around the store to see if I had recording devices in use while grasping her clutch at her chest. "Threat? I do not recall a threat. You must have misunderstood me." She grew silent and browsed more of my merchandise. "I would like to purchase something. What is the most expensive item you sell?"

I grabbed a pair of night vision goggles off the shelf behind me and set them next to the cash register. "Twenty-nine hundred dollars."

"I have no clue what it is, but I am sure it will make a lovely gift. Ring it up for me."

The profits from the sale would ensure I would eat, buy gas, and take care of other basic needs for a while. "I appreciate your purchase so much that the sales tax is on me."

Pam huffed, walked to the window, and stared across the parking lot. "You are not willing to guarantee to protect my husband, are you?"

"I don't make promises I can't keep."

"You are a man of honor, Mr. O'Reilly. That is unfortunate." She hurried out the front door without saying goodbye. I placed the twenty-nine hundred dollar goggles back on the shelf.

Sixteen

The cool, dry desert night gave relief from the heat wave that'd been pounding the city all month. It was late Friday night and the weekend gamblers had traffic at a crawl. Along the way, one billboard advertised *Native American Gaming*, while the rest labeled themselves as *Indian Gaming*. Casinos and sports teams had become the last bastions of political incorrectness. Once I got out of Riverside, the landscape was pure darkness until blue, green, and pink casino lights dotted the sky. I pulled into a near empty parking lot. Many of the fluorescent bulbs that decked the building had gone dark, and the entire word *Fiesta* was burned out on the *Fiesta Springs Casino* sign. I don't know where all those gamblers on the highway were going, but it sure as hell wasn't Fiesta Springs.

A placard at the entrance said *No Self Parking*, and when I tried to drive past it, the valets stopped me. I didn't like other people driving my car. True it was just a Honda Accord, but to a man in my financial situation, it might as well have been a Lamborghini. Besides, I had selected it after much thought and careful consideration. The car was as nondescript as they come, which made it perfect for tailing or stakeouts. One noticeable scratch or dent could easily spoil that for me.

"Sir, you've got to choose," one of the valets said. "You can either let us park it or go home."

"I always heard Vegas bends over backward for their customers."

"Yeah, I heard that too—from old people. Wasn't like that when I was there. And this ain't Vegas." The tall, blond, pimply-faced teen caught the car keys I tossed him. "Hold on while I get your ticket for your car."

"A ticket? There are hardly any cars here. I bet half of those are employees."

"Rules is rules." He handed me my stub, and I gave him my last dollar bill. He parked my car only three spaces down from where I stood.

I'd forgotten to ask Rod what games Warren played. The casino interior was cavernous, but with so few patrons, it shouldn't take too long to find him. Row after row of vacant slot machines emitted pings, pongs, and music to draw victims near. The sounds, mixed with the giant orange flowers woven into the red carpet, made me dizzy.

Warren didn't seem to be the slot machine type—not that I knew what a slot machine type looked like. If he was in financial trouble, I imagined that meant he liked the tables more. It was a lot faster to blow a grand on a poker game than on a slot machine. As I wandered briskly through the mechanical thieves on my way to the other game rooms, a minimum of three security guards had their eyes on me at all times.

I didn't find Warren playing roulette, craps, poker, keno, or baccarat. On my second round through the building, I spotted him. He was at the end of a row of slots playing blackjack—a card game I had played a lot while in the Army but wasn't any good at.

I purchased two five-dollar chips and sat down next to him. He kept his focus on the cards, and I wasn't sure if he realized I was there. He lost his hand. Without hesitation, he laid more chips down and was dealt two new cards. Three other men did the same.

I had expected the minimum bid to be lower, but it was ten dollars, so I tossed my two red chips in and was dealt my cards. An eight and a seven. Blackjack as a game was entertaining, but I never saw the appeal in gambling, so I wasn't sure how the betting system worked. "I'd ask for another card, but I have no more chips."

The dealer, a rigid man with square shoulders and a chiseled face, snorted. "You don't have to bid higher to get a card."

"Then hit me."

The next card was another seven. I busted. Warren also busted, and the dealer slid his chips away too. He immediately placed more on the table. I got off my stool and watched.

Warren leaned his head in my direction. "One word and I can have you tossed out on your ass," he whispered, keeping his eyes on his cards. "They know me here."

"So I've heard."

He asked to be dealt more cards. "What does that mean?"

"We all have our hobbies. I prefer ones that don't suck away all my cash. Word on the street is money was a bit of an... issue... between you two. In large part thanks to your patronage here."

Warren threw his cards down and glared. "And what are your hobbies, O'Reilly?"

I shrugged. "All work, no play for me these days."

He dabbed a handkerchief on his cheeks, his red combed-over hair, and across his forehead. "If you want to talk, come with me."

I followed Warren to a small bar in the middle of the room. He stood taller and broader than I remembered from the funeral. He ordered himself something called a rickey and a greyhound for me. There were small booths with blue upholstery that circled the bar. He struggled between the table and the seat but turned himself enough to fit.

"What's a rickey?" I asked.

"It's got gin. Are we done?"

"I'm surprised," I said. "At Victor's memorial service, you wanted to take my head off. Tonight, we're having drinks. Are you trying to fatten the pig before the kill?"

Warren held his jaw so tight that he was hard to understand. "We're not having drinks. You are having one drink. Just one. When it's gone, we're done talking, and I want you out of my life for good. What happened at the funeral was all your doing. You had no business interrogating me there."

"I wasn't interrogating you. I was trying to introduce myself."

"You had no business doing that either. I was mourning during a private ceremony. It was unprofessional and inexcusable."

"Don't forget ineffective." I didn't dare mention he couldn't expect privacy on one of the busiest beaches in the world.

"Now you have my full attention," he said. "If you have a lot to ask, I suggest you drink slowly, and don't piss me off."

I sipped my greyhound. "Let's start with why you've been so evasive."

"Let's start with you showing some compassion for the fact I just lost the man I loved for two decades. Let's start with the fact that it's too painful to talk about the terrible, painful way in which he died."

Warren finished his drink and called the bartender over for another. I fixated on my drink and swirled it around in its glass. "I'm sorry for your pain, but I still don't understand. I would think you'd want to ensure Victor's killer is caught and brought to justice."

"It's obvious Ernesto did it. It's only a matter of time before the police gather enough evidence to charge him and keep him in jail this time. Why don't you think he did it?"

"My job is to gather evidence about Victor's life and what happened that night, and hand it over to my client. That's it. At this point, I don't think anything. I'm just looking for clues. What makes you think it was Ernesto?"

"Ernesto was codependent beyond belief. It's no secret that Victor and I were having troubles. But it was for no reason other than we had grown to take each other for granted. Having an open relationship made matters worse. Instead of talking when problems hit, one or both of us would hook up with someone else so we wouldn't have to think about our issues at home. Men became a drug."

He took a sip and continued. "We were trying to work things out. We didn't want to toss all our years together in the garbage. He agreed to call it off with Ernesto and give monogamy a go. Ernesto was out to make sure that didn't happen."

"What do you know about Christian Freeman?"

"Who?"

"Christian Freeman. He and Victor were also seeing each other."

"Never heard of him. Who is he? What's he look like?"

"He's about six feet tall, built body, dark skin. He's a go-go boy at Euphoria in West Hollywood."

"This is the first I've heard of him." His face fell. "I'm such a fool. Our rule was no relationships. Just sex, and that's it. He broke that rule with Ernesto, and now you're telling me there was another guy? How many were there?"

I cranked up the heat. "I hesitate to say this, but there have been allegations you may have been involved in Victor's passing."

Warren tried to stand up but got stuck between the booth and the table. He mumbled obscenities and sat his ass back on the seat. "I wasn't even there, you bastard. How dare you imply I had anything to do with the murder."

"I know you were there that night. I also know you checked out early. I'm making no judgment. Just following all leads."

"It was Pam, wasn't it?" He slammed a fist causing some of my drink to splash on the table. "She put you up to this."

"I can neither confirm nor deny."

"You don't have to," he bellowed. "She's hated me from day one. She's always saying I was after her brother's money, but when we met, Victor had nothing. He was almost on the streets until I showed up. He didn't sell his first script until five years after we got together. Pam and Victor grew up poor in Barstow. Both of them worked hard and made good lives for themselves. I'll admit, I respect her for it. She's forgotten her roots, though. She's a pretentious bitch." He calmed down. "Have you noticed she never uses contractions?"

I placed my hands on the table and leaned back in my seat. "Contractions. That's what it is. I couldn't figure out why she talks funny."

"She sounds like a robot, right?" He gave a loud laugh that shook his belly, like a redheaded Santa. "She started doing that about the same time she met Rod, and she had to work hard at it. She thought it would make her more eloquent. Instead, it makes her sound foolish. Did you know Rod is gay?"

"No." I looked away.

"He was at Club Silver Lake when Victor was killed. You're either a liar or a bad PI if you don't know that by now. He's been able to keep it from Pam for years. Vic and I busted out laughing at first when we caught him years ago at a sex club. We were on vacation in Miami, of all places. He was there on business. It shook Vic up though. He wanted to tell Pam. Vic and Rod had a huge argument that night, and Rod swore he'd never do it again. Now there's someone to investigate. Rod has his reputation at stake."

"With so much for Rod to lose, are you still sure it was Ernesto?"

He thought about it for a minute. "Yeah, I'm sure. In the end, Rod wouldn't kill anyone—especially not his wife's brother. What would he get out of it now? It's been years since we found out. Ernesto's hurt was raw. He was a firecracker ready to blow."

"And then there's you."

Warren leaned in and grimaced while pointing a finger in my chest. "What are you insinuating?"

The bartender, who had been shuffling bottles in an attempt to hide his obvious eavesdropping, took a step back. He nonchalantly bit his lower lip and twirled his hair while scanning the casino. When he caught my gaze, he turned around and dusted the mirrored shelves.

I prepared to be pummeled. "There's no way to dance around the money issue. As I said earlier, gambling is an expensive hobby."

"You've got balls, you bastard."

"So I've been told."

Warren balled his fists and his face flushed. "It's time for you to pay up and leave."

"I thought drinks were on you."

He drank the last of his gin, squeezed his body out the booth, and pointed toward the door. "Leave, O'Reilly, or I'll call security and make sure you leave."

I didn't argue. It'd been a long night, and I had a store to open in the morning. I paid for my drinks and his and drove home, listening to Gorillaz as loud as I could.

Seventeen

I drove around Club Silver Lake for fifteen minutes before I gave up on parking, drove home, and walked the hilly mile to get there. I knew I was only going because Trent had invited me, but I worked at convincing myself attending the event was all part of my investigation.

My shirt was drenched by the time I reached the front door of the club. My body was on fire, but I noticed my hands were cold and clammy. I hesitated at the door a moment then stepped inside.

Seth leaned against the counter. "Trent was just asking if you showed up yet."

"I'll hunt him down."

"Whoa, hold up. You can't go wandering in there with your street clothes on." He tossed me a towel. "The place is fucking full. We're sold out of rooms, but I'll give you a locker for now and put you on top of the waitlist."

"No, thanks," I said. "A locker is fine. I'm just here to observe."

"So, you like to watch? Kinky bitch." Seth laughed.

I smiled, and he buzzed open the door to the back. Techno music blared through the halls while cobalt lighting flickered to the beat. The sound and color mixed with the

smell of sweat and sex aroused me in a way I hadn't felt in
a long time. I got a partial hard-on standing there taking it
all in.

The seats in the front lounge were taken by two naked
men and six others in towels. Animal Planet was on TV,
but no one watched. There were lots of wandering eyes, but
none were making the first move. They'd probably all go
home alone, each wondering why he didn't get laid.

I did a quick change into nothing but a towel in the
locker room and joined the party. Instead of pushing
through the crowd in the main hallway, I detoured through
the maze of private rooms to enter from the back. I had
never rented a room. When the club was one of my regular
spots, I was young, hot, and confident I'd find someone
sexy who had one. On the rare occasion I hooked up with a
guy without a room, we'd get it on in the open. Sometimes,
having an audience increased the thrill.

Halfway down a hall, a man with a curly black perm and
a cheesy mustache stopped me. He had an average build
and looked like a '70s porn star, except for a potbelly and
an odd set of pointy man boobs.

"Do you want to PNP?" he asked.

I brushed Mr. Party and Play aside and, without saying a word, continued toward the crowd. Behind me, he huffed and said, "Rude!"

The thrill of being there was enough of a drug that I didn't need someone dangling a bag of meth under my nose. It was electrifying. My last time there as a guest, it was a long weekend. I'd met a hot man on Friday night, and we'd fucked for hours. For three days I worked my way from one man to another, each with his own style.

I shook the memories and returned to the present when I reached the so-called playroom, with its sea of sweaty skin and white towels. Most were trying to dance, but there wasn't room to do much more than sway back and forth. There was a group of four obese men in their sixties who were pushed against three lean, muscular guys who couldn't have been older than twenty. The seven of them had their hands raised and were rubbing and bumping as they jumped up and down. They were having great fun, and it made me chuckle.

The giant cages had been converted for the night to DJ booths. In the large TV area, the screens were all turned off, and go-go boys danced above the crowd. There was a buffet dinner on the other side of the room.

I saw Christian Freeman dancing on a podium. He was in full performance mode, thrilling the crowd.

The food looked good, and I hadn't had time for dinner, but I couldn't bring myself to eat off a buffet in a bathhouse. I decided I'd grab a bite later—maybe a burrito from the vending machine up front. At least there I wouldn't have to worry about dozens of men dripping with sweat reaching across the food.

I pushed through the sea of men until I spotted Trent helping an employee add a tray of cheese sticks to the buffet. He wore a white T-shirt with Club Silver Lake in sparkly silver on his chest. Beside him was an overdressed man wearing blue jeans, a pink polo, and a tweed blazer. His clothes were two sizes too big, like a little boy wearing his older brother's hand-me-downs. He was frail. I was afraid at any moment someone would bump him and snap him in half. He kept turning away from the buffet to interrupt the customers who were dancing so he could introduce himself. No one seemed interested. Most seemed irritated. I presumed he was Gabe Quinto, the owner.

Trent finished refilling the hors d'oeuvres and noticed me. He grinned and nodded, but he looked busy. I worked my way toward him but lost him in the crowd.

Normally, it would be very dark, and men would quietly play cat and mouse while looking for the right guy to hook up with. This nightclub vibe was an entertaining change.

"Enjoying yourself?" Seth shouted from behind.

"Looks like a success."

"We've never been this fucking busy. It's amazing. Did you notice Christian up there dancing?" He pointed to him swaying on the podium and thrusting his hips.

"First thing when I walked in."

"I've got to get back up front. Make sure you stay for Christian's grand finale. It's an amazing sight."

Seth walked back to the front office. I searched for a quiet spot to wait for Trent when a hand grabbed my elbow. Instinctively, I snatched it away.

"Excuse me," a man yelled over the music. "Excuse me. I'd like to thank you for coming tonight. I'm Gabe Quinto, the owner of Club Silver Lake."

I turned. "Nice to meet you, Gabe." We shook hands. "Can we talk?"

He eyed me with suspicion then said something, but the room was too loud. I cupped my ear with my hand and leaned toward him.

"How may I help you?" he yelled.

"I'm Mitch O'Reilly, the detective hired by Ernesto Torres' attorney."

"Oh, yes." He leered. "Oh, yes, yes. Trent told me you were a hottie, and he was right."

He was even thinner up close. The perspiration from his balding top streamed into what little salt-and-pepper hair he had left. His mustache wax was melting onto his upper lip.

The mix of business and pleasure was awkward. It felt like ages before he lifted his gaze and looked into my eyes. His lips were moving, but he was speaking too low. "It's hard to hear you," I yelled.

Gabe took a few steps away from the crowd, leaned against the wall, and crossed his arms. "Trent said he told you that I'm allowing this investigation to proceed, with much trepidation. I expect you will not be disturbing our guests."

"Not a problem."

"Have you been here before?" he asked. "In your free time, I mean?"

"A long time ago, but a whole lot of life came my way. The war in Afghanistan, mostly. Then work keeps me busy. I haven't been around much lately."

He grinned, revealing yellow teeth. "Well, sir, thank you for your service. With that body and buzz cut, it looks like you're still on active duty."

I caught myself flexing and felt myself blush. "I'll take that as a compliment."

"As you should." He nodded. "Has Enrique been helpful?"

"You mean Ernesto? He's been helpful, but not as much as I'd hoped. He's in shock from the whole ordeal."

"Hmm." Gabe stroked his chin. "Maybe a sign of guilt, don't you think?"

"Maybe a sign of a man wrongly accused who fears for his life."

"Touché. You're the expert. Now that you're back in our club, I do hope we'll see you around. We never get enough hot men like you."

My towel loosened, and I caught it before it dropped from my waist. I tightened it, making sure not to expose the goods. "Thanks, but it's not really appropriate for—"

"While you're here, have some fun." He waved toward the maze of rooms.

"Maybe. We'll see." I had no intention of cruising for sex mid-investigation. "May I ask you a couple of questions?"

"Of course."

"You flew in from Chicago right after the murder. Anything you can tell about what you found when you got here?"

"There wasn't much to see," he said. "Everything the police were doing seemed routine, at least from what I see on television and in movies. Trent does a fine job running this place. I don't get involved in the minor details of my clubs unless they're not doing well. The one in Pittsburgh is giving me some trouble, but this location is profitable enough. I've never met any of the lesser staff, including Eduardo."

"His name is Ernesto. You don't seem all that concerned."

Gabe shrugged.

"As I said, I have full confidence in Trent. Between us, I wanted him to let it go. The police had a suspect, and I saw no need to retain counsel on his behalf. But Trent insisted we had to protect our employee from false accusations. I told him as long as it didn't distract him from his work, he could hire an attorney. The police and Trent keep me up to date as much as necessary. Now go cruise and have some fun." He faded into the crowd.

I ignored Gabe's suggestion and started toward the exit, but turned back to find Trent. He was talking with a group of men near the center of the party. I inched my way in his direction, but by the time I got there he'd moved on. I spotted him in a cage with one of the DJs. I pushed harder and faster. I reached him just as he was stepping out.

"Hey there. You're a busy man tonight," I said. "It's been hard to reach you."

Trent responded, but I shook my head to show I couldn't hear him. He reached around and pulled my drenched body up next to him. "Glad you made it," he said in my ear. His voice was emotionless. "I wasn't sure you would come."

His T-shirt was soaked, emphasizing his pumped chest and sculpted abs. His hardened nipples brushed against my exposed body. My cock snaked itself along his leg. He looked down, and for a moment we were the only two in the room.

"I accepted your invitation hoping to do a little investigating."

"Find anything new?" he asked.

"Not—"

"Hold on, my phone's buzzing."

I stood patiently while he placed a finger in one ear and yelled into his phone. He kept looking my way.

"Sorry," he said, putting his phone in his pocket. "There's a fight going on in the rear showers. It's a rare thing." He frowned and shrugged. "Enjoy the party. We'll talk later."

I faked a smile and watched him vanish in the mix. My stomach tightened. I stepped into a corridor intending to resume my investigation, but I couldn't think of anything else to look into. There was too much going on to ask Seth or Christian any more of my questions, and the party ensured I wouldn't be spending any quality time with Trent.

I headed for the hall of private rooms, aiming to leave the party quickly and quietly. A large roar came from the playroom, and I surmised it was Christian's grand finale. I could feel something stirring under my towel.

I found a bare wall next to an emergency exit and automatically slid into the traditional cruising pose—back against the wall, one knee up, bottom of that foot against the wall, the other foot planted firmly on the floor. It was like riding a bike—something I'd never forget. I stood for a minute then pulled my leg down and stood straight. My impulses had gotten the best of me, and my actions were inappropriate and unprofessional. I started to walk away and was startled when a thick hand gripped my arm.

The stranger released me when I spun around. "I apologize," he said. "It was rude to grab you like that, but it was a gut reaction. I couldn't let you get away."

He towered several inches above me and was a mountain of muscle. With his pale skin, golden hair, and piercing blue eyes, he looked as if he'd just gotten off the plane from Sweden. I allowed him to explore the contour of my chest with his fingers.

He had a scrunched up face with squinty eyes. It was a mean look that Josie and I called angry face—the male equivalent of resting bitch face. It didn't work for everyone, but in his case it was hot. Still, I reminded myself I wasn't there for sex. I tried to dart away, but he ran his finger along the top edge of my towel and paralyzed me. My eyes closed for a second and when I opened them, he smirked, nodded his head to the left, and started down the hall. I looked around to make sure no one was watching and followed him.

The man stepped into his room, smirked again, and disappeared into the shadows. It all came rushing back— that touch of danger, the thrill of validation, and pure carnal desire. I went in, and he leaned over me and closed the door.

He dropped his towel. The size of his body was both imposing and enticing. His hard cock stood at attention, looking as if it needed a room of its own. He was one of those men who was proud to have good control of his crotch muscles, and he used them now to make his dick throb and dance up and down. Guys who did that thought it was sexy. I found it silly but didn't give a damn. He pulled my body against his, ran his hands along the muscles in my back, and grabbed my ass, sliding my towel off.

This was what I craved—simple lust and fornication, with no unnecessary conversation. The anonymity was seductive, but I could get that on the net too. This was different. The heat, the pounding music, the smell of sex in the air, and the moans of men echoing all around me heightened the full experience. Until this moment, I hadn't realized how much I had missed being here.

He released his grip on me, took a step back, and smiled for the first time. His fingers drifted along my chest and abs, then one finger flowed down my happy trail, running from my navel to my cock. My balls danced as he fondled them and dropped to his knees. I closed my eyes in anticipation and leaned my back on the wall to avoid falling. My body shuddered, and I could feel my heart racing from the warmth that engulfed my shaft each time he swallowed me whole.

I gasped.

His hand had clutched my neck. He pulled my head down and slid his tongue between my lips.

"What the fuck?" I pushed his shoulders and stepped to the side.

"What's wrong?" He cupped my balls again.

Without a word, I snatched my towel off the floor and wrapped it around me. I stormed out the door, turned the corner, raced toward the lockers, and froze. Trent was in the hall.

"You're still here," he said, "I wondered why you left without saying goodbye."

I had no idea if he knew where I'd been, whether he'd seen me come out of that room. I felt myself blushing.

"Just hanging out," I said. "Gabe suggested it. I'm… I'm getting ready to head out now."

He gave me a suspicious look and glared. My muscles tensed and I clenched my jaw. I resented that I couldn't enjoy myself, that I felt shame and regret. It was unfair.

"Thank you for stopping in," Trent muttered. "I hope you enjoyed your research."

He walked away. As I watched him disappear, I wasn't sure what my best course of action would be. Should I try to smooth things over, or was it best to leave? I didn't even know if there was anything to clear up.

Before I moved, Mr. Party and Play came up the hall. Despite my obvious attempt to avoid eye contact, he asked, "You ready for a little fun now?"

"No, thanks."

"Are you saying no because you've become a permanent part of this wall?"

"No explanation required."

His jaw dropped, and he looked like he had more to say, but changed his mind. He huffed down the hall and into the darkness.

As he wandered off, my memory of that long weekend five years prior came to mind with a different perspective. The man I remembered as being hot was anything but. The only thing attractive about him was his glass pipe and stash. I had let my guard down with the garbage swirling in my brain. All I wanted was sex. It had become an obsession. A drug. After each round, I was unfulfilled. I needed another round. Another fix. I had moved from one room to the next trying to fill the hole in my soul.

Rehashing the memory made me repulsed and depressed. I was crashing at Josie's at the time, and it was after that weekend that she gave me an ultimatum to get my shit together or move out. She landed me the job with Regency Investigative Services. She helped me get my life back on track.

I opened my locker then slammed it shut. There was important business to take care of.

I returned to the playroom and pushed my way through, on the hunt for Trent. Gabe shrugged his shoulders when I asked where he was. The reaction from the DJ was the same. Finally, an employee who recognized me nodded in Trent's direction.

It wasn't easy to reach him, and I knocked a group of guys over in my haste. I grabbed his shoulder, and he gasped.

"Thank you for inviting me," I said. "I had a good time. I only wish you hadn't been so busy so we could have spent time together."

The edges of his lips turned up. "Me too."

"We still on for dinner next week?" I gritted my teeth, afraid of his response.

His shoulders relaxed, and the lines on his forehead softened. A grin spread across his face. "I wouldn't miss it."

By midnight, I was home and showered, with a bowl of Honey Nut Cheerios for dinner.

Eighteen

Fairfax Avenue from Rosewood Avenue to CBS Television City was a drab shopping district with an eclectic mix of bargain stores, thrift shops, and boarded up buildings. Eateries ranged from pizza joints to sushi, but located in the heart of LA's Jewish community, it was most well known for its kosher restaurants and delis. The most notable landmark was the long-standing Canter's Deli, open twenty-four hours a day. A few doors down was the lesser-known Olexi Greek Restaurant.

I arrived near dusk—twenty minutes late, as usual. The angle of the streetlights cast shadows across his face, but the broad shoulders and v-shaped torso left no doubt who stood there. Despite the restaurant's uninspiring exterior, two large blue double doors framed by thick, old-world gold molding welcomed guests. Trent, who was leaning against the wall, smiled and tapped his wrist.

He chuckled. "You got a lot going for you, but punctuality ain't one of your strong suits."

"It's this LA traffic."

He rolled his eyes and snickered. "Of course it is."

The traffic excuse was one I used a lot and living in LA, it usually worked. But the truth was I couldn't decide what to wear. Not something that typically worried me. Trent said the place was casual, so I chose a rarely worn, dark blue pair of jeans and a light green collarless pullover with a zipper in the front that ran several inches below the neck. It didn't show much, but a little definition and a tuft of hair. It was also baggy enough to hide the little bit of a pooch I had developed from surviving on junk food and skipping the gym.

Trent's lavender polo shirt, which clung to his olive skin, brought out the color of his amber eyes. He was hot, but what I felt was more than just physical. Josie was always good for a laugh, but I liked being around someone else for a change. None of my friends were gay. In fact, other than Josie, I had no friends at all, and I think sisters don't count.

It was clear by the way he smiled at me that he wanted more than to get laid. A nice dinner usually didn't equal just a good fuck. I wondered why such a good guy would be into me.

Though I had argued with Josie over the phone insisting that it wasn't a date, the second he held the door open for me, I realized I'd been fooling myself. I liked him, and it seemed that he liked me. Still, I couldn't allow anything to happen. I preferred my sex quick and anonymous—no romance, no attachments, no broken hearts. I couldn't pursue more.

"Let's go in. My aunt's waiting for us," Trent said.

"She's joining us?" He hadn't told me I'd be meeting the family.

"Not exactly. Aunt Ada runs the place. My family opened it in 1949."

We were greeted by a woman who looked to be in her mid-sixties. "Trent, my favorite nephew!" she squealed as if she hadn't seen him in years. They hugged and kissed each other's cheek.

She couldn't have been more than five feet tall. She was bony and a little hunched over, yet a force exuded from her that captivated me as much as her nephew had. Right away, I was eager to get to know her better.

"Aunt Ada, this is Mitch, the friend I told you about."

She pulled her brown cat-eye glasses down to have a look at me. Her smile deepened the lines on her cheeks, and I could see where Trent got his glowing face. "You didn't lie, Trent." She looked in my eyes and smiled wider. "*Eísai ómorfos!*"

"She said, 'You're handsome,'" Trent translated.

"Yes, you are," she said. "You're very handsome. My nephew has good taste."

Trent glanced at me, then dipped his head and blushed.

"Follow me," she said. "I have the best table waiting for you."

The entire restaurant was blue. A short, vague description, but that's what it was. Royal blue tablecloths, cobalt curtains, and teal chairs. She may have snuck in several shades, but everything screamed blue. It was like walking into a living Greek flag. Not having the gay decorator gene, the other tints were hard for me to define, but the carpet, the napkins, and the walls were all blue. The only prominent features that weren't blue were green plastic plants on white shelves suspended above each table and old watercolor paintings of Greek monuments that hung beneath them. Time had faded the pictures, but I could still make out the Acropolis, the Parthenon, and other ruins I couldn't name.

All the tables hugged the walls in order to give a belly dancer space to do her thing in the middle of the rectangular room. Silver strands draped from her neck over her shimmering blue bikini top and flowed down to hold medallions above her belly button. Another set of strands wrapped around her waist. Sheets of sheer fabric hung loosely from her small bikini bottom and fell to just above her ankles. I felt like she could swat me at any time as we walked through the restaurant.

Ada seated us and hurried to the door to welcome more customers.

"Look at that dancer," Trent said. "Isn't she beautiful?"

"Some find it entertaining, I guess."

He reared back and teased. "Oh, and you don't?"

Starting a date with a negative attitude is not good. Especially with someone as lighthearted as Trent. "I actually find it impressive." I lied. "The way she swings and sways and moves her arms like snakes. It's an art."

He waved a dismissive hand. "Oh, come on. One thing I like about you is you tell it like it is. This is our chance to get to know each other—there's no need to play games."

I fumbled with the napkin in my lap. "If you want honesty, I rate belly dancers right up there with mimes."

He guffawed. "That's bad. I mean, I like mimes myself, but I know I'm in the minority… Ah, the ouzo has arrived. My aunt always likes to kick off a meal with the official beverage of Greece."

A server held a small tray while Ada gracefully took two drinks off and placed them on the table.

"Thank you," Ada said to the server. "Mitch, enjoy." She winked at Trent, then excused herself and walked off to the kitchen.

I peered at my drink. "What's in this? Why is it white?"

"It's served here the way it's supposed to be, with icy cold water," Trent said. "That's what makes it milky."

I shrugged and swallowed it all in one gulp.

He protested. "You don't down ouzo like a shot of whiskey. Relax. Enjoy it. If you drink like that, you'll be a sick man."

"Sorry, it's instinct. I haven't had ouzo since college, and the point then was to get drunk." Heat rose to my cheeks. "Old habits die hard, I guess."

He laughed. "We're adults now. Take your time. Technically, you're not supposed to drink ouzo with dinner. It's to be savored slowly with appetizers prepared to complement the drink. It's practically an art in Greece. Americans are too impatient."

I chortled. "We do love instant gratification." I glanced at the menu. "I don't know much about Greek food, so you'll have to help me decipher the menu. It's all Greek to me."

"Relax, we'll get to that. How was your week? Did you recover from the party at the bathhouse?"

"The week was pretty slow," I said. "Business was down at the store."

"Yeah, the party was a bust," Trent said. "I mean, you saw that night. It was jammin', but it cost us a fortune and business has been way down ever since." He took a sip of his ouzo. "Have you got anything you can tell me about the case?"

"Not much has advanced over the past week. But that's normal—nothing to worry about. Things go fast in the beginning as we weed through suspects. After that, things slow down as we gather evidence."

Trent opened his mouth, but before he could respond, a server walked up with a tray and placed three plates on our table. He appeared to be in his fifties, with a pockmarked face and greasy, thinning black hair combed over to one side. All the servers wore black slacks and loose-fitting black shirts. The way they moved through the restaurant was quick and efficient. Aunt Ada would make a good master sergeant.

"Hello, gentlemen," he said, smiling. "Ada has chosen your dinner for this evening. Here are your appetizers."

Trent rubbed his palms. "That's just like her. Bring it on."

I seized the moment to toss in some business. "This works out great. Since I didn't gather new evidence over the week, this will give me time to ask some follow-up questions regarding the night of Victor's murder."

"Sure, sure. We'll get to that, but let's start with something less gruesome. I want to enjoy our drinks and our appetizers first. We have dolmades, garlic mushrooms, and *saganaki*. All delicious."

I said, "At least I know what garlic mushrooms are."

"You'll love everything. Dolmades are stuffed grape leaves, and *saganaki* is fried cheese. That's all I'll explain for the rest of the night. Think of this as an adventure. You seem like a man who thrives on adventure." He winked.

"Well—"

Two more belly dancers slithered out. One wore red, the other green. Both shook and swayed like the one in blue, who had now come to interrupt our appetizers. She motioned for me to stand. Oh, dear God, she wanted me to dance. I shook my head, but she wasn't fazed. She took my hand and continued to coax me. The other diners began hooting and clapping to get me out of my seat, but I wouldn't budge. The dancer in green found another man to join her, and the one in red grabbed a female partner. It was embarrassing enough sitting there with all eyes on me—I was not about to get up and dance. To avoid further torture, I shook my head again.

She ran her fingers down her cheeks and made an exaggerated frown, then took the hand of a woman at the next table. The three diners made fools of themselves, trying to mimic the dancers, and gave everyone a good laugh. Better them than me. Trent's furrowed brow showed his disappointment. He lifted a dolma and stared at it for a moment before taking a bite. He chewed slowly before speaking.

"You missed an opportunity to *tsifteteli*," he said.

"What's that?"

"A tongue twister of a word for Greek belly dancing."

I held out my palm. "Never do that to me again."

"What? I did nothing. She's the one who came up to you." He belted out a laugh.

"I'm suspicious by nature, which makes me well-suited for my job… and perceptive enough to know that you were behind this."

"I will neither confirm nor deny your suspicions, detective," he teased.

After finishing our appetizers and a second glass of ouzo, I could feel myself letting my guard down, having a bit too much fun. I should have let it stay that way but I couldn't resist getting back to business.

"Trent, listen. I've got Eve breathing down my neck for more information. I know we're here to have a good time, but I really need clarification on some things that happened that night."

He slumped in his seat and pouted. He opened his mouth to speak, then his eyes widened, and he grinned. "Just in the nick of time. Look who's brought us dinner. Aunt Ada, I love you!" He grabbed two platters from her and set them down.

"Enjoy," she said. "Mitch, I prepared a nice *pastitsio* for you, and here for Trent, we have his favorite, lamb *kleftiko*. Give Mitch a bite, yeah? I want him to try both." She looked at my empty glass. "A fresh drink will be right over."

Trent grabbed my platter and split our meals. I took a bite of each and gave him a thumbs up.

"New rule," he said. "No murder talk over dinner. Let's say we move on to some good old-fashioned conversation. What's your story?"

"My story? That's open-ended," I said.

"Intentionally... But let me think... Okay, this shouldn't be too hard. How'd you become a PI?"

"That's boring."

"So, bore me."

"When I left the Army, I was done with law enforcement, but I didn't want to go back to college. Being a private eye seemed like a good choice since my time served went toward experience credits. I had to work for an agency to get more hours in order to qualify for my license. Josie works for a place called Regency Investigative Services, so she got me a job there."

"Sounds like you left the military with a pretty good plan."

"Not necessarily. I glazed over those first few months while I was trying to figure it all out. I was, you could say, forced out of service."

"Oh?" He scooted closer.

"Not by a superior, but by circumstances. I requested a discharge. Too many friends were killed. People think all MPs do is drive around military bases arresting drunk soldiers, which—don't get me wrong—we do that too. I did it for two years at Fort Bragg, but I was also deployed twice to Afghanistan. During both of those tours, my job was to secure routes for troop movement and shipments. The enemy knows you can choke a unit by cutting off supplies, so we had to keep the roads open. That put us right in the center of shit. It was nothing like cruising around a domestic base or directing traffic." I cleared my throat and looked away. "Four years in the military was plenty, so I asked to come home."

I focused on the fork in my hand.

"I can't believe I deprived myself of Greek food all this time." I changed the subject. "This is delicious."

"I'm glad you enjoy it," Trent said, but he looked perplexed.

He watched in silence while I took several bites.

"Something wrong?" I asked.

"I'm confused is all. Four years isn't long, and they let you go? I can't imagine you'd get PI credit for service if it had been a dishonorable discharge. So... why did they release you?" He adjusted the napkin on his lap. "Sorry, I don't mean to pry."

I attempted a casual shrug and resumed feeding my face. Trent went back to eating as well, but after several minutes the silence was deafening. I fought from going on but felt compelled to continue.

"I was in a vehicle with three buddies."

Trent put his fork down, folded his hands, and gave me his full attention.

"We were on our way to investigate an IED that had been spotted, and ironically we ran over one." I bowed my head and laughed to keep myself from crying. "We were in a fucking MRAP."

"What's an MRAP?"

"That's what makes it so damn ironic. It's a Mine-Resistant Ambush Protected vehicle. They're better than Humvees but weren't as secure as the name implies."

"Oh. I'm sorry, you don't—"

"I blacked out instantly. When I regained consciousness, the vehicle was on its side, and I was covered in flesh and blood. I thought I was dead, but none of it was mine. My legs were pinned, but I survived. I was the only one."

"I'm sorry about your friends. Thank you for sharing that with me."

"You know, the last person I told that story to charged two hundred dollars an hour. It must be the ouzo."

"You've only had two shots, and half of that was water." He took a sip. "So, you came home after that? Discharged for your injuries?"

I nodded and took a bite of lamb.

After my story, we ate most of our dinner in silence. I wondered why I was so candid with Trent. I hadn't told him everything, but I'd said enough. I usually tried not to think about what happened, and here I had exposed my soul. Now and then, one of us would say something trivial, like how good the food was, and we hoped the drought would end soon. As we finished our last bites of the entrées, Ada showed up with a dessert platter.

"Sorry, ma'am, but I can't eat another bite," I said.

"Call me Ada," she said. "And Mitch, it's not an option. You're not leaving without trying some. We have *tulumba*, *ekmek kataifi*, and, of course, baklava. You must at least taste everything." She returned to the kitchen.

"Fried dough, bread pudding, and I'm sure you know baklava," Trent said. "Just a bite of each will make her happy."

As I reached for the baklava, an unintelligible announcement blared through the dining area. The speakers seemed to be as old as the restaurant itself.

"What's that about?"

"We're dancing now. Get up."

"You saw earlier. I don't dance."

He looked around the room. "Everyone is standing up. You won't stand out if you join in. You thought everyone put the pressure on you before to stand up and dance? Imagine sixty to seventy people standing up, all focused on getting you to dance. The only way you'll look foolish is if you sit there alone."

"And I'm fine with—"

"What are you still doing sitting here?" Ada cut in. "It's time to dance *syrtaki*."

"What's that?"

Trent chuckled. "Did you ever see *Zorba the Greek*? It's a folk dance."

Most of the other diners were on their feet, and true to Trent's word, they were cheering me on again. Trent and Ada glared at me.

"I don't like it, but what the hell?"

During the short lesson, most of us fell over each other and stepped on each other's feet. It was a chaotic mess, and I was miserable, but five minutes in, things fell into place. We weren't just dancing, we were doing it well. The smiles and laughter surrounding me made me laugh too, despite every attempt to refrain. As the dance neared an end, the woman next to me slipped and knocked me down, tripping Trent in the process. The three of us sat on the floor and cried from laughter.

Trent winked at me, and I understood his mission was a success. He got me to have fun.

The music stopped, and we returned to our table.

"That's the first time I've seen you laugh," he said.

"You've seen me laugh."

"Not like that I haven't. It makes me happy." He paused. "My place is over on Sweetzer Avenue. Come over for a drink and decompress?"

I snorted. "You're not very smooth, are you?"

"It's just a friendly invite." His crooked grin grew wide.

We said goodbye to Ada. I told myself repeatedly to turn around and drive home while following Trent's Jeep to his house, but it was as if my steering wheel had a mind of its own. When I pulled up behind him in the driveway, there were two things on my mind—one was that I should run like hell to get out of there, and the other was I needed to feel his body against mine.

Trent's place on Sweetzer was on a tree-lined street in the area behind the West Hollywood City Hall. There were mostly apartment buildings in a hodgepodge mix of different shapes and sizes. Detached houses were scattered in between the larger buildings. His mission-style home was midsize with a small front yard and well-trimmed hedges along the sidewalk.

The living room where he had me wait had a honey-colored wood floor, forest green walls, and an arched

entryway that led into a small sunroom. Another arched
entryway framed a hallway leading to the back of the
house.

Trent came out of the kitchen with two glasses of white
wine and sat next to me on the couch. I took a sip and put
the glass on an end table. I really didn't need any more
alcohol. He placed his glass on the coffee table. His eyes
never left mine. I wanted to run my hands across every inch
of his skin and rub the muscles underneath.

"Nice place you've got here," I said.

"It belonged to my parents. I got it when Mom died. My
life would be easier if I sold it, but I grew up here, and she
and Dad were so proud of it. Sometimes I think it's stupid
to keep it. I could sell it for a fortune, get a small place, and
live off savings while focusing on my writing, but I can't
bring myself to do it. Crazy, huh?"

"It's not crazy at all. Kind of sweet, actually."

Trent leaned forward to kiss me. I dodged and hugged
his neck. His scruff of beard felt good on my cheek.

"Relax. You're so tense." He kneaded my shoulders. "I
hope you like banana pancakes. I'll make some in the
morning."

Tension shot through my body. "Pancakes? Hmm."

He raised my shirt above my chest and kissed my stomach, working his way up toward each nipple. His tongue circled one while he rolled the other between his thumb and forefinger. He gently bit down, flicking my nipple with his tongue, making me groan. I reminded myself I should go home, but I was powerless. I pulled away and lifted his polo over his head. He tried to kiss me again. I ducked.

"No kissing?" he whispered.

"No kissing."

I turned his head and bit the base of his neck. He squirmed. Freckles scattered across his shoulders fit his boyish charm and made me smile. I kissed them while running my hands down his firm back, letting my fingers follow each contour.

Without warning, Trent took me by the hand and led me to the bedroom. He turned and unbuckled my belt. Once loose, he ran his hand down the inside of my underwear and stroked my cock.

I took my time sliding his zipper down, never turning my eyes from his. He wasn't wearing underwear, and I could feel his hard dick bounce free as his pants fell to his knees. He stepped out of them, put his hands on my hips, and dropped to the floor. He undid my pants and ran his tongue on my briefs along the outline of my cock before taking them off. I expected him to take me in his mouth.

He chuckled as he got up. When our eyes met, we smiled. I raised my hand to push him down on the bed, but he grabbed it and pulled, sprawling me on top of him. I raised myself up onto my elbows and leaned forward. He palmed my ass while I chewed his neck, putting him in that ticklish zone between pleasure and pain. I moved south and swiped a finger to taste his sweet precum, then ran my tongue around his cock head before taking it all in my mouth.

Refusing to allow him to cum, I moved on top of him and slid my ass up and down to tease his cock. He stretched his arm to pull open a nightstand drawer then put a condom in my palm. I rolled it on him, adding lube before backing up.

"You're amazing," I exclaimed, surprising myself. But God, he was, with a smooth, muscular body, square jaw, and those big amber eyes. What was I thinking? Again, I told myself to go home. I had never felt so conflicted.

"Quit teasing and take a seat," he begged. I chortled and continued to refuse, then eased my ass down, allowing him inside me.

He grinned and raised his hips, pushing his cock deeper within. I closed my eyes. "You okay?" he asked. I nodded. My jaw clenched. He remained still so my body could adjust.

I leaned forward, which Trent mistook as a kiss and responded in kind. He gave a brief look of disappointment when I turned away, then thrust harder. Without warning, he pulled me up and rolled us over, never allowing his cock to release.

He leaned forward and pressed his hips harder, driving himself deeper inside me.

"I want all of you. Balls deep," I cried.

He pinned me to the bed with each slow surge in and out.

"Oh, damn," he groaned as I tightened on his cock.

He moved faster, nearing release.

"Oh, no you don't." I twisted around and backed off his cock. The pleading looks vanished from his face when I grabbed another condom and put lube on my hard dick. I lifted his legs, pulled him to the edge of the bed, and teased his hole. He responded with an unintelligible grunt as I penetrated and pounded my dick inside him. A shudder rolled through me as his body locked tight and jerked, cum hitting his chest. This set off my orgasm, and I pushed deeper into him as I climaxed.

I collapsed and wheezed, clinging to him, but I didn't pull out. His legs and arms wrapped tightly around my body.

By 12:20 a.m., Trent slept soundly, with just a hint of a snore. Careful not to wake him, I grabbed my clothes and shoes and put them on in the living room. There would be no breakfast as promised.

I looked toward the bedroom while backing out the front door. On the drive home, I replayed the night and fought to convince myself it had only been lust, a momentary lapse in judgment. But I couldn't deny there was more to it than that. I felt it in my gut, and it scared the shit out of me.

I crawled into bed, but it took a long time to fall asleep. I couldn't stop thinking about what had just happened. The last I looked, it was 4:00 a.m.

Nineteen

Josie wanted to hear all about my date with Trent, so we met the next night at Celebración Cafe, a Cuban place on Santa Monica Boulevard in West Hollywood. It was one of my favorite restaurants, and yet I could rarely afford it. Their appetizers alone were worth more than my car. I didn't hesitate to accept Josie's offer when she called to invite me. Without her, it would have been another night home alone with my cereal.

The café was in a spot where nothing survived, but people kept trying. Every six months some new restaurant opened and closed until Celebración finally beat the odds. They had done a major renovation, pulling out the tired booths and closing off the kitchen. Four years later, business was booming. The place looked like a South Beach wonderland—arches and pastel colors everywhere. The linens and walls were a mix of soft red, orange, green, and yellow. I'd been told traditional Cuban décor had richer, darker colors, but it worked for them.

As usual, our conversation revolved around Josie—who she was dating, who she wanted to date, what she should do next with her hair. Near the end of dinner, Josie gave me the stage. I tried to discuss everything but Trent, but I hesitated enough for her to seize the opportunity to ask about him.

"How many times did he call today?"

"Twice. He wants me to call him."

"Twice, huh? Okay, so he could like you, or he could be a scary stalker."

"Pretty sure he's not a stalker. He sounded okay in his messages. I feel bad that I probably hurt his feelings."

Josie belted out a laugh then covered her mouth. "I'm sorry. You saying you hope you didn't hurt him is hysterical and doesn't sound like the Mitch O'Reilly I've known my whole life. Of course you hurt him. At least he's not obsessed or anything. I've had guys call a dozen times the day after. Two is sweet. He wants to talk, but he's secure enough to not make a fool of himself."

"Or he's too hurt to keep calling," I said.

"Oh, don't get me wrong, he has every right to feel hurt. You snuck out on him, you bastard. You're the insecure one, not him."

"You don't spend the night with the guys you go out with," I said. "Why are the rules different for me?"

"Because I make no pretense that I'm there for anything other than sex—something you didn't have the cojones to do. When he told you that he planned to make you breakfast in the morning, what did you say?"

"I didn't say anything."

"You had to have said something. What was it?"

"Hmm."

"Hmm, what?"

"That's what I said. Hmm."

"There you have it. If you're with a guy, and he offers breakfast, there's only two answers you can give. The first is 'No, thank you. I won't be staying.'"

"And the second?"

"Anything else!"

The waiter stepped to our table. "Would you care for your bill?"

"I can't leave now," Josie said. "My brother is too entertaining. Another set of drinks for us."

I waited until he was out of hearing range. "Trent manages a bathhouse. You'd think he understands the concept of a one-night stand."

"You had dinner, and you met his family. That doesn't qualify as a one-night stand. This isn't some guy you happened to fuck. He's the guy who hired the attorney who hired you. If you want to continue to work this job, and if you want to be considered for any job in the future, you need to call him and smooth things over."

Our waiter came back, and I shushed Josie until after he served our drinks.

"Okay, you convinced me. I hate it when you're right." I stood and pulled my phone out of my pocket. "Give me a sec."

Josie grabbed my belt and pulled me down in my seat. She took my phone and slammed it on the table. "You're calling him? Now? I don't think so."

I huffed. "A second ago, you told me to call him."

"Tomorrow. Later tonight. Whenever. But not now. We're partying tonight, Lil' Bro. It's been way too long since we've been out together."

"Josie, I love you, but you are clinically insane."

She laughed and finished her wine. "Come on, let's go dancing."

"Give me a minute to finish my dinner, will you?" I sighed. "Also, did you just meet me? Where'd you get this crazy idea I want to dance?"

"You said you danced at that Greek place last night. You're gay. You're supposed to like to dance."

"Yes, I'm supposed to like dancing, just like I'm supposed to be a hairdresser or an interior decorator, and I'm supposed to love Lady Gaga, RuPaul, and—"

"Now you're getting it," she said.

"When did I become a gay stereotype?"

She grinned. "The day I learned it would piss you off. Come on. I miss when you liked to dance. Ooooh, let's go to that club where you said that super-hot dancer works. What's his name? Something biblical."

"Christian. His name is Christian. He dances at Euphoria." I nodded at the window that faced the club across the street. "It's a bad idea to go there. He doesn't like me, and I don't like him."

"You talked him up so much. I've got to see for myself. It's not like you'll be socializing anyway. We'll be on the dance floor. Come on."

She grabbed her purse, slid her chair back, paid the bill, then returned to grab my arm and drag me away from the last of my *arroz con pollo*.

Once inside Euphoria, I ordered a greyhound for me, and a sea breeze for Josie. I pointed at an empty platform. "That's where he danced the last time I was here. He must be on break... Ooooh, but that guy over there ain't hard on the eyes." I nodded toward a dancer who was shorter and thinner than Christian, but well-defined. He was bald with a thick, well-trimmed beard.

"He's all right," she waved a dismissive hand. "He's just doing the standard gay dance—take off your shirt, throw your hands up, and bounce up and down. It doesn't get any easier than that. Not like the Greek thing you did last night."

"You're full of stereotypes tonight."

"Am I wrong?"

"Shut up." I chuckled. "Christian takes his breaks in there." I pointed toward the storeroom where I'd delivered tequila and a chaser to him on my last visit. I replayed how pissed off he'd been when I had interrupted his break, and snickered. "Why don't you go see if he's in there?"

Josie followed my suggestion, but no one answered when she knocked. She tried several times before she grabbed the knob and swung the door open. She put her hand over her mouth. Everyone around stopped dancing and stared, and for a second, dozens of gasps drowned out the music.

"Derek?" she said.

In the small room were two men. One was leaning against the wall while the other was on his knees, bobbing his head to the beat of the music. Neither was Christian.

"Fuck off, Josie." The one standing slammed the door. She clutched her stomach, bent over, and howled with laughter. The crowd behind her did the same. It took time for Josie and me to catch our breath.

"That's hilarious," she said. "Derek and I had a couple of dates last year. I hope the guy on his knees has a better time than me."

"Well, it looks like Derek's gay."

"Gay, straight, bi, whatever. Worst sex I ever had."

"I'll grab another drink and find out where Christian is," I said. "Want anything?"

Josie shook her head.

I ordered another greyhound and asked the bartender if he knew where I might find Christian, then pushed through the crowd and found Josie dancing with a blond flight attendant. He and I had met online but never hooked up. He put too much emphasis on wanting to cuddle.

"He didn't show tonight," I said.

"Then I'm ready to go. I stayed out too late last night, and it's hitting me."

I stepped back. "My God! You're getting old."

"Fuck you," she scoffed, then took one last sip of her sea breeze and grabbed my arm. I downed my drink before hitting the sidewalk. We strolled several blocks to where we had parked when I caught Christian's car out of the corner of my eye.

"Christian's somewhere around here," I said. "That's his Mustang—the light blue one with the *I'd Do Me* bumper sticker."

She pulled lipstick from her purse and giggled. "Hold on. I'm going to write something naughty on his windshield."

While she sped up, planning to write who-knows-what, I shuffled behind with my hands in my pockets. When she got to his car, she leaned over the windshield, lipstick in hand, and went perfectly still.

"Oh my God," she muttered.

I asked what was up, but she didn't respond. Silently, she stepped back and heaved.

I ran over and put my arm around her. "Are you okay?" Unable to speak, she waved her hand wildly toward the car. I reluctantly followed her orders. As soon as I glanced in the window, I had to fight from gagging too.

Christian Freeman's headed dangled forward on his chest nearly severed at the neck, his torso covered in blood. Crimson handprints throhout the vehicle conveyed a desperate attempt to escape as the life drained from his body.

For a few seconds, I wasn't in West Hollywood anymore. I was back in Afghanistan, bloody and screaming without making a sound. I snapped back to reality and stared at Christian's grisly corpse. I was fighting for each breath. Finally, I backed into the side of a yellow minivan, slid to the pavement, and stopped my hand from trembling long enough to dial 9-1-1.

Twenty

Within minutes, the police arrived and cut off the side street. Drivers had to swerve around the onlookers overflowing onto Santa Monica Boulevard. They were lined four deep outside the *Do Not Cross* tape. Once someone recognized his car, word spread like wildfire throughout West Hollywood. Christian Freeman was dead. There were a few tears among those in the mob, but most seemed to be there out of morbid curiosity. LAPD Detective Dirk Turner wrapped up questioning Josie.

The last time I'd seen the detective, he was in my store asking me to back off Warren. He had worn a suit and looked every bit the cop in his camel-colored suit jacket from the moment he'd walked in the door. Now he wore a blue tie with a white shirt. He'd loosened the tie and undone a few buttons. Lack of formality was forgiven during the record heat wave.

I was about to catch up with him when Attorney Eve Aiken yelled my name. Two officers were holding her back, preventing her from crossing the tape. I held my finger in the air to advise her to hold on a minute and told Detective Turner she was there. He waved to let her pass.

Eve wore a long yellow T-shirt and a pair of black
leggings. She looked haggard. Her wrinkles were deeper
than when I last saw her. Even her eyes were bloodshot.
One sleepy lid hung further down than the other. From the
smell of her, I figured she used the bags under her eyes for
carrying whiskey home from the store.

"What happened? What's going on, Mitch?" She
marched toward Christian's car. I rushed over and stopped
her.

"You want to hang back. It's an image that'll be etched
in my brain forever, and I've seen a lot." I shuddered.
"Christian Freeman was murdered."

"Who's Christian Freeman?"

"He was in the report I sent you—the go-go boy who
had an affair with Victor. They had a fight at Club Silver
Lake right before the murder. Victor led him on by
promising acting roles for sex. He was my number one
suspect—moody, angry, aggressive, and probably tired of
fucking for nothing. It's why I called."

Eve pulled me away from the crowd. Her neck and
cheeks were flushed. She gritted her teeth. "Suspect?
We've been over this, Mitch. You need to focus on
gathering enough evidence to keep the police off Ernesto's
back, and that's it. I don't give a rat's ass who killed

Victor. Play superhero on your own time and with your own money. I'm not paying for it."

"I planned to send you another report tomorrow," I lied. "At this point, there's plenty of reasonable doubt. Half the people at the bathhouse that night could've murdered Victor, and for some, the motives are glaringly obvious."

She crossed her arms, unamused. "How long were you planning on milking me before sharing this bit of news?"

"I haven't been milking you. You're the one who said this case could put us both on the map. Imagine how much exposure we'll get if we not only get the police off Ernesto's back, but we hand over the real killer? It's the only way to ensure we save his ass. I'm close. I know it, or I wouldn't bother."

"Close? You just told me your primary suspect is dead in that car."

"Doesn't mean he didn't commit the murder. We've both struggled long enough that we deserve a case like this. And now there's a second murder, potentially linked to the first. Let me keep looking into it, and I promise you we'll get more publicity than we could have imagined when this began."

"You're a smooth talker, O'Reilly. Or I'm a fool. We're going to take this week by week, and I want regular updates from you."

I was relieved she chose to keep me on the case. For a lawyer, Eve was easy to manipulate. No wonder she never made it past chasing ambulances.

"Now that that's cleared up, tell me what's going on here," Eve said. "How do you think the murders are linked?"

"I'm not sure they are."

Eve yelled at Detective Turner. "Hey, you, do you mind coming over here?"

He frowned and walked over. He pulled out a tissue and wiped his brow. "What is it?"

"How do you think this relates to the Victor Verboom case?" Eve asked.

"I can't say it does."

She nodded in my direction. "My associate says Victor and the victim here were bopping each other."

"He mentioned that."

"Eve, I never said the murders were related. They're just starting to gather the evidence," I said, trying to save face in front of the detective. He raised his eyebrows but didn't say a word, so I continued. "Victor had a quick slit across his throat from behind, which is easy. Christian here had his throat slashed, and his head nearly cut clean off. That's rage."

"You know your stuff, Mr. O'Reilly," Detective Turner confirmed.

"I was an MP, sir. Never worked as a detective or in forensics, but I learned enough to identify a brutal killing when I see one."

"And brutal it is," he said. "I'm no coroner, but this one is obvious. The cuts are rough, and the meat and bone are jagged with lots of slivers. Someone hacked away to kill this one. It's almost bestial. Whoever did this was in the backseat. By the time Christian knew what hit him, it was probably already too late."

"Do you think he was with more than one other person?" Eve asked. "With only two doors, why else would he have someone in the backseat?"

Dirk Turner stroked his mustache. "Someone may have gotten in without him knowing. They were waiting for him. If that's the case, as the blood smears suggest, it was a relatively easy kill. It doesn't take much to incapacitate someone by cutting their throat. Likely, the victim was flailing in shock while the killer continued to hack away at him."

I was nauseated and felt like I needed to sit down. My job required I stay and bear with it.

"When I speak with the DA, I'll let her know about the relationship between the two vics. But it's her job to do what she wants with the information, not mine. If that's all, Mr. O'Reilly, you'll have to excuse me, but I need to get back to processing. You and your sister are free to go. We'll be in touch if we have any questions. And I take it you'll do the same if you have additional information pertinent to the case, yes?"

I nodded, and he walked to the car to talk with an officer.

"I want a full report of your investigation first thing tomorrow morning," Eve said as she took off.

I found Josie mixed in the crowd with her arms wrapped around herself.

"Where's Eve?" she asked.

"Gone. She's thinking of pulling me from the case. I have to write a report before bed. Let me drive you home."

"No. I don't want to talk about it, and if we ride together, that's what I'll do. I'll be fine."

I shrugged. "It's your call, but text me when you get home, okay?"

"Okay." Tears rolled down her cheeks. "I'll never get that image out of my head, Lil' Bro. Never."

"You never do."

Twenty-One

My late night of writing the report for Eve took a toll on my body. The vodka in my greyhounds gave me a sour stomach. Visions of Christian's body were interspersed with the horrific things I'd seen in war. Aside from the massive headache and general queasiness, I could barely turn my neck from having fallen asleep in my chair. My morning began with a 7:00 a.m. call from Eve. She'd received the report but was not happy. Her screams made my head explode, even as I pulled the phone away from my ear. I missed most of what she said, but several times I made out that she wanted to fire me. She insisted she'd given me enough time to gather more information than I had. I convinced her to keep me on, but I had no idea how much longer she'd be willing to wait for concrete evidence clearing Ernesto.

Since I'd first opened the store, either Josie or I was there every Tuesday through Saturday running it. About half the time she got there after lunch, but she showed up. If ever there was a time for an exception, a second murder was it. I made a quick trip to hang a note on the door: *Closed For The Day*.

Once home, I took the hottest shower possible. Every square inch of my body hurt, and I let the jets massage the pain away before deciding how I'd spend my day off. Seth also lived in Silver Lake, just over a mile from my house. I needed to see him. It was too hot, and my body was far too tired to walk, so I got in my car and headed out.

Seth's landlord directed me to a stand-alone garage behind the house. I found Seth under an old hearse and wished him good morning.

"It ain't no fucking good morning." He slid out from under the hearse and used the door handle to pull himself upright. "Thought you'd show up. You here to talk about Christian?"

I hated those awkward moments where there was really nothing to say, so I stuck with the standard, "I'm sorry for your loss."

"Fuck that shit. I'll be hearing it for the next month, and I'm already sick of it." He grabbed a guitar that was propped on a sawhorse and took a seat in the rear of the hearse. He didn't play. He held it like a security blanket and rested his chin on the neck of the instrument.

"You play?"

"I was in a band in high school. We weren't half bad, but you know… we never officially broke up. One day, we all just stopped showing up for rehearsals."

"It happens." I didn't know what else to say about it. "When did you get the news about Christian?"

"Some friends called to tell me around midnight. I haven't slept since." The circles around his eyes told me as much. "I've been down here tinkering with shit to keep my mind from going there."

"What's the deal with the hearse?"

"It's my fucking car. It's comfortable, with a shitload of room to party. Christian hated it—swore he wouldn't be caught dead in it." Tears trickled down Seth's cheeks. He wiped them with his T-shirt. "That's not funny anymore, huh? What the fuck did that bastard get himself in to end up dead? Probably one of his old daddies." He saw I was about to ask a question and cut me off. "Don't get me wrong. He wasn't really into old guys, but he loved it when they showered him with money, gifts, and shit. He wasn't no fucking hustler. He didn't ask for money, but they gave him gifts, so he took them. The motherfucker didn't even have sex with some of them."

I let him keep talking. This was good information.

"Have you seen his new Mustang?" he asked. "You don't think he paid for that off tips, do you? That's one fine ass ride."

"Who bought it?"

"I don't know. Some dude who he played with down at a beach house. Shit!" He pounded his fist into his forehead. "He was supposed to meet that fucker last night after the movie—said he was going to stay the night."

I spoke softly, "Relax, Seth. Think about it. What was the man's name?"

"I don't know. I know nothing about the guy. He gave Christian that Mustang, and they'd fuck around at that beach house. That's all I can tell you." He paced. "You know, with all the things he got, he never told me why he stripped. He sure as shit didn't need the money, but he had a fucking ego. Christian thrived on being the center of attention. He only wanted to be an actor for the cash and glory. Between you and me, he was my best friend, but I know he was as much of an asshole as he was sexy."

While he talked, I looked around the garage. The walls held every type of tool imaginable—mostly car parts, but also a large selection of saws, knives, and other woodworking tools. From what I could tell, there weren't

any empty hooks on the pegboard. It appeared that
everything was accounted for.

Seth paused in his Christian homage, so I jumped in
with a question.

"Do you have any idea why this could have happened?"

"No clue." His voice cracked, and his eyes watered
again. He wiped them with his arm. "We were supposed to
meet at the theater to see *Human Extermination 3*. When he
didn't show, I tried to call, but he never answered. After the
movie, we had plans to meet up with some friends for
drinks at The Barge, but I went home instead." He looked
at me earnestly. "Do you know what time he died? I keep
imagining him struggling to get his phone to answer me,
but not having the strength to get it. It's eating at me."

"Seth, not to be morbid, but don't worry about him
feeling helpless trying to answer your call. He would've
gone into shock quickly." I could see he wanted to ask how
I could be sure. "I saw enough guys go from life to death in
the military that, unfortunately, I know a thing or two about
it."

Seth picked a wrench up off the floor and threw it at his
workbench. It smashed into a toolbox, spilling tools onto
the counter and nails all over the floor. He was moving into
the second stage of grief quickly.

"I'd hoped I could come offer some solace, but it looks like I've made things worse," I said. "I should probably come another time."

"You don't need to leave," he mumbled. "I've been under my car all fucking night trying to forget, but it ain't working."

"Listen, Seth. You know I hate to ask, but can anyone vouch that you were at the movie last night?"

Seth began to pound a fist on the floor of his hearse, but caught himself midway, and slowly lowered it down. "It's all good. You need to make sure it wasn't me." He pulled a ticket stub from his pocket. "Here. We were meeting at the Duchess Theater at 8:30. You can ask me whatever you want about the movie. I know it beginning to end by now. It was the third time I was going to see it—kick-ass film."

"Hang onto that ticket, okay," I advised him. "When we met, the first words out of your mouth were, 'Ernesto did it.' Do you still think he killed Victor?"

"You think the piece of shit who killed Victor killed Christian too, don't you?" He shook his head. "I don't know who killed Christian, but I'm one hundred percent sure Ernesto murdered Victor."

"Gut feelings don't produce arrests. You got anything solid to back that up?"

"It was Ernesto, but that's all I got. Christian pissed lots of people off… like you. He told me you were an asshole when you met him."

"But—"

"Don't worry. Christian thought anyone who didn't worship him was an asshole. He had plenty of haters—guys who were jealous of his body and his handsome face with those big dimples, and guys who were annoyed because he was so fucking cocky. But that's no reason to kill someone."

"Did he do drugs? Could it have been a deal gone bad?"

"Fuck no. Not even steroids. You know the saying 'your body is a temple'? Christian worked hard to look the way he does—or, did. He ran every day and worked out six days a week. He sure as shit wasn't into coke, crack, or meth. A lot of meth-heads come to the club, and it's amazing how fast they go from hot to not. The last thing he'd do is take something that'd put sores on his face or make his teeth rot."

Seth strummed on his guitar. He shut his eyes and hummed to himself for a minute, forgetting I was there. He stopped suddenly. "Anything else?"

"Just a couple questions—things that could help me make sense of what happened last night. When did you and Christian first meet?"

"We went to high school together in Barstow. We were best buds. He was fucking beautiful, and I was his lanky sidekick. I didn't have all the tats and piercings then. He wouldn't have had shit to do with me if I did. When I got my first ones, he said I had 'defiled God's gift.' Said I looked nasty. We can't all be perfect like that son of a bitch."

I took a risk.

"When did you first realize you had fallen for him?"

He cocked his head and sneered. "You bastard. You think we bonded, so now you're turning up the heat."

"I—"

"Chill, it's all good." He waved a dismissive hand. "I knew when I met Christian. He was the opposite of me. He was confident, sexy, and popular. I was a scrawny prick with low self-esteem. No one even knew my name. I could never be him, so I wanted to be with him."

"You don't seem like you have a self-esteem problem."

"I learned that from Christian. I realized one day that despite his looks, he wouldn't have gotten any attention if he lacked confidence. That's what people are most attracted to, even if they don't know it. My life started once I stopped giving a shit what people think of me. I made peace with myself. I'm still a scrawny, ugly fag. But I'm always having fun."

"Did you move to LA together?"

"No, but we were always close—like brothers. When we were juniors in high school, Christian's dad found some gay porn and threw him out on his ass. My parents took him in, and we shared a room. Nothing happened, but I got hard every night thinking about him. After graduation, I started college, and he moved straight to LA to be a star."

"Sad story."

"Depends on your perspective. My parents gave him a good home—a better life than he'd ever have gotten from his parents. He never showed any real appreciation though. You know, typical Christian. After two years of community college, I finally got tired of living in that piss-ant town. I had a hard time finding a job until I was hired at Club Silver Lake."

I stood. "I've taken enough of your time. Before I go, I have to ask again, do you remember anything at all about the man who bought Christian that Mustang?"

"Man, I wish I could—" Seth snapped his fingers. "I know what he drives. I was meeting Christian for lunch, and he had been down fucking that guy at the beach. I noticed he had one of those electric cars when he dropped Christian off. It was the opposite end of the parking lot, and the guy drove off, so I didn't see him."

"Was it a Prius?" I asked.

"No, it was the sporty one. A Tesla. It was a blue Tesla."

I was sure there were thousands of blue Teslas in the city, but one in particular came to mind—the one driven by Rod Hernandez. "Where is the house?"

"I don't know. Christian just always said they were at the beach. He never specified which one."

"I appreciate your candor. You've been a big help. Are you gonna be all right? I can't imagine hanging out under a hearse all day is the best way to deal with a friend's death."

"Yeah." He snickered. "A few of us are going to get shit-faced and toast to the motherfucker this afternoon."

"You sure you're up for that?"

"I'd rather be laughing with friends than crying alone."

Twenty-Two

Rod Hernandez wasn't answering my calls and wasn't in his office, so I drove to Los Feliz to pay him a visit at home. Pam answered the door, and I followed her into the foyer. She wore a turquoise sleeveless blouse with a collar and a salmon skirt that stopped just above her knees. Her hair was pulled back in a short ponytail.

"What is it you need, Mr. O'Reilly?" she asked.

"We're still sticking with 'Mr. O'Reilly,' huh? Can we sit down? I'm here to talk to Rod."

"No, you may not sit. You have unfortunate timing. Rodrigo is away, and I am on my way to a tennis tournament. I intend to put that braggart Octavia Oosterhouse in her place."

"I stopped by his work first, so I know he isn't there. Is he out of town?"

"There are times he needs a level of focus that his busy office does not offer. He goes elsewhere to strategize, make proposals, or whatever else he does. You must go. I am running late."

"Elsewhere? Do you mean the beach house?"

"Beach house?" Her eyes widened, and she walked across the foyer to a table next to the dining room entry.

She paused after picking up a pink water bottle. "Yes, that is where he goes. He says he is able to get more accomplished there. Now, please leave."

"I'm envious of people like you who live right here in LA and still have a second home minutes away on the ocean. Where is it? Malibu?"

"I will not be one more minute late. I have asked you kindly. You must go now."

She shoved me out, and I felt the air whoosh against my back as she slammed the door. It was ironic that Rod was at the beach house just when I was looking to question him about it. I pulled to the curb across the street as Pam sped out of the garage in her Thunderbird. I dialed Josie so she could search property records for me from her office. I hung up when I remembered she was in a training session for the day then shook my head to keep focused on the task at hand.

Without Josie, I'd have to run a property search on my own. It was an easy task, but one I usually let her handle. I pulled up the app and searched for property records in Rod's name and came up with only one house in California—the one I was sitting in front of it. The same result showed when I searched in Pam's name. I thought for a minute, and the obvious came to mind. Within a few clicks, I learned that Rod's company, Eureka Escrow, owned a place on The Strand in Hermosa Beach. Traffic was light for that time of day, and it took only an hour and change to get there.

Parking was tight in the town, and most streets required homeowner permits. Because I refused to pay to park, I left my car on a side street off Pacific Coast Highway and walked ten minutes to their home.

The house was typical of the community. Old bungalows were being razed one by one and replaced by boxy multi-million-dollar glass houses nearly identical in look and layout. Homeowners were separated from their neighbors by walkways no more than ten feet wide. Rather than take the main entrance off The Strand, I went to the primary family entrance in the rear. Despite its pleasant name, Beach Drive was nothing more than a back alley with garage doors, trash dumpsters and utility boxes—a stark contrast to the ocean and bicycle path on the other side of the beachfront homes.

I knocked on the door in the alley entrance and saw Rod's eyes widen when he peered out the window. He ducked away, and I had to wait a minute before he cracked the door open.

"What the hell are you doing here?" he asked.

"We have lots to discuss."

"Great, let's meet. Schedule an appointment with my secretary. I'm busy."

"Who are you busy with? Another go-go boy? Or a surfer, perhaps?"

"Excuse me?"

"I'm here to talk about your trysts with Christian Freeman." I paused a moment to allow my words to sink in. "Can I come in now?"

"Hold on. I'll be right back."

He shut the door. I waited for more than five minutes, until my impatience equaled my curiosity. I walked along the walkway to the side of the house facing the beach. I reached the patio just in time to see a young, shaggy-haired blond surfer pushed out from the accordion glass doors. The guy wore red board shorts and a blue tank top. He huffed, slung a backpack over his shoulder and gave Rod the finger before sulking away.

"I was joking about the surfer dude," I said as I stepped up. "Looks like I hit the target dead on."

He waved me in. "Come on."

Inside, the entire front wall and half of the sidewalls were large glass panels. I'd never been in any of the neighboring homes, but most of the ground level interiors were visible for all to see while strolling or biking along The Strand. The room, designed for entertaining, was like dozens of others I'd seen. It had an open concept with a contemporary seating area, dining room, and a kitchen with six chairs at a long counter bar.

"Beautiful place you have. How nice that your company pays for it."

"We entertain clients on the weekends. But I'm not interested in what you think of my house or any small talk. Sit down and say what you've got to say."

The blue-and-white-striped denim corner couch fit nine people. I sat at one end, Rod at the other.

"I thought you were only into risky sex in public spaces," I said. "Now I find out you like to entertain young men in the privacy of your company home too. Christian followed the money, and you helped him live better than your average club dancer." I waited while he shifted, then crossed and uncrossed his legs. "You two were having a little rendezvous here last night. Am I right? What time was he supposed to get here?"

"Look, I didn't hurt that boy. He said he had plans with a friend and would be here around midnight. I told Pam I had to work late and was staying overnight. I waited until 2:00 a.m., thought he blew me off, and went to bed. When I turned on the news this morning, I learned that someone killed him. I understand you were the one to find his body."

I got up and gazed at the sand with my hands behind my back. "Technically, it was my sister, but yes. It wasn't a pretty sight," I said.

"It's tragic. He was smart and had a lot going for him."

"How'd the two of you meet?"

Rod stepped into the kitchen, grabbed a beer from the refrigerator, and leaned against the counter.

"He introduced himself last year. Pam and I were downtown at a fundraising event for pet adoptions. She doesn't like animals, but it was the place to be seen that week. Christian was there with a theater director or producer, someone in the industry, and I noticed that he filled a suit nicely. I don't know how he knew, but he came over and talked with me. He had a gift. Before I realized what was happening, we were checking into a room at The Beverly Hills Hotel. After that, we'd get together a few times a month, he'd pretend he cared for a few hours, and then we'd both go home."

"Doesn't seem you cared too much. You didn't waste much time having that surfer boy over today for a little fun and frolic."

"I said Christian would *pretend* he cared, so I learned to do the same. We were only going through the motions, but it always felt good in the moment."

"How much did you pay him?"

"He didn't ask for money, but he did expect gifts—"

"Like brand-new Mustangs?" I asked.

"How do you..." Rod shook his head. "That was excessive, but there was an unspoken understanding." He took a large gulp of his beer and smacked it on the kitchen counter. "I had no reason to kill him."

"Could any of your neighbors confirm you were here last night?"

"What neighbors? Most of these are second homes and vacation rentals. They sit empty ninety percent of the time."

"You don't need to sweat it, Rod. You can prove it easily." After a pause, I waved my finger in the air. "Just show me footage from your security cameras."

He darted his head back and forth between the two cameras mounted in opposite corners near the ceiling. "That won't help. I turn them off when I get here. You don't think I want a record of the men I bring in, do you? I was here. You have to believe me."

I looked out the window then sauntered back to the couch. Rod remained silent while I dusted off my pants before sitting.

"I don't have to believe anything you can't back up," I said. "How well did you know Ernesto Torres?"

"Ernesto? You mean that little guy who worked at Club Silver Lake? All I know is he was there the night Victor was killed and probably the last time I was there, too, over six months ago. That's it."

"You knew Victor."

"That's a ridiculous statement. Of course."

"You knew Christian, but you lied about it."

"I never lied. You never asked."

He had me. "You're right." I leaned forward and stroked my chin. "But I'm asking now. Maybe just because I don't see a connection between you and Ernesto—"

Rod held out his arms. "Whoa. Whoa. Stop pushing it, Mitch. I don't know Ernesto Torres, and I didn't kill Victor or Christian."

"When did you get here last night?"

"Pam and I had dinner at a friend's home. We left around 8:30, and I came straight here."

"And she and your friend will vouch for you?"

"You can't ask questions. You told me you wouldn't out me to her. You can't out me to other people I know either."

"I told you I wouldn't out you unless absolutely necessary. It looks like we may have crossed that line."

Twenty-Three

I waited five minutes after hitting the buzzer before Lupe Torres came and opened the security gate.

"*Hola*," she said, her head raised, her lips turned down. "*Qué quieres?*"

"Are you asking what I want?"

"*Sí.*"

"I'm here for Ernesto. Uh. *Aquí por* Ernesto," I said. "*Lo siento* for not calling. Is he home?"

She started up the stairs and motioned for me to follow.

Lupe had me sit on the couch and pantomimed to make me understand that Ernesto was showering. She sat on a thick chair fitted with a gold slipcover and eyed me in silence. On the wall in front of me hung a painting of the Virgin Mary. She wore a white headdress and a robe with a blue shawl around her neck. She wasn't smiling and her eyes looked sad, but she had her arms open as she looked down from the heavens. With Mary in front, Jesus on a cross to my right, and Lupe staring at me from my left, I felt judged from all directions.

The chair I sat in was faded. It was brown with moss green paisley designs and topped with white crocheted lace doilies. The windows, covered with opaque white panels and olive swag curtains, gave little light. The only bright colors, other than the blue shawl in the painting, were the red, orange, and blue stripes in the Mexican carpet partially covering the scuffed oak floors. The only sounds in the room were the ticks echoing from the wall clock that hung beside the Virgin, and Lupe's occasional coughs.

As Ernesto strolled in, Lupe rose silently and left the room. He flopped down on the chair where she'd been sitting.

"Your grandma doesn't say much," I said. "I don't speak Spanish, but it seems like she's not talking to you either. She still upset?"

"She'll be this way a long time. She's still ashamed of me because I'm gay, and it makes me sad. Sometimes she talks to me, sometimes no. Her mood changes, but we never talk or laugh like we used to. I miss her."

"Sorry to hear. I hope you two work it out soon." I scooted to the edge of the couch and focused directly in his eyes. "You've heard by now that Christian Freeman was murdered this past weekend?"

"*Sí, es terrible. La policía* came and talked with me Sunday and acted like I kill him. They weren't nice. They made *mi abuela* cry. They ask her over and over where I was that night. Do you know who kill him?"

"No, no one knows yet. Except the killer, of course." I chuckled. Ernesto squished his eyebrows together and cocked his head. "Sorry, lousy attempt at a joke. I hope you can answer some questions, help me out."

He shuffled in his seat and clutched the chair's sides. "Okay."

"I hate to do it, but let's start with the question the police were asking you. Where were you Saturday night?"

"Here with *mi abuela* watching TV."

"What were you watching, and at what time?"

"*Inside Out* was on Telemundo around 7:00 p.m."

"*Inside Out?* The kids' movie about emotions? What else did you see?"

"After that, *Iron Man 2*. She likes action films. It's one of her favorites."

"Your Grandma can confirm you were here?"

"Now you're *ridículo*. I just say she was with me. We watched movies. I did no kill Christian. I never go to West Hollywood. Ever. Why I would go that night and kill him? I didn't know him, except for I see him at the bathhouse with Seth."

"Were you aware Victor was seeing Christian too?"

"I no like it, but Victor told me we were not exclusive. He'd meet guys at Club Silver Lake and around, so *es* no surprise he saw Christian. Everyone wanted Christian because he had lots of muscles and a real big dick. There were many places Victor could go. I never understand why he would go to the bathhouse where I can see what he did. I ask him to stop, and he told me no. It was no fair."

"I regret to tell you that Victor did more than hook up with Christian once or twice. They met at least once a week. It wasn't only you and Christian either, there were other men he saw, but I think he was with Christian the most."

"You're lying. You're trying to get me upset to trick me to confess." He wiped his wet eyes and stared at Jesus on the wall before speaking again. "I was here, watching movies that night. And Victor didn't see anyone else. He loved me. He loved only me."

The waterworks began, and he sobbed into his hands. Lupe came out of her room and stood in the doorway. She pursed her lips and darted her eyes back and forth between Ernesto and me, never making contact. When he pulled his arm away from his face and gasped, she returned to her room without him knowing she had been there.

"I hate I had to be the one to tell you, but it's the truth. When you two were together, did he ever talk about Warren? Did he mention money problems? I want you to stay calm and think hard. You told me you think Warren did it, but I still can't understand why."

He leaned forward and gasped. "He would no let me ask about Warren, but sometimes he talk about him. Not much, though. Sometimes, when we lie together, he say Warren made him sad. Mostly though, he say they used to fight a lot but stopped. They almost don't talk to each other no more. Victor said Warren asks about money too, but that's all he say. I know nothing."

"You have anything to add?"

"*Nada*. Except I know Warren kill Victor. I don't know how he did it, but he kill him."

I stood and said goodbye as Lupe came out of the other room. She had changed into a threadbare, peach-colored, short-waisted dress and black orthopedic shoes. She held at her waist a black Coach purse with a large brass buckle. The straps dangled to the floor. Ernesto jumped up and held his finger in the air for me to hold on while he spoke with her in Spanish. She shook her head several times then flung her hands up and huffed.

"*Abuela* is going to Mass, and I said you will take her," he said. "She go every night but I no like her out when it's dark. It's the Church of Immaculate Conception on James

Wood Boulevard. She usually take the bus, but it's only
five minutes by car. *Por favor?*"

I reached out to hold Lupe's elbow, but she drew it away
and hurried down the stairs. I caught up to her on the
sidewalk and had her follow me to my car. She didn't speak
at all during the short drive. She just stared straight ahead.

When I pulled up to the church, I expected her to sprint
out the door, but she continued to sit, holding her purse on
her lap. I figured she was waiting for me to open her door,
so I set a foot on the street, when she grabbed my elbow
and pulled me back.

She continued to stare forward and asked me very
slowly and carefully. "Are you gay?"

It wasn't like me to avoid the question, but she caught
me off guard. I allowed myself to feel the blood pounding
through my temples for a moment before responding.
"Yes."

"*No me gusta que* Ernesto *es* gay."

"I think you said you're not happy he's gay, and that's
okay. It's not what you expected, and you're shocked, but it
will get better." Lupe stayed in her seat fumbling with the
straps on her purse. "Did you like the *Inside Out* movie?" I
asked.

She looked away out the window. She was silent.

"Uh... *gusta Inside Out?*" She shuffled in her seat and remained quiet.

"*No casa* with Ernesto that night, *si?* Hmm, night is *noche? No casa* with Ernesto that *noche, si?*"

Lupe looked to me then back out the window for a long while. I fought the urge to continue talking, allowing her to collect her thoughts.

She looked at me. "Help him, *por favor.*"

Giving me no time to respond, she rushed out of the car, and slammed the door. I waited until she reached the top of the stairs and entered the sanctuary before driving off to Club Silver Lake.

Twenty-Four

With Seth out, the bathhouse didn't have the same vibe. It was too low-key. Ben Morris, a part-timer, was working behind the desk. He had that blond-haired, blue-eyed, "all-American boy" look. He was a bit thin for my taste, but his deep dimples and shaggy hair looked charming. He knew he was cute. The gleam in his eyes and his smug smile told me that much.

"Hey," Ben said. "You must be Mitch. Trent told me you were coming. Hold on while I find him."

Several minutes after being paged, Trent called the desk. He asked Ben to have me meet him in the game room where I found a familiar pair of brawny legs sticking out from under the pool table. His calves and thighs shifted with each move. I could have stood there all day and enjoyed the show.

I cleared my throat and got a reply. "Hey, Mitch. Give me a sec. I've got some balls stuck, and I'm trying to get them out." I forced back a snicker.

A moment later, I could hear the billiard balls rolling into the main chamber.

Trent got to his feet, and I held out my hand. He eyed it for a moment then gave me a brief hug. I forced my arms up and gave him a pat on the back. I feared if I returned the hug, I'd be unable to let go. He didn't appear angry, which I could have handled. His attempt at a fake smile failed. He was pouting, and I felt awful. The corners of his mouth turned down and quivered.

He crossed his arms and leaned his back against the wall. "Thanks for finally returning my calls. I was starting to think I wouldn't hear from you."

"Of course you'd hear from me. I'm working your case." Trent dropped his arms and sighed. I bowed my head. "I'm sorry. I know that's not what you meant."

"I had a great time the other night," Trent said. "You looked like you did too."

I raised my head. "I haven't laughed so hard in a long while. The best time I've had in years."

I rested one ass cheek on the corner of the pool table. Trent looked past me. I turned to see if he was watching something on a TV on the wall. There was nothing on.

"I'm confused," he said. "I like a one-nighter as much as the next guy, but that's not what we had... Well, I guess we did, but it's not what I was expecting. We had a great time." He stepped up next to me and put both hands on the edge of the pool table. "We planned to make pancakes in the morning. That doesn't sound like a one-night stand kind of plan."

"I never should have…" I drifted off.

"Did you lie about breakfast to get laid?"

I felt blood rush to my cheeks. "You haven't known me long, but I think you know me better than that. I meant everything we talked about. And I didn't lie about breakfast. I said, 'hmm.'"

Trent reached over and touched my wrist. "What happened?"

A rush of warmth spread through my body. I should have yanked my hand away, but I couldn't deny the sense of comfort and security it gave me. I pulled it back slowly.

"I had fun," I said. "I didn't want the night to end."

"But it did, and because of you." He stood upright and crossed his arms again. "What time did you leave?"

"Right after you fell asleep. A little after midnight."

Trent was silent. His eyes bored a hole through me.

"I'm sorry. I wanted to stay—I couldn't."

He huffed. "Don't even try 'it's not you, it's me.'"

"It may be a cliché, but it's true. It is me. I'm not ready for a relationship."

"Like it or not, we already have a relationship. Colleagues? Friends? More? We may not have defined it yet, but something is happening."

I owed him an explanation. "Trent, I have something I need to tell you about what happened in Afghanistan. I know it doesn't excuse my behavior, but hopefully, it will help you understand more what's going on with me." I paused to gain composure. "It has to do with Jackson."

"Jackson?" He stepped forward and placed his palms on the pool table. "Did you mention him before? Was he in that truck?"

"When I enlisted, I thought it was what I needed in my life, but after my first tour in Afghanistan, I regretted joining the Army. I was miserable until I met Jackson. We were stationed at Fort Bragg. We were together for almost two years, when I was shipped back to Afghanistan. He was too, but it was his first tour overseas." I felt myself choking up. I coughed. "We got engaged in July 2013. There was a lot of excitement that month. A whirlwind to say the least. On the twenty-fifth, we held the first deployed pride event at Kandahar Air Base."

"In Afghanistan? A parade?"

"No." I sniggered. "A panel discussion mostly, but more than sixty people were there, and we were stoked—it was a big deal. Two days later, we woke up to the news that the Supreme Court struck down the Defense of Marriage Act. They said The Department of Defense planned to give the same benefits to same-sex couples." I stretched my neck to release the tension and smiled. "I was so caught up in the moment that I proposed to Jackson on the spot."

Trent brightened. "That's awesome." His face fell. "Sorry."

"That's okay. You're right. It was awesome. It was the most awesome time of my life—for a very short time."

He put a hand over his mouth.

"August is when my buddies and I hit the IED. A few days later, my commanding officer came to my bed in the hospital at the air base. I expected to find out they were sending me home. That's when I learned Jackson had been killed... and that's how I wound up here telling my fucked-up story."

"I'm sorry."

"While I was in the hospital, he was killed by a sniper."

I sat in my discomfort, relieved to have finally told someone besides Josie the entire story.

"Why didn't you say anything?" Trent asked.

"We barely know each other, and I don't go around telling sob stories. Especially on a first date," I sighed.

"Listen, Trent, I don't think we want the same thing. Can't we be two guys who like to have a good time now and then?"

"I'm not looking for a fuck buddy."

"I didn't say that. Can't we be friends?"

"With benefits?" he asked.

"If that's what we both want—yeah. I can't give more than that. You seem like a great guy, and I'm so sorry if I hurt you the other night. But I just can't commit to anyone right now."

"I can't imagine the pain you've been through. I don't want to add more of a burden on you." He wrung his hands and gazed toward the ceiling. "I'm not trying to talk you into anything, but I need you to understand where I am in my life." He sat down in a wingback chair and waved his hand toward the loveseat across from it. "Please. Sit down."

I remained leaning on the table. "I think I have a good idea of what you want."

"Maybe you do, and maybe you don't. I'm not on the prowl seeking a husband, if that's what you think. Between writing and running this club, I don't have the time or space for that right now. All I want is to date. But, for me, dating someone means I believe there is a possibility to get serious down the road. I'm not looking for 'forever.' But I am looking for intimacy. It seems pretty clear now that's not what you're looking for. I like you, Mitch, but I don't do casual in the long-term."

He coughed, and for the first time since I arrived at the bathhouse, we held direct eye contact for more than a fleeting moment.

I stood and raised my arms. "Look around. We're in a bathhouse. There's guys everywhere having a good time. Why can't we do the same? Why does this have to be so difficult?"

I'd been with lots of men over the past several years, but Trent was different. I found his playful persona attractive—I needed more fun in my life, but I didn't want to get hurt. And I didn't want to hurt him either. I knew if I let him get too close, I'd just end up pushing him away.

Trent stood. "I'll back off, and when the investigation is over, I hope we can be friends."

I looked at him hopefully. "With benefits?"

"Just friends. No benefits."

"But the other night was—"

"If you're not open to dating, a friendly business relationship is about as far as I can go. I think it'll be best for both of us."

His words stung, but I knew he was right. "It was a mistake to muddle the two."

Trent frowned and slumped his shoulders. I hated that I had let myself cross over from business to pleasure, and hurt him in the process.

I cleared my throat. "I have every intention of proving Ernesto's innocence. I can assure you."

He nodded and raised his hands as if giving up. "That's all I can ask for. So, how's the case coming along?"

"Not much to tell," I said. "Christian's murder changes things. The police know he and Victor knew each other, so they're investigating whether it's possible the same person murdered both of them. Other than that, my lips are sealed. You know the drill: for Eve's ears only."

Trent stepped forward, and this time he was the one to offer his hand. We shook. "I've got to get back to work. I'm glad we had this talk."

He stood still as I walked away. I looked back, and his face was cool and resigned. When I reached the lobby, there were tears welling up in my eyes. I was furious with myself. Hadn't I got what I wanted—freedom from relationship and commitment?

"Have a good night, Mitch," Ben said as I walked out the door.

I waved without turning around. I couldn't let Ben—or anyone else—see me in that state.

When I reached the sidewalk, I took several deep breaths and leaned back against the building. A moment later, I wiped my eyes, stood up straight, and walked casually to my car.

My stomach cramped as I sat in the driver's seat, staring at the brick wall I had parked in front of. I replayed the conversation with Trent over and over in my head, trying to figure out how I felt about the outcome. I put the key in the ignition but didn't turn it. Instead, I leaned forward and laid my head on the wheel. Loneliness consumed me, but I refused to give into it. I sat up, turned on Green Day's *American Idiot* album, and drove off to meet Heather Verboom and Kelvin Daniels in Riverside.

Twenty-Five

My first attempt at a parking spot was thwarted by the remains of a used couch teetering off the sidewalk into the street. The next spot I attempted nearly resulted in smashing my front bumper into a cluster of abandoned shopping carts. I was almost giddy when I found two empty spaces on a side street, but veered away when I noticed the streetlights above were burned out. I didn't need the added risk of car theft from parking in the dark. After ten additional minutes of circling, I found a suitable spot.

Heather and Kelvin's small duplex was about sixty miles east of Los Angeles, in the city of Riverside. From what I could see, their home was the best place on the block, despite leaning to the side, dangerously off its foundation. The exterior walls were a soft shade of pink and the doors and window frames were lime green. The front yard of their half of the building was a mixture of succulents and flowers.

My drive time was better than expected, though I wasn't sure how they'd react to my popping in on them unannounced at 10:00 p.m. Since our prior meeting didn't end well, I didn't want to be rebuked by calling ahead.

Heather opened the door as Kelvin sat in the dining area playing a game on his cell phone.

"Uh, why are you here?" Heather asked.

"Hey, numbnuts, you got some nerve barging in here," Kelvin called without looking our way.

"I'm very sorry," I said in my most gracious tone. "I was in the area for a client and thought I'd stop in while I'm here. Somehow, I accidentally deleted your number from my cell phone. May I please come in? I know you want the man who killed your father caught, so I'm here to ask some questions which may help make that happen." I forced a toothy grin.

Heather turned back to Kelvin who continued to face the other direction, looking at his phone. She looked at me and waved me in.

The living space and kitchenette were combined in one room, and a single door led to the bedroom and presumably the bath as well. The weathered, pea green shag carpet was a flashback to an era long ago.

"Do you mind if I have a seat?"

"Yes."

"Kelvin, shut up," Heather said. "Sure, Mr. O'Reilly. Go ahead."

Rather than respond, Kelvin leaned back and put his muddy Nikes on the table. I sat on the couch. It was greenish-brown with a mix of red and yellow flowers. It was as uncomfortable as it was ugly, the broken springs stabbing my ass. Heather sat on a tattered recliner.

"Heather, your garden out front is beautiful."

"Thank you. It's actually Kelvin's garden."

"Really? Kelvin, I'm impressed. I didn't know you were the nurturing type."

He ignored me.

"Can I, um, get you something to drink?" she asked. "I have some Diet Dr. Pepper."

I looked to the kitchenette with its stack of dirty pots and pans and a dishtowel crumpled up on the floor. "I'm fine, thanks. I have to drive back home tonight, so I'd like to get down to business."

Kelvin looked up. "If you're in such a hurry, why don't you just go?"

Heather swatted in his direction and told him to hush.

"I appreciate you looking into my dad's death, but I'm not sure how I can help you. It's been less than two years since I started visiting him and even then, I rarely ever saw him."

"If you 'rarely ever' saw him, he sure spent a lot of money for nothing."

Heather sat up straight. "What do you mean?"

"Your father's been renting a hotel room for you about once a month. And an expensive one at that. In fact, he had a room in your name booked for the night of his death."

She blushed and bowed her head. Kelvin stood and balled his fists. "Been getting in our business?" he challenged. "Why don't you leave us alone?"

"Where your business and Victor's business collide, especially when it comes to the night of the murder, that is literally my business," I turned to face Heather. "I came to discuss this with Heather, but I'd be more than happy to tell the cops about your monthly visits and aggressive attitude. Is that what you'd prefer?"

Heather pulled her palms to her face. "No, no it's not."

I realized that fear and intimidation wouldn't get me any answers, so I tried kindness and compassion. "Don't worry. We'll do this slowly. No rush. Take your time."

"Thank you," she said.

Kelvin slumped back down in his chair and muttered. "Dickweed!"

I scooted forward and leaned toward Heather. "Why were you in town that weekend?"

"No special reason. He booked us a room whenever Kelvin and I had a couple of days off together so we could spend time with him."

"What did you usually do?"

"He and I would hang out… go to a museum, or just walk along the beach and talk. We had a lot of catching up to do."

"You said 'he and I.' What about him?" I nodded my head in Kelvin's direction.

"What about me?" Kelvin growled.

"Kelvin Z. Daniels, cut it out!" She stood and pointed toward the interior door. "Either shut up or go in the bedroom. You're stressing me out."

He jumped up, almost knocking his chair over. "I'm not stressing you out. He is."

She sobbed. "Will you please just leave us alone a minute?"

"Shitbag." He grabbed a skateboard that'd been leaning against the wall, then stormed out the front door, slamming it behind him.

"Sweet guy," I said, forcing myself not to smile at the absurdity of it all.

Heather stood, straightened her skirt, and sat down again. "Sorry about that," she said. "Ready when you are.

Let's, um, deal with one problem at a time." She bounced her foot. Despite her small size, the floor was shaking.

I placed my hand on her wrist. "Is it safe for you to be here?"

She slumped back into her chair. "Yes. He may act like an ass, but he'd never hurt me."

"Hurt isn't always physical."

"I said he's all right." She smacked her hand up and down on the arm of the chair. "Did you come here to insult my fiancé?"

"Let's start with how you really found out about your father's murder."

She sighed. "Aunt Pam called me while we were on our way home."

"But you were in town when he was murdered. Why did you lie before about being there?"

"That wasn't my idea. It was Kelvin's. I swear, sometimes he doesn't know anything but how to cause trouble." She glanced at me and corrected herself. "He wasn't doing it to make problems for anyone. He was trying to protect me. I know it looks bad, but we had nothing to do with what happened to my dad, and he was worried we'd have to be in LA meeting with cops nonstop if they knew." She looked around the duplex. "I'm not sure if you can tell, but we don't have a lot of money. Getting approval for the day off to go to my dad's funeral was hard enough, and neither one of us can afford to miss a day's pay. It was easier not to say anything."

"Trouble is right. What do you know about your father's friends at the bathhouse?"

She took a deep breath and exhaled slowly before responding. "Not a lot. I know he was having an affair with that Mexican guy."

"Easy. Everyone knows that. It was on the news. What do you really know?" I leaned closer.

"What do you mean? I don't know what kind of relationship you have with your family, but it's not like my dad was telling me every detail about the guys he had sex with. I knew the bathhouse existed. I knew he went sometimes. I didn't want to know more than that."

"What do you know about Ernesto?"

"That Dad was breaking up with him to work on his relationship. That's it."

"Did you ever meet him?"

"No. I never even saw his face until my dad was murdered, and that was just on the TV." She sniffled several times and blew her nose.

"Fine. New question. What were you and Kelvin doing at that time?"

"It was 3:00 a.m. We were sleeping." Her voice was harsh.

I had gone too far. I reminded myself to keep the questions sweet and simple.

"I understand it's hard to talk about this, but anything you can remember helps me get one step closer to figuring out what happened. What did he say to you that night? Did he seem agitated?"

Her brow furrowed, and her lips turned down. "I get it. You want to know what happened. But how can I give you a play-by-play when we weren't there?"

"I'm hoping to jog your memory of something your father may have said or done that could give us some unexpected clues. It's possible you were one of the last people to see him before he went into the bathhouse."

She huffed and waved a finger at me. "You're trying to figure out if there's a way we could do it. You actually believe I would kill my dad."

"I never said that." I leaned back. But she was right. I thought it. She stood to inherit a lot from her father, a man she herself admitted she hardly knew. How deep did the resentment of twenty years of abandonment go?

"It seems like you're fishing, but there's nothing to tell. Kelvin and I were sleeping when Dad died."

I gave her a minute to cool down. "I've changed my mind. I would like something to drink."

"Um. All we've got is Diet Dr. Pepper."

"How about just a glass of water?" I asked.

"I don't have any ice."

"Room temperature is fine." I had no intention of drinking it, anyway. I was forcing a break in our back and forth exchange, which was getting adversarial.

She filled a glass with tap water and set it on the table. I thanked her. She straightened her skirt again and sat back down.

"Heather, I hate to put you through this. I know it's a difficult time. I want to find out who killed your father. I need your help. I'm not making accusations. Sometimes people know more than they realize, and it's my job to bring that to the surface." I smiled. "I'm sorry."

"I'm sorry too. I guess you're only trying to help." She sat back up. "What more do you want to know?"

I thanked her for her understanding and got right back to questioning. "What can you tell me about Warren?"

She cocked her head. "What about him?"

"What about his relationship with your father?"

"My dad said they were once in love. They stayed together for twenty years—that's got to be a Hollywood record, right? But something went sour. It was bad before I started seeing Dad, and he said it got worse every month."

"I heard your father and Warren were trying to save their relationship, that it was the reason he planned to split up with Ernesto. Any truth to that?"

"Yes and no. Dad said they could barely stand each other, but neither wanted to flush all those years down the drain. They agreed a while ago to try and save their relationship, and they tried. Dad said things were improving, but Warren blew it by asking for money again. Dad had been bailing him out of his gambling addiction for years. He told me Warren's flower shop is in heavy debt because of it. When they agreed to work on their relationship, Warren promised he would stop. But he didn't. My dad told me at dinner that he had just asked Warren for a separation."

"So all those people who say he was breaking up with Ernesto because he was trying to salvage his relationship with Warren must not know the full story. If Warren was back to gambling, and they were breaking up, maybe Ernesto—"

"Listen," she cut me off. "I don't know much about this Ernesto guy or any other men my dad was seeing. God. I know he wanted to split up with Warren. And I know he wanted to split up with Ernesto. He did tell me he had to simplify his life. Maybe that was the reason."

"Hmm. When did Warren ask your father for the money?"

"I don't know, but Dad told me about it on the phone the week before he was killed."

"Did he say how much Warren wanted?"

"Not exactly. He did say it was more than he ever asked for before. He made it sound like it was a lot."

"Did he ever say he was afraid of Warren?"

"No. The opposite. Despite everything, he said he still cared for Warren. His hope was that once they separated and let the dust settle, they could be friends."

"What time did you see your father that last night you had together?"

"About 7:00. The three of us had dinner together at Bassanelli's on Sunset Boulevard. We talked for hours. We all had too much to drink, so he said he was going to take a cab home and paid a Lyft driver to get us back to the hotel."

"Your father didn't go home."

"I guess not." She shrugged. "It sounds like maybe he went straight to the bathhouse instead."

"I think reservations are required at Bassanelli's."

"Probably. My dad liked all those fancy places," she said. "Hey, if you want proof of when we were there that night, you don't have to call the restaurant. I took a selfie. You want to see it?" She reached for her phone and pulled up the picture."

"Yes, that's the three of you." Considering they left the restaurant long before Victor's murder, the photo wasn't that helpful. I stood and pulled my keys out of my pocket. "It's getting late, and I'm driving back to LA tonight. Unless there's anything else you'd like to add, I need to get going."

"I don't think so. I hope our discussion helped."

"I believe it did. Do you still have my number?"

"No. Kelvin tossed your business card."

"Here's another. If you think of anything, no matter how minor it may seem, give me a call anytime."

"I will. Thanks."

I had one foot out the doorstep when Heather grabbed my arm.

"Actually, maybe you should come back. There's something I need to tell you."

I stepped in and closed the door behind me. A few tears streamed down Heather's cheek.

"I lied when I said Kelvin and I were in our room when Dad was killed. I was there, but Kelvin was gone."

"Where was he?"

"Sleeping in the car. We had a fight, and he stormed out."

"You think Kelvin was involved?"

"Oh no. That's not what I meant. He wouldn't have any reason to go to the bathhouse or hurt my dad. I wanted to tell you so we wouldn't look suspicious if you found out somehow."

"You two don't have a good track record when it comes to honesty."

"Honesty is hard for Kelvin, and I wanted to protect us."

"And you're sure he slept in the car?"

"That's what he says."

"Looks like I'll have to speak with him again."

She scoffed. "Good luck with that."

"He doesn't like me much, does he?"

"No. Not at all. Don't take it personally. He doesn't like anyone."

"I noticed. I was almost surprised you guys made it out of that coffee shop without a fistfight, he was so worked up. Any idea when he'll be back?"

"He was angry. When he grabs his skateboard, he could be out all night."

"I'm leaving then," I said. "I'll leave it up to you if you want to tell him I'm looking for him."

"Oh no. I'll leave that between you two."

I was halfway to the street when I turned back. Heather was still at the door.

"One last question."

"Okay," she said.

"If you can't confirm that Kelvin stayed in the car all night. How can he confirm you stayed in your room?"

"Um—"

I turned back to the street. "Just something to think about, Heather. Something to think about."

Twenty-Six

"I'm trying to solve a murder. This is critical info I need."

Sharon Kirkland, Chief Loss Prevention Officer at the Willoughby Hotel on Hollywood Boulevard, was not being helpful. She was a short, light-skinned, freckle-faced black woman, with her hair tied up in a bun on top of her head. The green security jacket she wore was stretched out by her excessively large breasts.

Located a half block from the Hollywood & Highland Center, the Willoughby was built in 2004 as part of a plan to revitalize the whole area to its once glamorous era. The plan had proven more successful around the shopping center, and a mile down at the intersection of Hollywood and Vine. So far, there hadn't been much success developing the corridor between the two landmarks. Hollywood Boulevard was still made up primarily of check cashing shops, cheap clothing boutiques, and far too many empty storefronts. The world-renowned Hollywood Walk of Fame disappointed and scared many tourists with its gum-stained sidewalks, junkies, and pickpockets.

"I can't tell you when our guests come and go," Officer Kirkland was saying for the fifth time. "It's a privacy issue. Bring me a warrant, and we'll talk."

"I'm not a cop. I can't get a warrant. I told you, this man may be a killer. Doesn't that mean anything to you?"

"Of course it does. Have the police bring a warrant, and I'll give them everything they ask for, without hesitation."

I had hooked up with a guy once who was staying at the hotel. I remembered the rooms were all luxurious two-room suites and ran around half a grand a night. Thinking about the contrast between Heather and Kelvin's hotel stays and the ramshackle duplex they lived in made me chuckle.

"Let's compromise. I know you can't tell me if he left, but did he stay all night?" Maybe if I rephrased the question, I'd get a different answer.

She pulled her head back and scowled. "What kind of fool do you think I am?"

"I don't know what you mean. I don't think you're a fool."

"I can't tell you a damn thing. Now get your ass out of my office, or I'll be the one who calls the police."

After wasting thirty minutes with Security Officer Ballbuster, I walked the two blocks back to my car. Their parking garage cost twenty-six bucks. At the rate Eve was paying me, I was sure she wouldn't cover the expense, and I didn't have the cash to spend money to ask questions. I sat in frustration in my Honda, unsure of what to do, when an idea hit me. It was stupid, but I took a chance. I didn't have Kelvin's phone number, so calling Heather was my only option.

"Hello?" She was hesitant, as usual.

"Hello, Heather. This is Mitch O'Reilly. Can I speak to Kelvin?"

"Kelvin?" she called out. I could only hear mumbling as she covered the phone with her hand.

"I'm sorry. He won't talk to you."

"Tell him I have questions about the parking garage. He'll want to talk."

I heard more mumbling, followed by, "Hold on."

I waited a full minute before Kelvin came on. His voice was deep and angry. "When you showed up at our door, you said you lost our number."

He pulled the phone away from his mouth. "Heather, did you give him our number?"

"I need to talk to you about where you went after leaving the parking garage."

"What are you talking about?"

This was where I'd have to wing it. My tactic would either prove to be genius, or an epic fail. "I met with security at the Willoughby. They told me you left the hotel for a while the night of the murder. Care to explain?"

"Hold on."

I waited a long time before he got back on the line. "What do you want?" The sound was muffled like he was covering the mouthpiece with his palm to keep from being overheard.

"Is Heather still there?"

"I'm on the sidewalk. She's inside."

"Smart man," I said. "Now tell me why you left. And be honest."

"I didn't! I had to sleep in the back seat. Did you look at the friggin' validation ticket?"

Without cooperation from the hotel security, I didn't know what to say. He stumped me until I thought of more straws to grasp.

"I didn't have to see the ticket. The cameras show you left the garage on foot."

Silence on the other end.

I gave him enough time to collect his thoughts. My gut told me my bullshit was succeeding. "Did we get disconnected?"

"I'm here."

More silence.

"Kelvin, be honest. Did you go to Club Silver Lake that night?"

"I told you I ain't no knob jockey. I wouldn't go there."

"Then what happened?"

"I hooked up with a chick. Sofia. She's an ex-girlfriend. She lives around the corner on Orchid."

"Sofia who?"

"Her last name is none of your business. She's married, and her man was out of town. I don't want to cause her no trouble."

He was breathing heavily and starting to stutter.

"I'm not here to disrupt innocent people's lives. She can provide an alibi if you need her to?"

"Yes."

I could hear a woman's voice call out in the background.

"I'll be right there. Two seconds," I presumed he was shouting back at Heather. "Jesus Christ on a stick," he said to me. "Look, we're in a hurry to meet friends."

"Thanks for your time, Kelvin. I'm sure I'll be back with more questions."

"Come on, don't be a dickhead. Can't you leave me alone?"

"Not anytime soon, douchebag."

Twenty-Seven

I walked into Eye Spy Supplies a few minutes before closing. Josie was showing a woman a SeekerMax, our most expensive bug detector. With a high markup and priced just under a thousand bucks, I was tempted to jump in and close the sale. However, Josie was an excellent bullshit artist, so I let her showcase her skills.

Josie's phone rang. She grabbed it, looked at the number, and set it down.

"You know," Josie said. "With Homeland Security—and our government in general—overstepping their bounds, we must all stay vigilant and protect ourselves from this decay of our democracy."

The shopper's waist-length blonde hair lay flat against her back. She wore a thin, almost see-through, pink halter top that clung to her like a second skin, and jean shorts with daisies embroidered on the rear pockets. She nodded approvingly at Josie's every word.

"I couldn't agree more," Blondie said. "We can't sit back and watch our liberties be chipped away."

Josie's phone rang again. She looked at it and didn't answer.

"But I don't know," Blondie continued, "the price of that is awfully steep."

"You can't put a price on freedom," Josie replied.

"I'd say you're right, but my paycheck says otherwise. Let me get that Peek-A-Boo 386 you showed me instead. Fifty dollars, I can handle."

Another call came in for Josie. She refused it and went ahead and rung up Blondie's purchase. The woman took her bag, eyed me suspiciously, and walked out to her black pickup.

"Sorry, Lil' Bro, I thought for sure I had a big sale for you."

"Not even you can hit a home run every time."

She pulled the cash drawer out of the register while I locked the front door.

"I'll make it up to you tonight," she said. "Let me take you out to dinner."

"Nice offer." I pulled down the security gates. "But you can't afford it any more than I can."

"There's one big difference." She pulled a credit card out of her purse. "I can charge it."

Again her phone rang. After looking at the screen, she huffed and tossed it in her bag.

◆ ◆ ◆

I didn't want Josie spending too much money, so I chose a cheap place in Thai Town. Afterward, I was tired and could have gone straight home, but I went with her back to her place. She was still shaken from Christian's murder, and so was I, to be honest.

When we reached Josie's condominium complex, she jumped out of her car, raised her arms, and squealed. "It's our first rain in months."

"It's just a drizzle. Won't do much good."

She pushed me in my shoulder. "Don't be so negative. It's a start. Let's get upstairs before it starts really coming down. I can feel it."

When we entered her apartment, I went straight to her kitchen.

"You bought dinner; I'll pour the drinks. Have any tequila left from the other night?"

She laughed. "Do you really have to ask? A couple of shots would be perfect."

"Exactly what we need after a week like this. Limes?"

"It's all in the kitchen—limes, salt, and two large bottles of tequila."

I grabbed the necessities and set up our drinks. We each did two shots within a minute, then sat back and waited for the magic liquid to wash away our problems.

We were sitting on the couch, both nodding off, when her cell phone buzzed.

"It's that same number that's been calling all day. Can't they take a hint? I don't answer numbers I don't know."

"Someone is desperate to reach you. I'd take the call. If it's a telemarketer, you scream at them and then block them."

"Fine. Hello?" Josie answered. "Who is this?" She shrugged and handed me the phone. "It's someone who says he's a friend of yours."

"For me? Hello?"

The voice was robotic. The caller was using an inexpensive voice changer like the Garbler 1062 I sell in my store for forty bucks.

"Good evening, Mitch," the mystery caller said. "How is your sister?"

"Who is this?"

"I hear there is a special bond between twins. Something others cannot understand."

"I said, who is this?"

"I do the talking. You do the listening. It is important that you listen. Your sister is quite popular. A lot of people would miss her if she is gone."

Whatever he was leading up to wasn't good. My face was tense, and my hands were shaking. Josie looked concerned.

The caller continued, "I know where she lives. I know where she works. I know where she goes. I know her best friends—Winona, Kurt, Olivia. Stop asking so many questions about Victor, and direct your attention to other things. It is a big city. Lots of opportunity for a two-bit spy. Move on, and she will be okay."

Silence. Whoever it was had hung up.

I pulled the phone away from my ear and stared at it as if something would crawl out. I tried to stay cool, but Josie was looking at my hands.

"Who was it?"

"I don't know, but you're not staying here tonight." I went to her bedroom and pulled a duffel bag from the bottom of her closet. "What do you want to take? Grab your things. You need to pack."

"What are you talking about? What did he want?"

I faced Josie and put my hands on her shoulders. "I promise you'll be okay." She tensed. "The caller threatened to make you disappear you if I don't drop the case."

She hugged me. "Mitch, I'm scared."

I held her tight. "Me too."

"But you know you're not dropping the case, right? You're not going to allow anyone to bully you from doing your job."

"Let me think of somewhere you'd be safe. You should call work and tell them you won't be in for a while."

"I've taken too much time off working for you. I can't skip anymore. My boss will fire me."

"Call him in the morning and tell him everything. I guarantee he won't force you to work if you're in danger."

"You want to take me to Olivia's?" she asked.

"No. No friends. Whoever it is, he knows your whereabouts, your routines, the people in your life. Hell, he knew I was with you. You need to stay somewhere he won't suspect."

I pulled out my phone and started to dial a familiar number.

"Are you calling the police?"

"The cops are my next call. First, I have to find a place for you to go. Pour us a couple more shots, will you?"

The phone rang seven times before a groggy, raspy voice answered.

"Hello, Trent. I need your help…"

Twenty-Eight

"I wish I could put a squad car out front, but it wouldn't be approved," Detective Turner turned away from Aunt Ada's living room window and sat on her mint green Victorian couch. "Unfortunately, a single threatening phone call doesn't justify the time and expenses. I wouldn't even be here if you hadn't called me direct. Homicide wouldn't have sent me. This is a big city. There's a lot of threatening calls every day. We can't chase them all."

"Sir, I was told to 'move on and she'll be okay.' It doesn't take a badge to know what they were talking about," I said. "Josie is in danger."

"You're sure this is a safe place?"

"I took a lot of side streets and watched my surroundings. I'm certain I wasn't followed. We turned off her phone so no one can track her. She's not safe with any of her friends—the caller knew their names, and they knew where she works and hangs out. I don't think there's any way they can connect this place with Josie. She's never met Trent's aunt before, and I had only met her once. Not here. At her restaurant. No one would know to look here."

Ada was sitting on an overstuffed brown chair. Trent was patting her hand.

"I can assure you," Ada said, "she's in good hands. I've got a spare room, and I'll keep her well fed."

"What about when you work?" Detective Turner asked.

"She could come with me to the restaurant if you think it's best."

"No. It's better if she stays inside at all times. She shouldn't go outside, not even to the car."

Josie was sitting next to Detective Turner. She wrapped her arms around her stomach and leaned forward with her head down.

"I feel like I'm in jail. I don't want to be trapped here."

Ada frowned, but Josie continued.

"No offense, Ada, but there's no place like being in your own bed. I'm grateful for you sharing your space. I really am."

Ada smiled and bowed her head to look up into Josie's eyes. "Don't worry, dear. I understand."

Detective Turner nodded toward the kitchen. "Ma'am, may I take Ms. Weichselbaum in there to talk privately?"

"Of course. This is her home now too."

I followed Josie and Detective Turner into the kitchen. He raised his hand. "Sorry, Mr. O'Reilly, I'd like to speak with her alone."

"You okay with that, Josie?" I asked.

"I'm fine."

I joined Trent and Ada in the living room. Trent kicked the leg of a wingback chair, causing it to scoot into a wall. Ada jumped.

He stood up and started to pace. "I'm getting so I can't stand people anymore. Cheating, lying, killing, making threats—people suck."

Ada placed her hands on her forehead, "Oh Trent, I don't like it when you're like this." She turned to me. "It's so rare he gets angry. It upsets me when he does."

"The murders have made me cynical," Trent said.

"A lot's been going down. You're forgiven," I said.

Ada stood and put an arm around Trent's waist. "I'd bring you some coffee, Mitch, but I can't go in the kitchen."

"To be honest, ma'am, I'd rather have a little ouzo," I said.

She looked at me. Something told me she knew about our fallout and could sense my presence was making him more nervous. "I know you," she gave a thin smile. "You want more than a little."

Detective Turner stepped out of the kitchen and shut the door. The hands on the grandfather clock had barely moved since he and Josie stepped in together, but in my current state, minutes felt like hours. "She doesn't know anything about the case, does she?"

"She knows some," I replied, "but none of the nitty-gritty. She helps me run Eye Spy Supplies, so she's overheard some conversations in my office, and she's taken off work to cover the store when I'm out asking questions. But she doesn't help with investigations."

"Let's talk privately." He waved me over and asked Josie to step back out into the living room. She was shaking. I'd never seen my sister look so vulnerable. She's always been nothing but fierce. "After you," he said. I took a seat at the small kitchen table. It had a red laminate top that fought with the canary yellow walls for attention.

Detective Turner poured us some coffee before sitting down. Just as he opened his mouth, the little bird in the hallway popped out of the wall clock and cuckooed twice. "I never get any sleep," he grumbled. "Anything you can share since our last conversation? Who are your primary suspects, for instance?"

I hesitated. "No disrespect, sir, but what's in it for me?"

"Not much other than my gratitude."

"How about a surveillance team watching this house?"

"That's not my call, but I'll do what I can."

"Not very reassuring, but if it's all you got. My primary suspect was Christian Freeman."

"The arrogant go-go boy your sister found murdered?" He sat across from me and clasped his hands on the table.

"You or one of your guys had talked to him already. By the time I talked to him, he was agitated, defensive, and evasive. Not enough to throw the book at him, but he was also seeing Victor on the side." Detective Turner nodded his head. I couldn't tell if he was acknowledging he knew this information, or if he was taking it in. "Being dead doesn't mean he didn't do it, but he's not my focus anymore. It's easier to investigate the living than the dead. I'm looking at Rod Hernandez, Warren Barone, Seth Snider … and Ernesto Torres, of course. Everyone except the six guys who have witnesses to back up their alibis."

He scowled. "Ernesto is on your list. Isn't that who you're working for?"

"Just because he's marginally my client—via Eve Aiken, via Trent—doesn't mean he's not guilty."

He nodded toward the living room. "In that vein, what about Trent Nakos? You didn't mention him."

"Of course not. Ernesto was already jailed for the murder. If Trent killed Victor, he'd have been ecstatic to leave Ernesto there and wouldn't have paid for an attorney to protect him."

"Ernesto was jailed for drug possession."

"Come on, you don't hold a guy for forty-eight hours for a little bag of meth—not in this city. You were upfront with Eve that he was a person of interest. You were buying yourselves time to nail him, but you came up empty-handed."

"Trent hiring Ernesto's attorney is the only reason you don't consider him a suspect? Is that it?" Detective Turner raised his eyebrows. "You must be pretty close for him to take your call at this hour and offer your sister a place to stay."

I hesitated when I realized I was feeling defensive. "Let's say he's not a strong suspect," I finally said.

"Hmm. Can't leave any stone unturned. Some people do crazy things to cover their tracks when it comes to murder. What evidence do you have on Rod, Warren, Seth, and Ernesto?"

"That's where our conversation ends, sir. We aren't in court yet."

"It was worth a shot. Can't blame a guy for trying, can you?" He sniffed. "You know you have to turn over evidence if it implicates someone."

"You'll be my first call. You have anything you want to share?"

"Not much different, except Trent's definitely on our list." He paused, weighing his words carefully. "If he did it, and the threat was related to the murder, I don't have to tell you that Josie's in real danger here. She's your sister. I'll trust you've thought it through."

I looked at him deadpan. "She's safe."

I stared into my cup. Detective Turner had made me realize I'd never considered Trent in my investigation. He was right. Trent did leave his office. He had the chance, and Rod had seen him in the bathroom washing his hands right after Victor's time of death. But, I had no clue what his motive would be. And, more importantly, I trusted him. I closed my eyes for a moment and allowed the thought that I could have had sex with a murderer to clear my mind.

"You're being awfully honest with me. What gives?" I asked.

"The heat's on us. The public never likes it when a murder makes the headlines and no one sits in jail to account for it. I was hoping you'd come across something we hadn't seen, something that could point us in another direction or break open the case against Ernesto."

"Wish I could, but not yet. When I get anything conclusive, I'll call—err, Eve will."

"Well, you must be getting close. Someone's spooked enough to involve your sister."

We sipped our coffee and sat in silence, trying to find something to say. We both jumped when Detective Turner's phone rang. He excused himself and walked into the dining room. Tired, I lay my head on the table and was immediately out. I was back in Afghanistan dodging sniper bullets when someone shook my shoulder.

"Hey, Mr. O'Reilly. Wake up."

I had been in a deep sleep for just dozing off. I raised my head.

"You said you prefer to investigate the living rather than the dead?"

"Yeah?"

"I got a call from homicide. You can scratch Ernesto Torres off your list."

Twenty-Nine

By the time we reached Club Silver Lake, the sprinkling of rain had turned into a deluge. Despite it being the middle of the night, crowds were huddled at the entrance to the side alley of the club. Detective Turner escorted Trent and me through the sea of umbrellas and around the police tape.

He stopped momentarily and put his hand up. "The two of you can come in the alley, but stay back from the crime scene. I may need your help with identifying possible suspects. Until then, stay out of the way." He stopped us about twenty feet from the crime scene, which was covered with a pop-up canopy. He handed Trent his umbrella, then walked over and looked inside the dumpster before talking with some cops. He glanced inside the dumpster again, then jogged back to us.

"What happened?" I asked.

Turner removed his glasses to wipe away the water droplets, looked at Trent, and bowed his head. "It's Ernesto Torres all right."

Trent kept his composure for a few seconds, then put his hands to his face and sobbed.

The detective pulled me a few steps away and whispered. "Ernesto's throat was cut too. This one's more gruesome than the others. Three bodies, all associated with this bathhouse, all with their throat slit, each murder more horrific than the last. It's too early to jump to any conclusions, but… I have to mention the possibility we're dealing with a serial killer here."

"Can I—"

We hustled back next to Trent as a team of officers rushed by, carrying a second large pop-up canopy. The three of us watched, bunched together under the umbrella, as they constructed another cover to keep the investigators dry.

"Sir, can I see the body?" I asked.

Trent took a few steps back while I followed Detective Turner to the dumpster. I placed my hands on its edge and took several deep breaths.

"Hands off! You'll contaminate the scene!" one of the forensics officers yelled.

I dropped my arms to my side. The rain had washed most of the blood down into the trash underneath Ernesto's body. His head was twisted backward, attached to his body by only a few tendons. There were cuts and scrapes on his arms. I asked a forensics officer if they got there before the heavy rain started. She stepped back and looked at me with disdain.

"No," she said. "God only knows how much evidence was lost."

I looked at the body again and felt as if thousands of insects were crawling beneath my skin. Then came the flashbacks, but worse than ever before. My past, present, and future collided in one vision, and I lost everything. This time it was not only my Army buddies in the truck. Trent and Josie were there too. When the vehicle hit the bomb, it was their blood and their flesh that coated the interior of the vehicle and much of my body. My knees buckled. I grabbed the side of the dumpster again to keep from falling. I puked in my mouth but was able to swallow it. It burned as it went down.

Detective Turner escorted me back to Trent.

Trent leaned me against a wall to keep me from falling. "You've lost all the color in your face."

"Trent—I'm a mess."

He placed an arm around me and pulled me against him. "Yes, you are a mess. In many ways. And yet, I care about you."

He held me, and I let him. Exhausted, we slid down to sit on the pavement, not realizing there was a small puddle where we had been standing. Our asses became soaked. I was too disoriented to care. He kept an arm around me

while holding the umbrella with the other. Despite the
rainwater on his face, I could see tears rolling down his
cheeks.

"You okay?" he asked.

"I should be asking you the same question." I felt the
blood rush to my face. "I don't seem like much of a
detective, do I?"

"You seem like a man who's been through hell. What do
you think is going on?"

"I have no idea, but every time I think I know who
murdered Victor, they die."

"You thought Ernesto did it?"

"I shouldn't have said so, but yes. He had a strong
motive and the best opportunity. I didn't have proof, and of
course I was doing what you and Eve hired me to do and
looking into other suspects. But yeah, I thought it would
turn out to be him. It was just a hunch." I shrugged. "I'm
learning my hunches don't mean much." We both looked
around the crowd blocking the alley. "Can you think of
anyone who might have done this?"

"I can't imagine anyone wanting to hurt either one of
them."

I thought about telling him it appeared Ernesto had put
up a fight to defend himself against whoever killed him but

decided against it. Instead, I curled up tighter against him and watched the rain splash against the pavement.

Thirty

Where am I?

I sat up and looked around my office at Eye Spy Supplies. My head was playing tricks on me. I couldn't remember much of what had happened, and the days and nights were starting to run together. I remembered taking Josie to Aunt Ada's. I remembered seeing Ernesto's body. I remembered being with Trent, letting him hold me. He had made me feel safe in the midst of chaos.

After that, it was all a blur. I supposed I must have driven straight to work and crashed on the couch. I was drifting off again when a loud noise came from outside the store. I grabbed my gun. Someone was banging on the window. It was 12:05 p.m. I was two hours late opening. I shuffled to the front door just in time to see a white Ford pickup drive away. It was my landlord.

After washing my pits and crotch, I put cash in the register, opened the security gates and stepped out the door. Frank was still sleeping. I reached down to give him a shake but instead grabbed the envelope that was taped to the door. I opened it. Jeff McAfee, the owner of the plaza, was giving me thirty days to get out.

"Jeff, what's the deal?" I asked over the phone. "Give me some time, and I'll get you the funds. I've got a major job I'm working on. I'll get you the rent."

Jeff was a heavy mouth breather. When he talked, you could hear the wind whistling through his teeth. "I don't know when you get paid for your 'major job,' but I hope it's within thirty days, cause that's what you've got."

"You can be more generous than that, can't you?"

"A thirty-day notice is the norm for residential units. For commercial leases, the law only requires I give you three. I am being generous, especially since you're already two months behind."

Just as I was starting to process what was happening, Eve Aiken pulled up in her rusty Mercedes.

"Do I hear a car pulling in?" Jeff asked.

"Yes, but—"

"Take care of your customer." He hung up.

"Asshole," I muttered as I stuffed the phone in my pocket.

Eve strode into the store and placed her purse on the counter. "You look like shit."

"Thanks. The sun was rising when I fell asleep. It was a long night."

"I'm aware." She dug into her purse. "Here's your check."

"This is a surprise. You said I'd get paid at the end of the month."

"I did, but since you're not working for me anymore, I thought I'd make a personal delivery."

I stepped back. "You're firing me?"

"No. The case is over. You were hired to investigate Ernesto Torres. He's dead, and so is the case."

"But we still don't know who did it."

"That's your issue, Mitch. Trent and I talked this morning. He says he doesn't need me anymore. Therefore, I don't need you. Case dismissed."

I stood, staring at my check. It was just enough to cover the store's rent but would leave little else for the necessities of life. "Sucks to be me, huh?"

"Not as much as it sucks to be Ernesto Torres."

"You're damned sweet, Eve. Got any other jobs for me?"

She pointed at the check, still in my hand, and chuckled. "Have you looked at that check? You must be desperate at that rate."

"I could use the work."

"I can't help you, Mitch. I don't have any jobs that require a snoop."

"Well, in that case… are we done here?"

"I guess we are."

"You'll let me know if anything comes up?"

"You'll be first on my list." She walked out the door, and I phoned my landlord back.

"Jeff? Mitch O'Reilly here."

"You must have made a sale. I know you wouldn't waste my time if you didn't have the rent."

I stepped back into the office and plopped onto the desk chair. "I've got one month's worth."

"You owe two, plus this month. If you don't have three, we have nothing to talk about. No more extensions."

"The place is a dump," I stammered. "It's not like people are lined up to move in. You've got what… four empty storefronts?"

"Sorry, I'd help you, but this has gone on long enough. It costs me money to have a store open. I feel for you, but I'm not running a nonprofit. Get the rest you owe me, and you can stay. Otherwise, start packing."

The check waved up and down as my hands shook violently. "You used to be a nice guy, Jeff."

"You used to be a good tenant, Mitch."

For the rest of the morning, I scoured my accounts for any way to come up with the rent. I knew the search was a waste of time, but I didn't know what else to do. Giving up on a buried treasure, I spent a couple hours checking websites where I could sell my merchandise online. I took note of some options.

By midafternoon, the only person who came in wanted change for the laundromat around the corner. I usually told people to go to the bank, but I was feeling generous, so I exchanged his ten dollars for a roll of quarters. My eyes followed the man out the door and past my window. My hands started shaking again, and I could feel the blood rushing to my face. I needed a drink, but when I reached for the tequila, the bottle was empty. With everything else in my life going to shit, the last thing I needed was to be out of booze. I grabbed the empty bottle and sent it flying across the room. It shattered dead center on a picture on the wall, knocking it to the floor. I hated the photo. It was a bridge over a babbling brook, and I felt no connection to it at all. Josie had hung it after I ignored her suggestion to liven up the place.

I reached for the broom, said *to hell with it,* closed the security gates, and locked the door.

Exhausted, I flopped on the couch, took a series of deep cleansing breaths, and stared at the ceiling. I couldn't get the case out of my head. Victor. Christian. Ernesto. What connected the three that they all suffered the same fate? Victor used Christian, which gave him a motive. He dumped Ernesto, which gave him a motive. But what tied Christian and Ernesto together? My investigation had revealed little connection between the two, other than both being in the club when Victor was killed. Whatever that link was, it could lead to solving the case.

In my head, I reviewed my list of living suspects. Warren Barone. Seth Snider. Rod Hernandez. Trent Nakos? Detective Turner was right. I had spent no time investigating him. I had gotten too close and let my guard down. With the exception of Warren, they all had the opportunity to kill Victor, but only Warren and Rod had motives. And if the murders were connected, what did either of them have against Christian and Ernesto? Warren could've wanted them dead, but he didn't stand to gain anything from killing them. With Victor, at least he stood to get money out of it. Someone had to be hiding something. I wondered what I didn't know yet about Seth and Trent.

I started to drift off, but the feeling of falling just before reaching deep sleep jolted me awake. My doctor said they were called hypnagogic jerks, probably related to my war experience. I rolled back over and fell asleep within minutes.

My frequent nightmare began again, but this time I wasn't there. Inside the MRAP, Victor was at the wheel, Christian rode shotgun, and Ernesto was in my regular seat in the back. The scenery kept moving past, like a screen in an old movie, or a badly animated cartoon. They kept driving over the place where the IED was buried, but nothing happened. Over and over again, like an endless loop, until the bomb finally went off. Just like what had happened in my real-life experience, the two in the front were killed instantly. But Ernesto was doomed to a different fate from my own. He had deep gashes in his body. Blood was pouring from his chest, and he was pinned under the truck. I showed up just as he died. I casually walked up to him, pulled out a clipboard and took notes. I walked around the perimeter, stopped at what was left of Victor, and took more notes. I did the same with Christian's body. When I circled around to where Ernesto had been, there was nothing left but a large pool of blood. I bent down for a closer look, and a pair of hands reached from behind and covered my eyes.

I startled awake and tried to shake any meaning my mind wanted to draw from the dream. I stared at the ceiling for nearly an hour while I mulled the case over in my head.

When I woke up again, it was the middle of the night. I drove home in a downpour, grabbed some cereal, and flipped through the TV channels, looking for something mind-numbing. I stopped at *Gilligan's Island*. It was the episode where a rock band goes to the island to get away from their fans. Getting away from the world sounded like a good deal. I laughed at the absurdity of my thought. An island? I barely had enough money to buy gas. As the final credits rolled, so did the tears on my cheeks.

Thirty-One

The rains had ceased, and the city gleamed, matching
the false image most of the world had of Hollywood. Los
Angeles is at its most beautiful the day or two after a storm,
when the sky is blue, and the mountains are visible. There
was even a little green in the trees in the Hollywood Hills
while I drove to Warren's home. It was my second time at
his house, but my first time through the front entrance. The
doors stood open, and Warren called out for me to enter
when I knocked on the frame. He was waiting for me on
the couch in the formal living room. I sat on the chair
closest to him. It was shaped like a tilted white infinity
symbol. I planted my ass on the lower loop and leaned all
the way back to rest on the top loop. Not a good idea. The
base of my spine felt like it would snap, so I leaned
forward.

"Did you have trouble finding the place?" he asked.

"No, it was quicker than last time."

He raised an eyebrow. "Last time?"

"Well, the last time I was in the area, of course. My
sister and I drive through the hills on sunny days. Great
way to chill, you know, and I've noticed your home before.
The glass cobalt doors stand out against the stark white

walls. It's a beautiful place." I lifted a seafoam throw pillow. "The interior accents and the tchotchkes are nice too."

Warren stood, walked across the room, and raised his arms. "Vic hired the designer. I look forward to selling it… not only because of the painful memories. It's not my style, and after twelve years it still doesn't feel like home. The entire house is filled with this same modern, sterile design. Except for the den down the hall. He let me handle that one. Unlike the rest of the house, there's color, and the furniture is actually comfortable to sit on."

"Sounds homier," I said. "Truth be told, I like a room with some color."

"I didn't peg you as a man who'd care about design, O'Reilly." He sneered. "I can't express how thrilled I am that you like color." He sat back on the couch. "Now that you're here let's get to it. How may I help you?"

"Straight and to the point, skip the small talk, I like it. But you called me. So, let's turn the question around. Why am I here today, Warren?"

"I had no choice but to call you. You've tracked me down at the memorial service, Bloomers, my favorite casino. You've left messages. Somehow, you convinced the police not to let me file for harassment against you. But mostly, I want this resolved."

"Go on."

"When Victor was killed, I was sure Ernesto did it. It's not smart to say, but I'll say it anyway—good riddance to Ernesto Torres." For a second, he held his hands in the prayer position. "I was raised never to wish harm on anyone, but I will not miss that man-child. Vic and I were mending things when he showed up. That bastard clung to him no matter how hard Vic tried to break away… At least, I thought so, until you told me the truth."

"So, you called because—"

"I'm not telling you anything new. I called because it seems like there's got to be a link between Ernesto's and Victor's murders. When the police came, they said the same thing."

"Throw in Christian Freeman's murder, and the odds become epic."

"I asked you to come because I'm no fool. I know I'm a suspect, but I'm also a potential victim. I don't want to be next, O'Reilly. I need the real killer to be caught."

"We both do," I said. I could see the fear in his eyes, and wondered whether he was telling the truth or putting on a really good show.

He looked at a framed photo of him and Victor on a shelf near the fireplace. "I never fell out of love with him, no matter how bad things got. I loved him as much on the day he died as the day we met. That sounds maudlin, but it's true. He felt the same. We had grown to react like oil and water, but we both wanted to go back to the way things were." He clasped his hands and hung his head. "I want to help with the investigation."

The edges of the hole in the lower loop of the infinity chair dug into my glutes. I had been shifting my weight throughout our conversation, but there was no relief from the discomfort. To top it all off, I felt foolish. Without armrests, I had tried keeping my hands in my lap, which wasn't easy because of the chair's angle, and ended up dangling them by my side. It was a ridiculous way to sit.

"I'm not sure how you can help, other than to cooperate," I said. "The cops are on it, and so am I."

"What about more money? So you can dedicate more hours to the case. How much do you need, O'Reilly?"

"I'd love to take your cash, but that won't speed things up. I'm still surprised you called me. I would've guessed you'd hire another PI."

"I considered it, but with the police and you already working the case, it'd be too many cooks in the kitchen.

Besides, I like you. You're a royal pain the ass. In fact, you excel at it, but you know you're an ass. You own it. I like bastards who are upfront and don't play games."

"I guess I'll take that as a compliment. So let's talk. Where—"

"I was at The Thrust."

"What?"

"You were going to ask me where I was when Ernesto was killed, and I was at The Thrust in Silver Lake. A detective said someone murdered him at 9:00 p.m. It couldn't have been me because I was at the bar."

"Not gambling for a change?"

"There you go being a smart-ass again. I said I like you, but don't push it."

"The time of the murder is more of a best estimate," I said. "A bathhouse employee found his body a little after midnight. The cops based the time on all the employees' schedules—seeing when they were out back—and when guests came and left the parking lot. It's hard to pinpoint since business was slow."

"I guess everyone was at the bar. It was busy… I got there just after dinner. Right around 7:30 p.m."

"When did you leave?"

"I can't say exactly, but sometime after 10:00 p.m. I stayed longer than I should've. The Thrust is a sleazy bar, and between us, more Vic's style than mine. He called it a cocktail bathhouse." He chuckled. "I felt out of place, but they're not judgmental. A lot of bears and bear chasers, but none were interested in me. I don't think people find me approachable."

I coughed to force myself not to laugh. "Why would you say that?"

"Don't be so damned sarcastic," he said. "I was there too long because I thought it'd be a quick way to meet someone and have fun. I'm stressed out, and I just wanted one night to kick back and forget about everything else going on. I should've gone online like everyone else."

"I hear that's popular." I hadn't seen his picture on any of the sites I visited. No need to admit to him that it was my preferred method. Or, it had been, until I took this case.

"What can I say? I'm out of step. It's why Vic played around more than me. He liked bathhouses and seedy bars. I didn't go online, and I don't like cruisy clubs. That left me fending for myself a lot of nights. Don't get me wrong. There's plenty of nice bars to meet people the old-fashioned way, but I end up drinking alone wherever I go. I like gaming because it's a solitary sport, and yet I don't feel alone when I'm there."

"Let's veer back on track. I want to talk about the night Christian was killed. You—"

"I was home that night. I watched TV and went to bed early. The police talked with the neighbors, but no one can back me up. Living in the hills is great for privacy, terrible for an alibi. I never wished more for a place where everyone snoops on their neighbors."

"Yeah. Between the garages, the hedges, the security gates, and the slopes of the roads, it's no surprise they didn't know if you were here. Tough break. What about the night Victor was murdered? You left a half hour before it happened. Where'd you go?"

"I came home. Trent woke me when he called around 4:30 a.m. Ninety minutes seems like a long time to wait to call someone after a murder, but I understand it was chaos."

"You didn't go back after?"

"You mean after they found him dead? No, I couldn't deal with it. I sat right here alone until the police arrived, and then I went to the mortuary."

"Let me rephrase the question. Did you go back to the bathhouse after you left, but before Victor was murdered?"

"What the hell kind of question is that, O'Reilly? You do know they have security cameras and a guy at the front desk to buzz you through, right?"

"Silly question, but I had to ask."

"I don't find it silly at all. I thought we were working well together, and now you're asking stupid questions that imply things I wouldn't think of. I confided in you, O'Reilly. I trusted you."

"Sorry. Can anyone verify you were at The Thrust the night Ernesto was killed?"

"You don't have good comprehension, do you? No one even noticed me."

"Now who's being the smart-ass?" I said. "What about the bartenders? Did you use a credit card?"

"I don't know the guys behind the bar. I prefer to pay cash—better for tipping. And you're pissing me off. The guy who made my drinks is a tall, thin, African-American guy with a goatee. I think his name is Gary. What else do you need?"

"I'll cut my losses while we're on good terms."

Warren grumbled.

It was 8:00 p.m. when I left his house—the perfect time for an ice-cold beer.

◆◆◆

Silver Lake had seen an influx of gays and lesbians move in during the 1970s when real estate agents promoted it as the eastern alternative to West Hollywood. Because of its hilly terrain, the neighborhood had earned the nickname "The Swish Alps," and shops and bars that catered to the neighborhood's newest residents sprung up throughout the area. Things changed when the AIDS epidemic swept the community, and by the 1990s, hipsters buying and remodeling homes jacked up prices. Silver Lake remained popular for those who were LGBTQ, but nothing like its heyday. Most of the old bars had closed, and many of the ones that stayed reinvented themselves to cater to straight and gay clientele alike.

The Thrust was a stronghold that had been running continuously for more than forty years, and one of the few places left that proudly promoted they were as raunchy and seedy as ever. When I arrived, there was a midsize crowd. Large enough to keep things hopping, but not so busy that I had to elbow my way to the bar to reach a bartender. It had never been one of my favorite spots, but from what I could recall, the red cement floor and black painted walls accented with corrugated panels hadn't changed a bit.

All eyes were on me. Fresh meat. I hated being the center of attention, so I focused straight ahead to avoid eye contact. I didn't want to send anyone the wrong signal. A tall, thin, black man with a goatee, fitting Warren's description, mixed drinks.

"Mitch!" he exclaimed. A full smile spread across his face while he shook my hand. "I've never seen you here. What are you having? First one's on me."

I was faced with a situation where I had no idea who I was talking with. It was not one I looked forward to, but an inevitable part of the online scene. I grinned wide enough that I bared my teeth. "I'll take a Rolling Rock. It's good to see you, Gary."

He grabbed a beer from the cooler, put it down and laughed. "Gary?" He leaned in close. "Who's Gary? Is he cute? Maybe we can all get together."

Before I responded he placed a hand on my shoulder.

"No worries, we only met once. The name's Grady." He stood straight and eyed me. "You don't recognize me. I came to your place two months ago. We met on studs4studs.com. Does that ring a bell?"

No, but I could fake it with the best of them. "Of course. I remember now. I'm sorry, I've been so busy, it's hard for me to focus."

"If you're here cruising, I get off in two hours."

"Sounds great, but I'm here on business tonight. I'm a private investigator." On my phone, I pulled up the About Us page on the Bloomers website, which had pictures of Warren and his staff. "Does this guy look familiar?"

"Oh yeah, him," he said. "Big guy. Ordered a rickey. It's an easy drink to make, but I remember it because not many men order them."

"Do you remember when he was here?"

"Not really. Why?"

"Someone he knew got hurt," I said. "I'm asking people who may know about it."

"You mean witnesses?"

"Yes, I'm looking for witnesses."

Grady sniggered and pointed at my phone. "He the guy who hurt somebody?"

"I can't give details, but no."

"I don't remember which night he was here, but it was definitely on the weekend."

"Saturday?"

"Yeah, that's right. It was a Saturday because we had nothing going on," he said. "Have you heard of the gay cowboy group, the Rainbow Broncos? They had an event scheduled. We sold tickets at the door and everything, but none of them showed. Not even the DJ. I heard they were dying out, but you'd think they'd call. That's why I remember. Plus, he was hard to miss." He pointed to a table in a dark corner. "He sat there looking like a serial killer. Not the jolliest of fellows, is he?"

"I've met friendlier. Do you remember what time he was here?"

"He got here early. Not much of a crowd yet. I don't know how long he stayed, but it was longer than I would've liked. It was depressing watching him and his sour face. He brought the whole place down… but once it got busy, I forgot about him."

"Anyone else here who might know when he left?"

"Hold on. Maybe."

Grady left the bar unattended for five full minutes before he came out with another man following behind. He stood as tall as Grady, with bronzed skin and a shaved head. I fixed on his sculpted abs and pumped chest. He wore a leather harness with a silver ring at his breastbone.

"Hey, Mitch," he said. "It's been awhile." We shook hands. "Remember me? I'm Randy."

"Sure, I do. How you been, Randy?"

The mixologists laughed. Grady turned to Randy. "I told you he wouldn't remember."

Randy continued to chuckle. "It was a long time ago. Grady said you asked about that ginger bear who was here Saturday."

Grady walked away to pour drinks, and I pulled up Warren's picture on my phone to show Randy. "Yeah, this guy. You remember him?"

"Mm. Oh yes, I do." Randy stroked his chin. "I'm into gingers, and he looked all mean and shit. He's hot. What'd he do?"

"Mitch ain't going to tell you," Grady said in passing. "He wants to know what time he was here."

Randy placed his hands on the bar and looked up. "He was here when I started my shift, but he left at—hold on a second." He pulled his phone from his pocket, scrolled for a few seconds, and tapped keys. "He left at 9:13 p.m."

"How could you possibly remember that?"

"Here." He showed me his screen. I didn't know what I was looking at. "I was out back having a cigarette, talking to my boyfriend. You see here, I called him at 9:07, and we talked for six minutes. When I hung up, that ginger bear got in a car with a tatted dude."

"Tatted dude? Can you describe him?"

"He was tall, but I didn't pay him much attention. The bear was hot, so my eyes were on him. They came out when my break ended. The lucky bitch."

"You and your cell phone are a PI's wet dream. I can't thank you enough."

I neared the door. Randy yelled, "Hey Mitch, come here."

With hesitation, I walked back. Grady got a twinkle in his eye, raised his eyebrows, and wrapped his arm around Randy's shoulders. "Do you want a three-way later?"

"Great offer, but I've got to run. Besides, what would your boyfriend say, Randy?"

"He'd love to join. We can have an orgy."

"Is it an orgy or a four-way?"

"Good question. Grady, what do you think? How many men do you need for an orgy?"

"I'll let you two figure it out," I said. "You've been a big help. Have a great night."

Grady scratched his head then shrugged his shoulders. "I don't know, man. The more, the merrier. Who cares what you call it?"

I couldn't help but laugh as I walked out the door.

Thirty-Two

I was out of ramen. I considered closing the shop for
lunch but convinced myself I couldn't afford to. Two
breakfasts never hurt anyone. I reached for the Honey Nut
Cheerios, pulled milk out of the mini fridge, and poured big
spoiled chunks of it right into my bowl.

"Shit!"

The rancid smell permeated the room, and my lunch fell
to the floor. After a quick cleanup, I ate dry cereal with a
spoon while browsing through one of Josie's magazines. I
read an article titled "Men's Top 5 Erogenous Zones,"
laughed, and tossed it aside. They weren't even close.

A call came in just as a muscular, six-foot-tall, black
man wearing a blue Dodgers jersey came through the door.
I held up a finger for him to give me a minute.

"Hello?"

"It is a pleasure to speak with you again, Mitch," the
caller said. "Remember me?"

Pain shot through my palm as I clasped the phone.
Pressure built behind my eye, and my heart raced.

"I remember you," I muttered.

"Excuse me," the Dodgers fan interrupted. "Could I get some help over here?"

I raised my finger again and turned away.

"How is Josie?" the caller said. "I hope she is comfortable at the home of your friend's dear Aunt Ada."

I waited to answer until the caller wouldn't hear my voice quiver.

"Hey!" the customer said. "Are you going to help me or talk to your girlfriend?"

I ignored him. "Who is this?"

"Poor, poor Josie," the voice said. "She must get lonely while Ada is at the restaurant. All alone and vulnerable. In fact, I believe Ada is working now, is that right?"

I turned to the customer and mouthed, "sorry." I tasted salt as silent tears rolled down my cheek. He rolled his eyes and stormed out the door.

"Listen—" I said.

"No. No. We have talked about this. That is not how it works. You are the one who needs to listen. I told you to move on, and you did not. You need to understand what I am saying."

"Yes?" The truck explosions, gunfire, and suicide bombers I'd experienced in the past were no match for the fear that grasped me.

"I will be more clear. If you want your sister to live, you will stop your investigation." The caller paused and breathed heavily. "If you do not, might I suggest that you hug her now while you still can?"

They disconnected.

My cell hit the floor. Panicked, I scooped it up to check if it still worked. I bolted for my car, called 9-1-1, and then phoned Josie. I made three more calls during the drive to Ada's house. Detective Turner and Ada answered, and I left a message for Trent. I was at the house within fifteen minutes.

Two police officers stopped me at the sidewalk. Josie dashed from the house and wrapped her arms around me. Her tears drenched the front of my shirt. The cops grabbed us and pulled us inside.

"Mitch, I'm scared. I don't know where else I can go? How'd they know I'm here?"

"Remember, I track people for a living. I wish I could tell you it's hard to do, but if you know what you're doing, it's actually pretty easy. Even taking the precautions we did... But we'll get you somewhere safe, I promise."

"What about Ada?"

An officer stepped forward. Her nametag said Jimenez. "If you're talking about the woman at the restaurant, she's okay. A car is already there."

"They're taking this more serious than the last time," Josie said.

"That's what happens when you have a second threat, a third murder, and the very real possibility that they're all linked."

I walked her to the couch and had her sit next to me. She raised her head off my shoulder and rubbed her eyes. Then she sat quietly, hands on her lap, as I stepped across the room with Officer Jimenez to give my statement. I whispered so Josie wouldn't hear the exact words from the phone call. The officer and I were still talking when Detective Turner arrived. I repeated the same information to him.

"We have two options," Detective Turner said. "Your first option is that Ada and your sister can stay here, and we'll post an officer."

"What's the other choice?" I asked.

Turner brushed his fingers across his mustache. It had been cut in a straight line directly above his lip and no longer fell into his mouth. "We take them to a safe house and keep an officer there at all times."

"I like that idea better," Josie spoke up.

"It's a deal," Turner responded. "We'll take care of it. They'll both be okay with Officers Jimenez and Franks for now. What do you plan to do, Mr. O'Reilly?"

"I'm done, sir. The case is over for me. It's yours now."

"Hell no!" Josie yelled. "This is too important for you. You are not letting that sonofabitch take you away from it. Don't try to argue with me. We'll be fine."

"It's not up for debate," I said to her, then turned back to Detective Turner. "I'm dropping the case, sir. I'll share any information you may find helpful."

I turned my back to Josie, who was still trying to talk me out of it. When she'd had enough of me ignoring her, I could hear her blowing raspberries behind me.

"As I was saying," I took a few steps to distance Detective Turner and myself further away from Josie, "we can meet and discuss the three murders once I get my files together. Where will you take Josie and Ada?"

"Don't know just yet," he said. "Protocol is we don't tell you. It's for everyone's protection."

I stayed with Josie until Ada and Trent arrived. While Detective Turner and the police officers figured out where to take them, the rest of us comforted each other. Once I felt like things were in control, I drove back to Eye Spy Supplies to close it properly for the night.

After I locked the security gates, put my paperwork in order, and cleaned the shop, I sat at the computer to write up a report for the detective. I couldn't focus on it.

I wondered why the killer would threaten to hurt Josie or Ada to stop my investigation when they could just do away with me. The only way to guarantee I'd end it would be to end me.

After ten minutes, the only thing I'd typed was "Dear Detective."

Josie may have been right—after that asshole had murdered three people and made Josie and Ada into frightened pawns, bailing would be foolish and dishonorable. If the military had taught me anything, it was to proceed in the face of fear.

I called Turner and told him I had changed my mind.

Thirty-Three

The forecast called for more storms that night, so I savored the fresh air as I drove to work. Halfway there, I made a U-turn and headed back to Silver Lake. I would need to question the remaining suspects again, starting with the bathhouse office supervisor, Seth Snider.

When Seth didn't immediately answer the door to his apartment above the garage, I banged harder. I knocked so loud that his landlord screamed at me to stop. He said he didn't know where Seth was.

When he didn't answer his phone, I called Club Silver Lake directly. They said he was off work for a couple of days. With no other direction to take, I gave Trent a call.

"I don't know where he is," he said when I asked. "Why do you need to talk to him so bad?"

"What does he do in his free time? Do you know of any bars he goes to?"

"He talked about hanging with Christian in West Hollywood sometimes, but I don't think going to clubs is really his thing. He's never said what he does other than working on cars."

Seth didn't fit with the West Hollywood crowd. He wouldn't get much interest from the typical twinks who

clubbed there. I reminded myself to stop making
assumptions based on stereotypes.

"No bars? No clubs? No restaurants? No hobbies?
Nothing?"

"I don't have a clue."

"How's Josie?"

"The last I talked with Ada, she said Josie is okay.
Upset, but making the best of it. Ada was even giving her
cooking lessons."

"Thanks." I disconnected without saying goodbye,
realizing after the fact that I'd been rude.

With Seth out of reach, I turned the car around and
headed to Bloomers. Warren was locking the door when I
pulled in. He'd hung a handwritten sign on the door that
said *Closed Early. Come Back Tomorrow.*

"Sorry, O'Reilly," he shouted through the door. "Come
back tomorrow. I'll have fresh flowers in the morning." He
wasn't rude. He was upbeat but insisted he was too busy to
chat.

"Come on, Warren. I only need a few minutes of your
time. I really need your help."

He smiled, then grimaced, and let me in. "Give me a
minute. I'm all alone today, and I have to wrap things up."

While he put flowers in the coolers, I browsed a wall display of trinkets for sale. I had no idea what a mystical pocket stone was, or why someone would want a stuffed fuzzy hamster with Girl Power on its belly, but there was a buyer for anything.

After I had wasted ten minutes, looking through sappy greeting cards, a man walked out from the backroom.

"How much longer are you going to be?" he asked Warren.

He was as tall as Warren but lanky, with a gruff face, a ragged brown beard, and a mustache. He also had tattoos. A lot of tattoos. They covered his arms, shoulders, and his neck.

Warren gave me a quick glance then back at the inked man. "I'm going as fast as I can. Turn on the TV in my office if you want."

The man sulked into the back.

"Who's your friend?" I asked.

"Not that's any of your business, but that's Don. He and I met years ago at a studio party with Vic. He's a costume designer." He tossed a bouquet into the cooler. "How can I help you?"

"I'd like to ask you some questions about your relationship with your stepdaughter, Heather Verboom."

He scowled for a second, then the smile returned to his face. "I don't know how I can help. I told you I know nothing about her, but go ahead."

"I heard a rumor that Victor had changed the sole beneficiary of his will and insurance from you to Heather. Any truth to that?"

A broad grin spread across his face, followed by a guffaw. There was a twinkle in his eyes. "Where would you hear such nonsense?"

I didn't dare tell him I had guessed it from breaking into his home. "You know how rumors get around."

"I assure you there's no truth to it. I met with Victor's attorney yesterday, who also is his executor. I'm the sole beneficiary of his insurance and ninety percent of his estate. He left the rest to Heather. He said he'd call her before he left his office."

"Hence the good mood."

Warren's face dropped. He stuttered. "I know it looks bad being happy so soon after Vic's death. I lost the love of my life, but this store has been a chain around my neck for a long time. I can finally get rid of it and move on. I need a fresh start."

"Any chance you'd like to invest in a strip mall spy shop?" I muttered under my breath. It was worth a try.

"What's that?"

"Uh, nothing. Bad joke." I cleared my throat.

"Am I still a suspect? I'm sure my enthusiasm doesn't look good if I am, but right now, I don't really care."

"Probably not—hold on." I called to the back, "Hey, Don, could you come out?"

"What the hell? What are you calling him for?"

Don lumbered out to the storefront. "Yeah?"

"Don. Warren was telling me he met you years ago. It's good to meet you, I'm Mitch O'Reilly. I'm a private investigator."

We shook hands.

"You look puzzled—I understand. I need to ask where do you like to go out? Any particular bars or clubs?"

Warren groaned. "What is this, O'Reilly? What business of this is yours?"

"I want to know where he was on Saturday."

"Why do you care?" Don huffed.

Warren's shoulders slackened. "It's all right, Don. I know what he's getting at. This isn't about you—answer the man, if you would."

Don put a finger to his chin. "That was the night I bumped into you at The Thrust." He pointed to Warren.

"Why didn't you tell me this?" I asked Warren.

"I told you I was at The Thrust. What more did you need to know? Don saw me, we went to my car, and we talked."

Don chuckled. "We did more than talk."

In a flash, Warren's face turned red. "That's true. We were there for a while. We talked, and we kissed too."

"We did more than—"

"That's enough," Warren snapped. "O'Reilly has all he needs to know. I'll be back shortly."

Don shuffled to the back.

"I think I've got what I need," I said.

"I'm surprised you're still pursuing this. I had heard a rumor they had dropped you from the case. What a pity to see all that time chasing me around come to a waste." He winked and pushed me out the door, locking it behind me.

Thirty-Four

After leaving Warren's flower shop, I got in my car and called Seth again. He didn't answer, so I searched for Rod Hernandez. He wasn't at his office, and his cell went straight to his voicemail. Pam answered their home phone, snapped that he was at the beach house, and hung up.

Traffic was backed up on the I-10 freeway, so I took surface streets. It didn't help. What should have been a one-hour drive to Hermosa Beach took almost two.

I jumped when Rod threw open the patio door. I expected the glass to shatter.

"I'm busy, Mitch. What can I help you with?"

"If you have a friend over, you'll need to tell them to wait," I said. "We have things we need to talk about."

"There's no one here. I'm working."

"Then it's the perfect time for a break." I stepped past Rod and sat on his couch with him growling behind me. "Have a seat. I have some questions to ask starting with Saturday night. Where were you?"

Rod hesitated—he sat down. "I was home and came here. Why?"

"Ernesto Torres was murdered. He had his throat slashed too. See it on the news?"

"The janitor at the bathhouse? I've had a lot going on, and with work so busy I haven't seen anything. I was home with Pam most of the evening and then came here around midnight. I told you before, I don't know the guy—didn't." He pointed to his chest and shook his head. "I hope you're not looking at me."

"I had hoped you'd come up with something better than being here. Pam can back you up?"

"What time was he killed? I told you I was with her most of the night. She can give me an alibi. The whole neighborhood can." He stood and paced the floor. "She knows."

"Knows what?" I played dumb.

"I'm gay. What else do you think I'd be talking about? She told me Saturday afternoon." He eyed me. "I know she came to the store and tried to buy your silence. She's known for years. I can't believe she could live with my lies for so long." His shoulders shook. "It turns out you're good at keeping secrets too."

"Listen, Rod, I know it's scary now, but you'll be glad the truth came out in the long run."

"I don't need to hear, 'It gets better.' We fought the entire night, and she told me to get out. Not that I wanted to stay there, anyway." He grabbed a couple of Sam Adams beers from the fridge, tossed me one, and sat on the couch. I put the unopened bottle on a table. "You need to know I've been lying to you. It's kept me up for nights, and it's about the case. I saw the guy from the front desk walk back to the sauna that night."

"Seth?"

"Yeah, I think that's his name. Weird skinny dude with all the tattoos and piercings."

"What time?"

"As I was going to the bathroom where I bumped into that muscular guy."

"That's Trent, the guy who hired me to clear Ernesto's name." The flash of doubt that Detective Turner had planted in me about Trent popped up again. I pushed the thought away. "Tell me more about Seth."

"I was walking from my room to the bathroom, and he ran into me," Rod said. "He stuttered and continued down the hall."

"Why are you telling me this now?"

"Now that I've said something, I'll likely end up in court to testify against him. I didn't want that to happen. I didn't want the entire world to know I'm gay. I have two sons to think about. Pam and I will tell them now that it's out in the open. No point in keeping secrets anymore."

"If it comes to it, you're willing to testify?"

"It's been on my conscience too long." He looked to the floor. I gave him time to get himself together. "Are you calling the cops?"

"No. I'll let you tell them. It's your responsibility. But please, do it today."

"How will this affect the case? Does it change anything for you?"

"Don't worry about that. Thanks for telling me. You make that call, and I'll take care of things on my end. Now that you're being so honest, are there any other details you failed to give me?"

"You should go now." He stepped to the door and slid it open. When I was within inches from him, he placed his hand on my chest and closed the door again. "There is one more thing. Sit down."

I paused. The fear in his eyes caused me to shudder. I sat.

"I'm sorry about your sister." He paced again.

"My sister?"

"She's been threatened, right?" He stopped. "It was Pam."

I jumped off the couch. My full body tensed. "What the fuck? What the hell did my sister do to that bitch?" I shook my fist. "Did you have anything to do with this?"

Rod held up his palms and took several steps back. "No, I had nothing to do with it. Please, don't hit me." He sat on the couch. His hands bounced off his shaking knees. "You know how she is about propriety. She didn't want you digging any further into our business. She didn't want it to get out that I'm gay. She wanted you to back off."

"I should have known it. I knew the caller sounded funny. Pam and her lack of contractions bullshit." I smacked my head. "I'm an idiot." I started calling Detective Turner on my cell.

His voiced trembled. "She hired a private detective to follow your sister. Apparently, they'd been following me for some time. When he gave her the details of your sister's routine, she called and made the threats with a voice changer thing like you sell in your store—who are you calling?"

"The police. Is she still at home?"

Detective Turner's voicemail came on.

"She's flying to our condo in Honolulu. I don't know the flight."

I disconnected. I would call the detective after I called the police.

"I don't know if the police will want to meet us here or at your home," I said. "Either way, you're not going anywhere without me."

Thirty-Five

The police caught Pam Hernandez as she was checking her bags at the airport. She was jailed overnight, and they let her out on bail the next morning. Josie and Ada were free women, and we celebrated with too much Greek food and ouzo at Olexi's. Regency Investigative Services gave Josie back pay and said they would seek reparations from Pam. Josie talked to an attorney about suing as well.

Seth Snider didn't show up for his shift at work. He'd been missing for three days. Calls to his phone said his voicemail was full. He had ties to Christian and Ernesto, though I was unable to come up with a motive. I had no idea why he would murder Victor since there didn't seem to be any personal connection between the two. There was always the possibility he murdered Victor on Christian's behalf, but that didn't seem likely. There was great risk killing Victor in a public place—the odds that it was planned were remote.

There had been a monsoon during the week that caused flash flooding throughout Los Angeles County. It had slowed to just a hint of a drizzle by morning when I pulled into the strip mall parking lot. Frank was curled up in my store's doorway under a blue plastic tarp. He was spooning with a woman I'd never seen before. She had short gray hair that looked like it hadn't been washed or combed in months, and she was wearing a filthy, puffy, blue dress. It was so ugly I could only assume it had been tossed out after a prom in the '80s. I decided to wake Frank and let the sly devil wake her up on his own.

I shook him. "Frank. Time to get up."

He grunted a few times, then looked down at her, back up at me, and smiled. "This is my new friend. We met yesterday in front of McDonald's. I was waiting for the bus, and she was sleeping on the bench."

"Glad you made a friend, but—"

"I was tired, so I told her to get her ass up so I could sit down."

"That's romantic."

"I think I love her. We had relations right here last night."

"I'm happy for you, Frank." Thank God I had bleach inside. "Now scoot out of the way. You can wake her up while I open the store."

He moved his legs so I could step past. After unlocking the door, I looked back at the happy couple. The sleeping bag I had given him was tattered, with little stuffing left.

"We need to talk more often, Frank. Let's start with a new bag for you."

He nodded and proceeded to wake up the new woman in his life.

By the time I set up the store, the rain had returned with a vengeance. I looked out the door for Frank and his woman. No one was going to drive through this mess of a storm for spy supplies, so I wanted to let them in, but they were nowhere to be seen. The rain was pounding so hard against the windows that I half expected them to explode at any minute.

The weather would give me time to focus on solving Victor's murder. Warren was off the hook. I had thought there could have been a way for him to get back in Club Silver Lake to kill Victor. It was a shot in the dark, but I had pursued it since he had so much to gain. With Don to back him up during Ernesto's murder, there seemed no point in pursuing him any further.

Rod was nowhere near being in the clear. He had reason to kill Victor. I didn't know why he would butcher Christian, but there was no telling if there was more between the two than just their rendezvous. I had no idea why he would kill Ernesto, but his alibis were weak in all three cases. Trent had seen him at the bathroom, but the times were vague, so he had the possibility.

Trent also had to be taken into consideration. I failed at establishing motives in any of the three murders, but he did have opportunity.

In between the time spent evaluating the suspects in my head, I made a couple of small sales during the day. Nothing that put a dent in my financial problems, but good to see some money come in. I sold a couple of my bigger items on eBay and hoped Jeff, the owner of the strip mall, would be satisfied with what I would be able to give him. I took a hit selling the products below cost, but these were desperate times. The rest of the day I spent calling former clients to try to drum up a little extra surveillance work, with little luck. Deborah Halverson said she'd take me on for a few hours. Nine months prior, she'd believed her husband was cheating and hired me to track him. I came up short, but she wasn't convinced he was innocent. She agreed to have me follow him again but said he was out of town on business for three weeks. That wasn't going to help my immediate need for groceries. I tried to tell her he was most likely to cheat on his trip and get a little all-expenses paid weekend out of it, but she didn't bite. We agreed to get started when he got back home.

As I brainstormed former clients to call, the door jingled, and Trent stepped in. Every stitch of clothing clung to his wet body. He was a beautiful sight, and I had to fight to take my eyes off him.

"This is a nice surprise," I said. "What brings you in?"

"I was on my way to work when there was a break in the storm. It hit hard again when I was around the corner, so I'm seeking shelter. It's really bad out there."

I tossed him a towel from the bathroom. "Here, dry yourself off. You're messing up my floor."

I watched open-mouthed as he ran the towel around his body, stretching every muscle as he went. He looked up, caught me a couple of times, and smirked.

"Do you know if Seth and Heather Verboom know each other?" I asked.

He scrubbed his hair hard with the towel. "Heather Verboom? That's an odd question. Why would you think so?"

"No reason really, just… something's bugging me. I've got a hunch."

He sniggered. "You and your hunches that I'm not supposed to ask about." He took the towel back to the bathroom. "I don't know how they would know each other, so I guess I'd say no."

I realized since Eve had dropped the case there was no need for confidentiality. "The reason I'm asking is... In passing, Seth said he grew up in Barstow. Heather was born in Barstow before Victor moved to Los Angeles. It's not much to go on, but it's a small town over a hundred miles away, and it reveals a connection between two of my suspects—Heather and Seth."

"One degree of separation."

"Exactly," I said.

"Why don't you ask them directly if they know each other?"

"You know Seth is AWOL, and Heather's not picking up her phone. Plus, I don't trust they'll be honest with me." I flopped down onto my desk chair. Trent followed suit and sat on the couch.

"They seem like they're about the same age," I said. "I found on several of Heather's social media accounts that she graduated from Barstow High in 2014. Seth is nowhere to be found though. It looks like he started a Facebook account at some point, but there are no details. No picture or bio, just his name and where he lives."

"That's no surprise. Seth is kind of a Luddite. He's a get down and dirty kind of guy. Computers are a necessary evil. I doubt he'd spend much free time online."

"I haven't run a social trace report on him yet. I guess I can do that now, but I don't know how much that will help. It's a given they both went to Barstow High since it's the only game in town—assuming Seth, and Christian for that matter, went to public school. They're all in the same age range, so the odds that there wasn't at least some overlap are small, but knowing whether they attended the same school at the same time still won't tell me if they knew each other well. The best that I can think of is to drive out there and ask around."

"You don't need to drive up there for that. You can find anything online. Let's try chalkboardchums.com." Trent leaned across me and started typing on my keyboard. His side felt good rubbing against my shoulder.

"What is Chalkboard Chums?"

"It's a social site that has old yearbooks. I guess it was popular before Instagram and Snapchat. I never heard of it until a friend wanted me to see an old picture from when I was a sophomore." He stood upright and put his hands on his hips. "It's a funny story. I went to Fairfax High, and our mascot was 'the lions.' My buddy Joshua and I made a two-man lion suit, and we—"

"We need to focus, Trent."

"Sorry," he said as he tapped on the keyboard again. "You have to create an account, but I wonder since I have one if it will let me search another school."

He clicked through chalkboardchums.com, and within a few minutes, he had navigated to a page listing fifty years of Barstow High yearbooks.

"Do you know what year Seth graduated?"

"No idea," Trent said. "It's on his application in my office, but he probably would have graduated in 2014 or '15. I'll try 2014."

He scrolled through the pages to the senior class pictures. "Bingo! There he is."

I took over the keyboard and jumped to the index and found that both Heather and Seth had photos on page ninety-seven.

"Look at that," Trent said.

"It's a safe bet they knew each other." The picture was of Heather and Seth laughing as he gave her a piggyback ride down a hallway. "I think I just found myself a new prime suspect," I told him. "Look at that." I pointed to Christian walking behind Seth and laughing.

"Holy shi—this has to be a coincidence."

"You think so? We need to find out where he is. I have a few questions I need answered."

Trent tried calling Seth several times but couldn't get an answer. "Nothing. It goes straight to voicemail and says it's full. He must be out of range."

"Or, more likely, he has it turned off."

I tried to call Heather a few times with no luck. I started to put the phone down, but figured I'd give it one last try. I expected to reach her voicemail again, but she answered after the fourth ring.

"Um. Hello?"

"Heather, Mitch O'Reilly here. Is Seth with you?"

"I'm sorry, I'm busy. I need to go—"

"Hold on, hold on," I yelled into the phone. She didn't speak, but I could hear the rain in the background. She hadn't hung up.

"Heather, where are you? It's important I speak with Seth. Is he with you?"

"I'm home." More extended silence. "You mean Kelvin?"

I paused momentarily. "No, Heather. I mean Seth. Seth Snider—the guy you went to high school with. The guy who was working at the bathhouse the night your father was murdered. I have a feeling you know who I'm talking about. And you probably know where he is."

Trent and I watched the clock as the seconds ticked by. I could hear Heather breathing, but she wasn't talking.

"Heather, I need to find Seth, and we need to talk about your father's murder. I think you know more than you're telling me."

"I had nothing to do with it. I promise. Nothing."

"Where is Seth? What did he do?"

She didn't respond. She was weeping on the phone. I tried to be patient, but the longer I waited, the more nervous I got that she'd end the call and I'd miss my chance to get my questions answered.

"Heather, what do you know?"

I could barely understand her through her wailing. "It was Seth. He killed my dad. He murdered him."

I stayed calm and carefully considered every word before speaking. I wanted to get information, but not scare her. "I want to help you, Heather. Why did Seth kill your dad?"

She came back on the line and sounded more confident. "You're going to think I'm a terrible person, but just remember, I never thought he'd take me seriously."

"Go on," I said.

"We joked about plans to kill him so I could get my inheritance and move out of this crappy place I live in. I said I'd give Seth a cut for always being there for me when we were growing up, and I had all my millions of 'daddy issues.' But I thought he realized I wasn't serious." She paused. "I admit, I was pissed when my dad told him he was working things out with Warren and taking me out of his will. I called Seth to complain, like old times. But then he overreacted and just did it. He said he had to act fast before the will was changed. It wasn't supposed to happen."

"I've never found murder a good subject to joke about." I needed her to tell me more, so I decided to soften my approach. "I'm so sorry, Heather. You must feel awful. We'll find him, and he'll pay for what he did to both of you."

I waited for her sobs to slow.

"Heather, do you know why your dad changed his will to you then back to Warren?"

"They were getting back together, and he said he didn't trust Kelvin with his money. That it'd all be spent on drugs and alcohol." She started crying again. "Kelvin doesn't even drink or use drugs."

I muted my phone and said to Trent, "Call Seth now. He murdered Victor. And who knows about the others? I'm worried Heather's in danger."

Trent said, "Seth did it? Are you sure?"

I nodded and turned off the mute button. "Heather, what about Christian and Ernesto?"

"I feel so bad for Ernesto. He didn't do anything."

"Ernesto knew what Seth did too?"

"No. Seth had been telling everyone Ernesto did it, which Ernesto said 'destroyed his honor' or something like that. They got in a fight in the parking lot, and Seth killed him too. He said it was easy because Ernesto was so small. I think he enjoyed it." She got quiet. "Mr. O'Reilly, I'm scared. He's gone crazy. What if he comes after me next?"

I tried to stay calm and took a big swallow. I needed her to keep it together and continue talking. "I know you're afraid. I want to help you, but you didn't say anything about Christian. What about him?"

"Christian knew," she said. "Seth told him. Seth always told Christian everything, but Seth wouldn't hurt him. He loved Christian like a brother... even more." Her voice became distant as if she pulled the phone away. She wept. "I had to ask him if he did it. I didn't want to, but I couldn't ignore the possibility. He was so hurt that I asked, and he swore he couldn't even think about it. I felt bad for asking."

"Does Seth have keys to Christian's car?"

"He did to the Kia because he did the maintenance for him. I don't know about the Mustang."

"Do you know where he is now?"

"No, the last time we talked was when I told him about the call from Dad's attorney. He lost it and started screaming when he realized he killed my dad too late. The will had already been changed. I haven't been able to reach him since. I think his phone is off."

A door slammed on her end of the call. Then I heard Heather say, "What are you doing here?" The phone disconnected. I called back several times.

"She won't answer," I said. "Someone walked in, and we were disconnected."

"Do you think Seth's with her?" Trent asked.

"That's what I'm afraid of. Try reaching Seth, and I'll call Riverside PD. Be prepared to drive out there."

The phone at the Riverside Police Department rang many times before anyone answered. Rather than a long explanation, I gave them Heather's address and said that a man was attacking her.

Trent directed his phone to call Seth several times, but the phone didn't understand. It was probably because his voice was shaking. He dialed frantically. "He's not answering. I even tried the club."

"Let's go," I said. "We're driving to Riverside."

I rushed to the front door. Trent was still on the couch. "What are you doing?"

"I'm calling his landlord. He may know something. Hello, Mr. Apple. How are you?"

"Cut the formalities," I screamed.

"Mr. Apple, this is Trent. I can't reach Seth on his phone. Is he home? … Oh, okay. Do you know where he is?"

I was gritting my teeth waiting for a response.

"Gentle Slope Road?" Trent said finally. "No, I'm not sure why he—"

I grabbed Trent's arm. "Come on. We need to go." Trent shrugged off my hands. "Hold on, he's still talking."

"Warren lives on Gentle Slope Road."

"He says Seth rushed to the house from his apartment. Seth told him he had lost his phone and asked Mr. Apple if he could use his computer to pull up a map."

"Let's go. Now!"

I let him out of the door and locked it without closing the security gates. Trent followed me to my car.

"Where's Gentle Slope Road?" he asked.

"In the Hollywood Hills. If we don't get there fast, Warren might be our next victim."

Thirty-Six

My wipers were useless against the heavy rain. It was only through instinct that I was able to navigate my way down Hollywood Boulevard. Traffic was lighter than usual but still crawling at a snail's pace. I hoped whatever route Seth was taking was worse than the one we were on.

I yelled to Trent seated beside me, "What the hell is going on?"

His face was flushed, and he was sweating and gritting his teeth. "I've been disconnected twice, and now I'm on hold."

"How can 9-1-1 put you on hold?"

He waved his free arm dramatically at the windshield. "Take a look around. I'm lucky to get through at all. Goddamn it." He smashed his phone against the dashboard.

"What? What the hell?"

"I got disconnected again." He looked at what remained of the phone. "Quick. Toss me your cell."

"Be careful with it," I ordered. Trent caught my phone and furiously dialed again. I was listening to him give the 9-1-1 operator Warren's address when I heard a high-pitched screech. An oncoming car sideswiped me, and I bounced off the curb. Trent yelped as his head struck the side window. I overcompensated and nearly lost control, but regained power over the vehicle and continued slowly forward. In the rearview mirror, I saw the car that hit me stopped on the sidewalk. I had to decide—stop and exchange numbers or save a man's life. I continued driving.

"Did you tell them about Seth?"

"I didn't invite them over for tea."

"I just got clipped. It's kind of hard to focus."

He had one hand clutched on the door handle and the other on the dashboard. "They radioed the police, but the city's a mess. I don't see how they'll get there before us. We should have taken my Jeep."

"Thanks for stating the obvious. We were in kind of a rush."

The storm let up a little, and we were making better time until we reached Laurel Canyon Boulevard leading up to the hills. A lane closure had bottlenecked traffic, resulting in an accident that blocked the intersection. Trent was panicking as he repeatedly called both Warren and Seth. Neither answered.

I drove up a median, knocked a sign into another car, and tore up the hill as fast as I could safely go. My Honda was not built for such abuse but took it like a champ. Streams flooded from the hills onto the street. It got worse when I turned on Gentle Slope Road toward Warren's house. Waves of water tore from the hills above, turning the road into a river. There were several moments the car nearly stalled.

"There they are!" Trent pointed.

In front of the house were two shadows, faintly visible through the rain. One large figure—Warren—was huddled down on the driveway, while the other—Seth—stood over him. Before I could stop the car, Trent jumped out and ran through the water. Seth turned the gun toward him.

I braked in the middle of the street, stepped out of the car, and strode to Trent's side. The water rushed across my feet and ankles. It was hard to see with the rain and wind batting at my eyes.

"Seth, put the gun down," I yelled.

"Fuck you!"

Trent moved forward, so I blocked him with my arm.

"Don't do it, Trent," I said. "You'll get yourself killed."

"There's no reason for him to kill me."

"There's no reason for him to kill Warren either, yet there he is. He's scared and running on pure adrenaline. I've seen this in combat. You can't reason with him."

"Put that down," Seth screamed when I drew my gun.

"You need to put yours down and back off, Seth. You have nothing to gain."

"This son of a bitch ruined my life. Fuck him and fuck you."

"Warren didn't ruin your life. Heather did."

Trent leaned into me. "I thought you said there was no reasoning with him."

"I did," I said, "but now that I've got a gun on him, it's worth a try."

Warren started to get up, and Seth turned his gun back at him. "Get back down in the mud, you fat bastard."

Trent called to Seth. "Don't pull that trigger. Heather told us everything. Aren't three lives enough?"

"Don't lie to me. She didn't know anything about Christian."

Trent spun his head to look at me then back at Seth. "Think about your own life. You don't want to ruin that."

"It's too late for that, you fucker." Seth kept the gun trained on Warren's head.

Trent looked stunned. "He's never talked to me like that before."

I shrugged. "I told you so."

Trent waved his arms, trying to get Seth's attention. "Hey, when I lived in Atlanta for a year, I had a neighbor in a similar situation—"

Seth laughed. At the same time, he and I replied, "Similar to this?"

"Kind of. He was a high-strung guy, and his girlfriend dumped him. Well, she didn't really dump him. He walked in and caught her in bed with another guy. I mean, he shouldn't have been that upset because they weren't that serious, but sure enough, he was. You know how that is, right? So, anyway, when this guy walks in and catches them—"

"I'm not in the mood for one of your bullshit stories. Shut the fuck up." Seth was swaying back and forth, fighting to keep his aim on Warren.

Trent stiffened.

It didn't seem possible, but the rain poured down even harder. We all stood silent, staring at each other's blurry outlines. The gusts fought against my arms, which were growing weary from holding my gun straight in front of me, but I remained steady, ready to take Seth down.

We heard sirens coming up the hill. Seth stepped directly over Warren and placed the barrel of his gun on Warren's head.

"Seth, trust me. You don't want to get into a gun battle with me."

He froze, his gun still pointed at Warren as he stared straight at me, considering. "You're right," he finally said. "I don't."

Seth pulled the gun away and held it to his side. Warren was sobbing on the ground, tears and rain rushing down his face. Seth continued to stand and face my way for another minute. I fought against the gusts for good aim. Flashing lights bleeding through the downpour distracted me.

"No!"

Trent screamed, and I turned just in time to catch Seth placing the gun in his mouth.

"Stop," I yelled.

Warren reached out, snatched Seth's legs, and pulled him to the ground. The gun flew from Seth's hand and splashed several feet away.

I bounded across the driveway and grabbed the back of Seth's shirt. We both fell, and his shirt ripped as he tore away from me and ran toward the side of the house. I leaped forward and sprawled on top of Seth as the raging waters knocked him down. Two police cars parked in front of the driveway. Their flashing lights bounced through the heavy drops. I couldn't see any officers, but it was hard to make anything out, even at that short distance.

Seth crossed his arms and wailed.

"Help me," he whimpered.

I grabbed his hand and pulled as I got up on one knee. That's when we heard it. Seth and I frantically looked from side to side, unsure of where to run. The ground shook, and a rumbling came toward us. The rushing river of mud and rocks and twigs came from the hills above and slammed into us like a locomotive, knocking us backward and dragging us down the hill behind Warren's house.

Unable to see, I foolishly reached out to grab anything that came my way. My arm struck a tree, and I screamed, certain it had been ripped from its socket. My eyes cleared enough to see Seth spiral off my chest and slam into a thick tree. At the speed we were going, it was certain death.

Something ripped at my shoulder again, and my mouth filled with mud when I tried to scream. I spun around and continued downhill headfirst, prepared to have my skull crushed at any moment.

When I was revived, the EMTs were holding my head upright. My curiosity overpowered my pain enough for me to turn and see the trees, cinderblocks, and boards mixed in the sludge beside me. I grabbed one EMT's arm to pull myself up and was ordered to get back down.

"You need to stay put," she said.

I collapsed onto the murky road and gasped, "How?"

"You only have eight lives left, Mr. Lucky. You were lying under the mud when we found you here on the street."

As they wheeled a stretcher over, my stubborn nature got the best of me, and I tried to rise to my feet again. The last thing I remember was the searing pain that shot through my body as I fell on my damaged arm.

Thirty-Seven

After three nights in the hospital, I was relieved to be discharged. There had been a steady stream of visitors during my stay, and I needed to be home to rest. It was interesting how many casual acquaintances suddenly became great friends after seeing me lauded as a hero on the news. Josie's visits were fun, but she caused waves of pain to shoot through my body each time she made me laugh.

Trent rarely left my side. He and the others were at the edge of the mudslide, so they were knocked into the house but suffered only minor injuries. Two neighboring homes were destroyed, and a police car was pushed into the side of Warren's garage.

Each night, Trent slept on a cot in my room and brought his meals up from the cafeteria. He was like having a dedicated full-time nurse, regularly asking me what I needed and if I was okay. There were moments I wanted to sit quietly and watch television but couldn't focus because—despite his best efforts—he was unable to refrain from telling his long-winded stories. I didn't mind. It was comforting to have him there.

My arm was broken in two places rather than ripped from its socket as I had assumed. I suffered from a concussion, several gashes in my shoulder, and deep cuts on my arms and legs. My entire body was covered in scrapes and bruises. Not bad, considering what had happened. Had the cause of my injuries been different, I likely would've been sent home the next day. My fifteen minutes of fame paid off, and I got extra special care, despite not wanting to be there.

Josie took even more time off from her job to work at my store. As much as I loathed her boss, Nat Phelps, I'd have to suck it up and thank him for being so flexible. As usual, my bullshit-fluent sister made more sales than when I was there. She saved the store from closing for the time being.

Eve surprised me by giving me a hundred-dollar gift card. It seemed unlike her until Trent showed me a newspaper ad she placed touting her goodwill. It was laughable, but a kind enough gesture that Trent convinced me to invite her to my "celebration party."

The party consisted of the three of us—plus Josie—in Trent's living room, having a few drinks and some cake. Trent was going through the motions, trying to lift my spirits, but I knew it wasn't a celebration for him. Ernesto was dead, and other than in court, he'd never see Seth again.

While I was lucky to be alive, Seth's survival was nothing short of a miracle. The tree he crashed into left him with two broken legs, a few broken ribs, a broken nose, and the loss of many of his teeth. He had to stay in the hospital for several days longer than me. After that, he was going to be transferred to the jail infirmary. Before finding out he was a killer, he had seemed like a nice guy, so a small part of me felt sorry for him.

The morning after the Hollywood Hills incident, Kelvin tipped the police off to Heather's hiding place. She was staying with a friend in Riverside. The police arrested Heather. They questioned her friend but decided she didn't know about Heather's involvement. Heather confessed that Seth had called her when he started working at the bathhouse. Verboom wasn't a common name, and he called to ask if they were related. That's when she had reached out and reconnected with her father. She wasn't the innocent victim she had professed to be. Seth was nothing more than the initial hatchet man. Heather was the one who cooked up the whole scheme.

From her point of view, Heather was honest when she said Seth didn't have anything to do with Christian's murder. He lied when she asked if he had killed their friend. While not involved, Christian knew what they had done. He had panicked and was going to the police. Seth was left with no choice but to take care of that problem.

It seemed the mix of guilt and terror over murdering Christian had been too much for Seth, and he had lashed out in response. That's what sealed Ernesto's fate when he confronted Seth.

Eve held up a glass of bourbon. "I was wrong about you, O'Reilly. You really came through. Thanks for keeping it quiet that you were no longer working for me when things went down."

"It's all good," I replied. "Although my phone hasn't been ringing off the hook with new clients like I'd hoped."

"It hasn't even been a week. You've got to give it time for the news to spread."

"I'm not a patient man."

Josie laughed. "You sit in your car for hours snapping pictures of people."

"Yes, but I hate every second of it."

Trent tapped a spoon against his glass. "I have just a few words to say. Nothing fancy. I want us to raise our glasses in Mitch's honor for ignoring common sense." He winked and added, "And sticking with the case."

We raised our glasses and clinked them all together.

"Time for me to go," Eve said.

"Me too," Josie said. "I have a date."

"A date? As in a 'date' date?" I asked.

"Third time. That's a record for me lately."

Eve shook my hand. "I'm sure I'll be calling for another job."

I smirked and refrained from wiping her clammy sweat onto my pants. "You know where to find me, but I don't know if you'll be able to afford me."

Josie gave Trent a tight squeeze, then turned. "Are you ready?" she asked me. I'd forgotten that she'd given me a ride.

"One minute," I said to Trent. Josie and I stepped out on to the front porch. "I'm gonna stay. I can call Lyft later."

Josie squealed, wrapped her arms around my neck, and said, "Have fun, Lil' Bro."

I yelped from the pain of her grasp against my aching body. Once she was safely in her car, I stepped back inside. Trent stood there waiting for me.

"I hope you don't mind if I stay. Josie would be more than I could handle right now."

"I was hoping you would." He looked me up and down. "Care for another beer?"

I nodded and eased myself onto the couch. "You and I have been too stuck in the middle of all the insanity to talk about things," I said. "I'm sorry for everything that happened."

Trent sat next to me, exhaled slowly, and placed his face in his hands. I raised my cast to put my arm on his shoulder, which sent a streak of pain down my neck. I gritted my teeth and leaned my body against his. He exhaled again and wiped his arm across his eyes.

"I'm glad you're here," he said.

"I am too." I smiled. Trent leaned forward and pressed his lips against mine.

It was our first kiss. I felt a release of tension from my body. My gut reaction was still to turn away, but I didn't.

When he pulled back, he grinned. "Thank you."

I blushed again, looked away, then turned back, looked him in the eyes, and smiled.

I lay on Trent's chest until he fell asleep, just before 1:00 a.m. I continued to stroke my one free hand along the contours of his muscles, then rolled onto my back and stared at the ceiling for what seemed like hours. When I got the energy, I tried to prop myself up but collapsed from the pain. I twisted and looked at the clock. Only twenty minutes had passed. I wanted to curl back up with him and feel the warmth of his skin against mine. I tried to convince myself it was just sex, but I knew that wasn't true. At the very least, we were friends.

When I could no longer stand the squabble in my head, I gently rolled out of bed, grabbed my clothes, and limped into the living room, cringing as the hardwood floor squeaked with each step. I sat on the couch, and with my one good arm, I fumbled putting on my underwear and socks. I grabbed my pants and edged one leg up to my knee.

Then I stopped. Despite my misgivings, I couldn't leave.

I let my pants drop and stripped myself naked again. I stepped over my clothes and continued toward the bedroom, stopping suddenly in the doorway as the floor gave a loud creak. Leaning against the frame, I grinned as I watched Trent sleeping. He had curled up on his side facing away from the door. I shuffled in and stood over him. The streetlights from the window cast shadows across his back. When I crawled back into the bed and put my arm around him, he grabbed my arm and wrapped it tighter around his body. I didn't care that he stretched my aching muscles.

"I'm glad you stayed," he whispered.

"Me too." I brushed my lips across his ear.

I tightened my grasp around him and listened to the soothing rhythm of our breaths.

I didn't want to break the silence. "I won't be staying in the morning."

His body stiffened. "No?"

"There's a PTSD support group at the hospital at 9:00."

He relaxed, rolled over to face me, and beamed. "I can't think of a better reason to miss breakfast."

I ran my thumb across his lower lip, placed my hand softly on his cheek, and brushed my lips against his.

I tried to lie back on his chest, but the strain on my muscles was too intense, and I slithered off onto my back.

Trent jolted upright. "Are you okay?"

I reached up with my one good arm, placed it on his cheek, and smiled.

"For now, I am. Goodnight."

The Next Mitch O'Reilly Mystery

A Body on the Hill

Coming Fall 2019

For news about this and other releases, sign up for
Brad's Monthly Newsletter at

www.bradshreve.com/signup

While it's fresh on your mind, please take a moment to leave a review for

A Body in a Bathhouse. It'd be greatly appreciated.

Review on Amazon at

https://www.amazon.com/author/bradshreve

Review on Goodreads at

https://www.goodreads.com/bradshreve

About the Author

After growing up in Michigan and North Carolina, Brad crisscrossed the country working in the hotel industry. In addition to working as a bellman, front desk clerk, and reservation call center director, he managed coffee houses, waited tables, sold potato chips off a truck, and even hawked pre-burial funeral plans.

He credits *Where the Wild Things Are* by Maurice Sendak for developing his interest in art and storytelling. He'd spend hours on the floor sketching and painting and writing stories. *My Side of the Mountain* by Jean Craighead George gave him his first inkling that he'd like to be a novelist someday.

He developed his love of mysteries from Lawrence Block and Sue Grafton.

He's a proud dad, beach bum, and coffee house squatter.

He currently lives in the South Bay of Los Angeles with his husband, Maurice.

www.bradshreve.com

www.studs4studs.com

Made in the USA
Coppell, TX
04 January 2020

14088120R00238